Sailing Beyond the Sunset

ALFRED P. DOBLIN

Rattling Good Yarns Press
33490 Date Palm Drive 3065
Cathedral City CA 92235
USA
www.rattlinggoodyarns.com

Cover Design: Rattling Good Yarns Press

Library of Congress Control Number: 2026935645
ISBN: 978-1-968983-00-0

First Edition

In memory of Rick Unterberg.

The Stories

"*Death closes all: but something ere the end,*
Some work of noble note, may yet be done,
Not unbecoming men that strove with Gods.
The long day wanes: the slow moon climbs:
the deep
Moans round with many voices, Come, my
friends.
'T is not too late to seek a newer world.

~ Alfred, Lord Tennyson

An Early Spring

David opened his bedroom blinds. He sipped his first cup of coffee as he stared out the window, looking up the street. The arc of morning sun reflected off the windows of the brownstones across the street. In the summer, a thick canopy of leaves muted the early morning light from the east, but in winter, the bare tree limbs offered no resistance.

There had been little snow this year. Although only mid-February, temperatures were expected to climb into the 50s. Joggers were already out, some moving in twos, others running solo. David watched the morning show.

An elderly woman using a walker waved at a runner, a woman in her thirties. The female runner stopped to talk with the older woman. They laughed at something, and the runner, before returning to the rhythm of her jog, gave the older woman a quick hug. The older woman looked at the runner for a moment and then resumed her slow, deliberate walk.

A few parents with children headed north toward the elementary school five blocks away. The unmodulated sounds of seven and eight-year-olds talking to their moms and dads carried through David's double-paned glass.

An SUV pulled out of a parking space along the street as an equally large SUV approached. The ongoing dance of city street parking continued, with one car following another. David called this the "Fred and Ginger," after Astaire and Rogers, because the car that followed had to navigate the space backwards, but as David noted, paraphrasing Ginger Rogers, the driver following "didn't have to do it both backwards and in heels."

David looked out from his fifth-floor window at the trees. If temperatures remained warm, buds would soon begin to show. It would be an early spring. David looked forward to the arrival of spring, the switch to daylight saving time, the longer days, and the smell of flowers everywhere. Working from home, much of his day was spent indoors. It was the show outside that provided the needed distractions from whatever publishing deadline he faced.

He wrote until 11 a.m., when he stopped, poured a fresh cup of coffee, and sat on the sofa to listen to the music. At 11 a.m., Monday through Friday, he would hear the footsteps above in Leon's apartment. He couldn't hear Leon's door opening and closing, but the moving of chairs and music stands, with the attendant shuffling of four old men, was the prelude of the daily concert.

Originally not a fan of classical music, David acquired a taste for chamber music, particularly string quartets, as he grew to love the morning concerts. Leon had been a professional concert cellist. Now retired, he and three other musicians—two violinists and a violist—met in Leon's apartment on weekdays for an hour of making music. They played for themselves, and when the weather warmed up and the windows were open, for the people on the street, who would linger on the sidewalk below to listen to the quartet.

One of the violinists and the violist lived in the same brownstone. David would see the two men come out of the house across the street, arm in arm, gingerly walking down the nine steps of the stoop to the sidewalk. David didn't know if the two men were a couple or just neighbors. The other violinist lived in the adjacent brownstone. He was spry, carrying his violin case in one hand while he waved his cane like a conductor's stick, beating out time in the air.

Thirty years ago, this street was filled with musicians—symphony players, chamber music artists, singers, and a few conductors. It had been a tight-knit community once, but as real estate prices soared, the aging musicians were either priced out of their apartments or those who lived in co-ops like David cashed in their profits and moved to warmer, less highly taxed places. The apartment windfalls made up for the lack of retirement cushions that would have allowed them to stay in New York.

But these four men had stayed. Whether they invested wisely or were living on cat food, David didn't know. It wasn't that kind of street anymore, where everybody knew everyone's business. The faces were familiar enough, but they were like the facades of the stately brownstones, revealing only an exterior and nothing more.

David had imagined how each of the four men looked as they played—who smiled, who looked intent, who anxiously awaited the page turn, and who frolicked across the measures like a toddler in a field of flowers—that was Leon, David was sure.

There was something childlike about Leon. Maybe it was that he always smiled in the elevator or the laundry room. Maybe it was a fearless quality he had when he left the building wearing a beret and tapping out a beat with his walking stick, which, to David, seemed more like an affectation than an actual necessity, as if Leon had decided this was how a musician of his age should look. Leon's embrace of the moment—of his moment—was what intrigued David most.

For David, moments were defined by the omnipresent clocks placed throughout his apartment. For Leon, it was the crinkles and creases in the skin around his eyes and mouth that marked laughter and tears—the two fundamental elements of life.

He and Leon talked casually whenever they ran into each other in the building or on the street. But in the four years David had lived at his current address, he had never been inside Leon's apartment or Leon in his. People kept to themselves.

It was the music that broke through the walls—the collective voice of these four old men playing notes written by men long deceased. Haydn, Mozart, Beethoven, and Schubert were resurrected as four bows glided over strings, as if the notes shouted, "Lazarus, arise, arise."

David turned away from the street life below and began writing; the piece was due at the end of the week, and it was already Wednesday. For the next three-plus hours, he worked nonstop, lost in the rhythm of his words forming as he struck the keys on his laptop with a force that had not diminished from his college years on a Remington manual. The shuffling of feet signaled it was 11 a.m. David looked out the window and saw the spry violinist scurrying across the street, marking time with his cane.

Within 10 minutes, David knew all the men were upstairs by the movement of chairs. And then—the music. David refilled his mug, sat on the sofa, and listened. He didn't know the composers; he only knew the music was beautiful.

Two weeks passed before David ran into Leon in the elevator.

"The music today, what was it?" David asked.

"Was it too loud?" Leon asked. "We were a little more energetic."

"It's never too loud. It's not like I'm listening to a bad tenor singing opera."

"There are no good tenors singing opera," Leon said with a chuckle.

"I really wouldn't know. I never could get into opera—too many words in languages I don't understand."

"Yes, I get that. That is the beauty of the string quartet. Four voices speaking in one universal language. When I was younger, I enjoyed the attention that came with being a soloist. Now, not so much. The older you get, the less you want to go solo—there is an eternity of solos getting closer and closer. The quarter is perfect—not too many, not too few."

The elevator reached the lobby. They passed another resident wearing purple rubber gloves. She stepped back as they walked by. The two men continued talking as they neared the front door.

"I guess she is getting concerned," David said. "Some people are getting fearful about this virus. I'm trying to take it in stride. I'm not sure of what lies ahead."

"You know, Davey...it's Davey, yes?"

"Yes, well, David. And you're Leon. Everyone knows you."

"That may be true enough. Not everyone in the building likes Mozart in the morning, but I say, 'Screw them!' I know when I can play and when I can't. But what was I going to say?"

"I said that no one is sure of what lies ahead..."

"Yes, yes. It's like looking at a new piece of music—something you've never heard before, and then you start playing. Maybe it will be good. Maybe not. Maybe easy to play or sometimes not just hard, but impossible, beyond your skills. I wouldn't trade any of those experiences. So, I'm trying to be careful about this virus, but I'm not going to wear rubber gloves. I'm a cellist, not a proctologist. There's a reason they only use one finger."

David laughed. "Well, there's a statement." They stood outside, with people passing by heading north and south. The "Fred and Ginger" took place right in front of them. "He's never getting that car into that space," David observed.

"Oh, ye of little faith," Leon said. "You just have to push it a bit. Physical contact is how we make everything fit."

The two men watched as the driver made several attempts at the spot, with each one worse than the last. Traffic was backing up, and horns blared.

Leon crossed the street and signaled to the driver to open his window. "Move over, and I can park this."

"Are you crazy, old man?" the driver said.

"Maybe. But look, I'm an old man wearing a beret. Do I look like a carjacker? I know how to park. Do you want this space, or do you want to drive around for another forty minutes?"

The driver thought about it, looked at David standing under the co-op canopy, opened the driver's side door, and slid over into the passenger seat. Leon got in, adjusted the mirror, moved the car forward, and then pulled into reverse. He parked the car on the first try. As he got out of the vehicle, he turned to the closest driver who was honking and gave him the finger.

"That was amazing," David said as Leon rejoined him under the co-op's canopy. The honking driver rolled down his window and returned Leon's gesture.

David and Leon laughed and waved at the man who sped off.

"I parked cars from college through my mid-twenties. Some skills last forever."

"Apparently," David replied. "You are amazing."

"Yes, I am," Leon replied.

David didn't know Leon well enough to know whether that was a joke or a statement of fact. All he knew was that he should have invested more time years ago in getting to know his neighbor.

"I'm late for an interview," David said, "but what was the music this morning? It sounded modern, not very harmonic in the beginning, but then it sounded almost like Mozart."

"Because it was Mozart's String Quartet No. 19. It's nicknamed 'Dissonance,' for its seemingly atonal opening. Herbert, he's one of the violinists, insisted we play it today because of this virus news—it's all confusion at the beginning, but just wait and see, it all ends in C major."

"I wish I understood what you just said," David said.

"So do I," Leon laughed. "We'll find something happier tomorrow."

"I look forward to it."

With that, David headed east toward the subway, and Leon turned south. The streets were crowded with workers grabbing lunch. Double-parked delivery trucks slowed traffic, and horns sounded.

⁕⁕⁕

David looked out his window. The cloud cover was blocking much of the morning sun. The trees were beginning to show signs of new life. The weather stayed warm, and rain, not snow, was in the forecast. There was a light drizzle. Parents walked their children toward the elementary school. One child held up an umbrella shaped like a frog, while his mother held a Burberry. Both wore masks. Another mother and daughter—neither wearing masks—approached heading south. The Burberry and the frog crossed over to the other side of the street before the other family got too close.

The familiar female jogger could be seen coming from the park at the end of the block. The old woman with the walker was making her way north. She wore a dark green waterproof jacket with a hood. She waved at the jogger, who pointed up to the sky and the light rain. The elderly woman waved her hand, as if to dismiss the weather.

A "Fred and Ginger" had started across the street in the very spot that Leon had navigated weeks earlier. David sipped at his coffee. He turned back to his computer and started writing.

At 11, he heard shuffling above. He looked out the window and saw the spry violinist scurrying toward his building. The noise of chairs and stands being moved around continued for another five minutes. And then the music.

David didn't know much about instrumentation, but he sensed something was off. He heard Leon's cello, a violin, and, he thought, a viola, but it sounded less—something was missing. It was still beautiful, but it sounded somehow diminished. Maybe one of the violinists had gotten sick, David thought. He had been following the news like everyone else, but no one in the city was particularly concerned. Schools remained open. Bars were packed. Broadway played on.

He sat on the sofa and listened to an unfamiliar piece. Sometime after noon, the music stopped, and the chairs moved again. David went to his bedroom window to see who was leaving. He saw the spry violinist marking time with his cane as he walked south toward his apartment. Then he saw one of the old men who lived across the street walk past the building's canopy. That must be the violist, David thought, because he was sure he had heard a lower-tone string instrument.

The old man looked both ways before crossing. He walked across the street and held tightly to the railing as he climbed the stoop without the aid of his companion. His gait seemed sad—or so David thought. David was feeling sad because he had always seen the two men together. Something was wrong seeing only one.

Later that day, he ran into Leon in the laundry room.

"Your group sounded different today," David said as he loaded a machine next to Leon.

"You have a good ear. Herbert is gone," Leon said. Seeing David's crestfallen face, Leon quickly added, "Gone upstate. He has a grandniece who insisted he get out of the city. She's nervous about this virus. It's supposed to have our names on it."

"The elderly are most at risk. That is what they say," David replied as he poured detergent into the machine. "It makes sense to leave."

"Bull," Leon said, pulling clothes from the dryer. "We're all in our eighties. We survived purges, wars, and AIDS. Christ, we survived Giuliani! A virus isn't going to chase us from our homes."

"I like your spirit, but this could get bad," David said. "We probably shouldn't be standing this close."

"It's just an excuse for the snooty people to not get in the elevator with me."

"I wouldn't say that," David said defensively.

"That's why I did. I'll be careful, but music is life—it's my life. Kill the music, and you kill me. Herbert will be back. In the meantime, trios are fine. Between you and me, Herbert tended to get lax with his personal hygiene. It's refreshing without him, if you know what I mean."

David nodded. He was in the same place he was weeks earlier, unsure if Leon was joking or serious, because he didn't know him well enough. Leon pulled the last of his laundry from the dryer and stuffed it into a laundry bag.

"I'll see you around, Davey."

David wanted to correct Leon; he disliked being called Davey, but he let it go. He turned back to the washing machine. As he pulled his cash card from the machine, he heard the elevator open and close. When he turned around, he saw a neighbor from the seventh floor at the door. She let out a shriek. It might have been louder if not for the mask. She was also wearing rubber gloves.

"I was surprised to see someone," she said, embarrassed. "I'll let you finish."

"I'm just about done," David said. "All the other machines are free. I can't remember when so many machines were free on a workday afternoon. Usually, there is some cleaning lady filling them all up."

"A lot of people are leaving town, going to their country homes," she said, still standing in the doorway. "My husband and I are heading to our farm in Connecticut tomorrow. Just wanted to get the laundry done first."

As David approached the doorway, the woman stepped back and up the hall. David smiled. "Well, stay safe," he said from the elevator cab as she started to move away from where he had been standing. As the doors closed, he realized people were now doing the "Fred and Ginger."

✳ ✳ ✳

The ambulance siren pierced the afternoon quiet. David looked out his window and saw it had stopped across the street. The view was slightly obscured now that the trees were just beginning to bloom. EMTs got out of the vehicle with medical equipment and a gurney and went into the brownstone where Herbert and the other old musician lived. A couple stood on the opposite corner looking at the scene. David noticed a few neighbors were looking out their windows as he was.

The EMTs came down the stoop. There was a man on the gurney with an oxygen mask or something similar on his face. David wasn't sure, given the distance, but he thought it was the violist. The EMTs lifted the gurney into the back of the ambulance. The siren started anew. The ambulance pulled away. Silence fell on the street.

David wanted to do something, but he wasn't sure what to do. He didn't want to knock on Leon's door and ask whether his friend had just been taken away. What if Leon didn't know? What if he did? He couldn't comfort him and go inside Leon's apartment if he had had close contact with someone infected with the virus. He decided to wait and see. Tomorrow at 11, he would know for sure. If the music continued, all would be OK.

David needed the music to continue. It surprised him how much it mattered to him. Usually, not one to give in to the anxiety of the moment, the ambulance siren made it feel all too real.

David stopped working the next day at 10:30. He looked at his watch like an anxious bridegroom, realizing he might be stood up at the altar. At 11, he heard a shuffle. Not much of a noise, but something was being moved around.

He heard Leon's cello clearly, but the violin was heavily muffled. David went to the window and opened it. The unseasonably warm March air felt good. David could see the spry violinist leaning out of an open window on the fourth floor of the brownstone across the street. The violinist was playing to Leon, who must have opened his window as well.

At 7 p.m., people banged pots and made noise on the streets in the city. On social media, David had seen housing projects in Italy where neighbors stood on balconies or hung out windows and sang popular tunes. This was not that. It was only two old men—a cellist and a violinist playing a soulful duet.

Other windows opened along the street. Some of the faces were old, some young—none were familiar to David. It was as if the brownstones and apartment buildings on his tree-lined street had turned themselves inside out. No longer showing their facades but rather exposing the lives lived behind the stone.

Leon and his friend—David wasn't sure if he ever knew the name of the violinist who waved his cane like a conductor's baton—played to one another, each from a window, the sounds of their instruments meeting somewhere above the street. The concert lasted only thirty minutes. The logistics of leaning out a window must have been trying for the old violinist.

When the two men finished playing, David burst into applause, as did the other people leaning out their windows. Probably some of them had heard the quartet in warmer and better times, when they were on the street looking up at Leon's apartment. There was no one on the street today.

The window recitals continued for another two weeks, and then another siren sounded across the street. The ambulance, the EMTs—it was too familiar, not just on David's street, but in other neighborhoods, in other states. David was sure it was the violinist. He wanted a definitive sign, as if the old man on the gurney with the mask on his face would raise his cane and beat out a rhythm as the EMTs lifted him into the ambulance.

But there was no sign. The following day, David heard Leon's cello. It sounded like Chopin, one of the piano preludes, David thought. It was a sad piece, funereal. David knew he had heard this on a piano, but the piano didn't do it justice. The cello humanized the prelude. It was as if Leon, through his instrument, was pleading to God, reciting a psalm that needed no text.

David sat on the floor of his living room, as directly below Leon's instrument as he could surmise from the sound. There were no words for his emotions. David knew that he would likely be fine through this crisis; he was young, healthy, and stubborn enough to endure.

He began to cry as a child cries, a downward slide of emotion that gains speed the farther it goes down the steep slope. David didn't know when he would stop. He could not stop. And then he did. Leon had ceased playing for some time, and David became angry with himself for getting so lost in his own emotions that he had not savored the music that morning. What if today were the last day?

It was not. Leon played for another week. The musician who didn't want to play solos in his old age embraced his new reality. The music was all sad. David knew he could not see Leon, but he went upstairs to the sixth floor and slipped a note under Leon's door. He didn't want to knock because he was afraid Leon might be resting.

The next day, there was a note under David's door. "Davey," it began. David smiled and winced. "Thank you for the note. I am doing OK. I have plenty of food. I have arranged to have it delivered to my door. Your offer is appreciated. I had some sad news from Herbert's family. He passed yesterday. He was 83. It was a good life.

"When you're young, you don't see the ending, but the ending is always there. It's like a piece of music. It has an ending. Beethoven got it right. His last symphony isn't just the best symphony. He ends it big. Ode to Joy. The ending can be more exciting than the middle or beginning.

"Don't know why I'm sharing all this. Probably because you always seemed like a nice man who didn't have enough friends. Stop playing solos. Make a quartet. That's my advice, Davey. You're too young for solos. Make a quartet.

"Best, Leon—by the way, I know you don't like to be called 'Davey.' You need to be needled."

David read the note several times. There was something hopeful about Leon's note, even though Leon and he knew that the odds were not in Leon's favor. Leon saw an end not just to life, but to the virus.

Intellectually, David knew the virus would eventually become less lethal. Maybe it wouldn't go away completely, but go into hiding like racism, homophobia, and fascism, only to resurface generations years later in a new form. It or something else would come back in another 100 years, if he were lucky, or in a generation or two, if he were not. But that was still some time in the future. People were dying now. Nearly 800 people a day in the city.

When would it all end, David thought. As to the music, the answer was four more days. Then silence. A cold silence, as if a heavy snowfall had blanketed the floor above which once vibrated with music.

A note was posted in the elevator three weeks later stating that longtime resident Leon Schneider had passed. His death was attributed to the virus. David assumed Leon must have gone to an ER and been admitted to a hospital, where he died.

The day after learning of Leon's death, David got up as usual and began writing. After some time had passed, he opened his window and looked down at the street. It was late April and warm. There should have been children with their parents going to school. But all the schools were closed.

He looked for the old lady with the walker, but he hadn't seen her since mid-March. The female jogger who used to chat with her still sprinted by early each day; nothing had stopped her stride. He saw a young man carrying groceries walking across the street. The frog and Burberry umbrellas had disappeared when his apartment building mostly emptied out. There was no traffic—no cars looking for parking spaces. Fred and Ginger were dead.

David glanced at his watch. It was past noon. He had worked through the entire morning, no music from above to interrupt him.

He leaned his head slightly out the window to take in the air. It was a clear day. A benefit of the ban on most travel was less pollution. The sky was cloudless, a brilliant blue. The trees were now all green; their blossoms had fallen.

It was quiet. So damn quiet, David thought. He read somewhere that sound waves eventually become another form of energy. Maybe the late April warmth was what had become of the quartet's music. It was all around him. He breathed it in through the window.

"Make a quartet," David said aloud into the stillness. "Make a quartet."

The only sound was the rustle of the breeze through the leaves. A gust swept up a few of the remaining blossoms on the sidewalk. David watched four of them pass his window. They swirled before him in the warm air and then were gone.

It had been an early spring.

Last Call for Don

Don was dead. That was still a fact 17 months after, well, the fact. His picture sat on the piano where the tip bowl usually was. Alan thought they should have kept the tip bowl there. Don would have liked that. But Don was dead, and Don, Alan was sure, did not like being dead more than the placement of the tip bowl on the piano. So what did it matter about the tip bowl anyway?

Dead or not, Alan knew Don would like there to be a cake. A big cake. That was another issue with Don—one from a long, long list of real and imagined grievances with The Edwardian.

Over the years, Alan had heard them all. But the cake thing was a religion with Don. It was never big enough. Yeah, that sounds like a bad joke. Well, maybe it could be in another context, but the size of the birthday cake The Edwardian brought out on Don's birthday every year mattered more to Don than the size of a man's dick. A therapist would have something to say about that, for sure. Alan mused that several shrinks had something to say about that to Don, who had been in therapy for as long as Alan had known him. And that was a long time.

A two-man comedy routine began playing in Alan's mind about how therapy was as addictive as a narcotic:

Man 1: "I want to break with my therapist."

Man 2: "Drop dead."

Man 1: "That was harsh. It was only a question. How do I break with my therapist?"

Man 2: "Your first statement was not a question. It was a statement."

Man 1: "You're missing the point. How do I break with my therapist?"

Man 2: "Like I said now—twice. Drop dead."

Man 1: "You're pissing me off."

Man 2: "I'm pissing you off? You asked, 'How do you break with a therapist?'"

Man 1: "Yes."

Man 2: "Drop dead."

It would go on like that for some time, Alan imagined, until finally Man 1 realized the only way to break with a therapist was to drop dead, which he would then do out of exasperation. Alan liked his comedy dark, and truth be told, not all that funny. Alan was a sucker for Chekhov. He was also in therapy.

The back room was empty. It was not yet 6 p.m., which was early for The Edwardian crowd, but nothing was the same anymore. Or at least, not yet, some 18 months after this second plague in Alan's lifetime had hit. It felt dangerous to be inside the bar without a mask, like being convinced by a very hot, muscular man to lie down on your stomach while he pounded you without a condom. There was PrEP. And there were COVID vaccines now. But did either come with a 100 percent guarantee?

It was unavoidable, this thinking about death, about the 800-a-day-deaths in the beginning, back when Don died. He had played that last big weekend before everything shut down. Alan had stopped going out to places like The Edwardian a few weeks earlier. Alan was cautious by nature. That got him through the '80s and the '90s, so he could now be working his way through his 60s.

Not Don. There was irony for you. Don had lasted long enough to receive the magic drugs that saved him from death 20 years earlier. But eventually, the piper must be paid, like in those film franchises where a group of teens cheat death on a roller coaster or a plane only to fall victim to some other fatal occurrence.

Alan thought, although he did know that part of Don's history, that Don had always assumed he could dodge the bullets even back in the early '90s. But he couldn't then; that virus found him. So, it was no different in the spring of 2020. The new virus found him, and this one wouldn't take "no" for an answer.

Alan looked at the text in his phone dated March 16, 2020:

"I'm okay. Already stir crazy, though. Out of work for at least 8 weeks. Ugh! Hope you're holding up OK."

That was the last text message. Five weeks later, Don was dead. Alan had texted him frequently after that first text at the beginning of lockdown. No response. The weeks went by, sirens screamed through the streets, and pots banged at dinner time. The pot-banging was more than a communal event celebrating first responders and healthcare workers. It was also a loud reminder of where we all were and where we might end up: in a refrigerated truck in the back of a filled-up mortuary somewhere in a downtrodden part of Queens.

In New York City in the spring of 2020, Broadway theaters were empty, but funeral homes were SRO, horizontally speaking.

When Alan finally tried a landline number he had for Don five weeks into lockdown, he feared the worst. When a woman answered, he knew his fears were about to be confirmed. She was a friend of Don's who was staying in his apartment. Don was dead, dead that morning.

The months passed. New York Governor Cuomo gave daily televised updates. Trump told people to drink bleach, or something to that effect.

Fauci was glorified. Fauci was vilified.

Through my Fauci, through my Fauci, through my most grievous Fauci.

The dead piled up. Crime rose.

Shots in the arm.

Shots in the streets.

America had gone crazy, and the only thing muted was your co-worker talking without sound on Zoom.

To Alan, now in September 2021, standing with a drink in the backroom of The Edwardian, it felt surreal, as if someone else had lived through it—a backstory in a novel about post-World War I New York City. But it was Alan's backstory to process. Don didn't have that burden. No backstory. Just dead.

The Edwardian was a sanctuary for Alan, Don, and the thousands of queer people who passed through the three main-floor rooms of the old brownstone. The bar's name was a nod to its pretensions, and perhaps to the townhome's history. From its birth, The Edwardian lived in the past—a place somewhere between Miss Havisham's dining room and Belle Reve.

No one took that all in on their first visit, or at least back when Alan first came to The Edwardian nearly 30 years ago.

Before he moved to New York, Alan had heard about The Edwardian from his friends in Los Angeles, Robbie and Jim. They said The Edwardian attracted his kind of crowd—mostly professional men in suits, a good mix of ages, and there was a piano in the back. The Edwardian wasn't like those cheesy Village piano bars where everyone tries to be discovered singing the same goddamn songs from *Les Miz*, unaware that most of the patrons were people like themselves: struggling actors with little money. The Guffmans they were waiting for would mostly be bridge-and-tunnel gays, singing out their Louise, or straight people from Ohio wanting to look at "the gays" in their natural habitat, which they had been told was a subterranean piano bar with little ventilation. The Edwardian was nothing like that.

Alan remembered walking east toward the bar that first night. He knew he was close because he saw a small cluster of suited men standing on the sidewalk smoking and talking. They glanced at him as he walked past toward the steps leading up into the bar. Alan was new meat.

The polished brass plaque announcing it was The Edwardian to the right of the door was unnecessary because the men on the street gave it away, just as the politically incorrect jockeys lining the wrought iron railings of the now-defunct 21 Club once had for that establishment. Up the stairs, Alan went. A tall, bald man in an impeccable grey suit, white shirt, and bright red tie and matching pocket square stood sentry. He had a small clicker that counted the men as each entered.

"Welcome to The Edwardian," the man said. He looked at his people counter and added, "69."

"Thank you," Alan said. "I'm not sure I'm that flexible anymore."

One of the men on the street heard Alan and said, "I could fix that."

Alan realized that Robbie and Jim had been right; these were his people. He walked into the foyer. The air shifted immediately from the coolness of late April to a sultry July. This was the 1990s, and people still smoked inside bars. A grayish fog was drawn into the air filters in the ceiling, zapping like insect traps catching flies. Two men, around 40, were heading out as Alan was walking in. They brushed against him, both smelling of gin and cologne.

Alan didn't smoke, but he liked his gin almost as much as his men—slightly scented. He took in a deep breath and pressed further into the front room of The Edwardian. Men in suits everywhere. To his left, a long bar coursed the length of the room. Men of various shapes and ages pressed against the men who had snagged coveted seats along the bar. Conversations were loud. Cosmos and martinis were the libations of choice. Lit cigarettes made the walk slightly dangerous as Alan moved through The Edwardian's first gauntlet. Men stood on his right against a half-wall that revealed a stairway downstairs.

He took in the faces as he walked: *Handsome. Average. Cute. Too old. Too drunk. My type, but unattainable. Crazy young. Crazy. I could marry him. Why is he fanning himself with a Madame Butterfly fan, and where can I get one?* Alan had some unresolved issues.

As Alan moved further toward the back of the bar, he saw a line down the stairs that was divided by a long brass railing. Men going up on one side; men going down on the other; a metaphor for the mating rituals underway. He learned later there was a pay phone—it was still the '90s—and an ATM at the bottom of the stairs, in addition to a coat check. Alan pressed on.

An anteroom opened up with a small sofa and chairs to his right. The cigarette haze was thicker here, like a Los Angeles valley depression where the air gets trapped.

Three men were chatting and drinking on a sofa that could comfortably seat two. A young guy, maybe 24 and polished like a cubic zirconia, sat at one end of the sofa. He had longish black hair that fell onto the collar of a black-and-gold Versace shirt, open low, revealing a tanned chest covered in thick dark hair. He sat next to an older balding man—older than Alan, at least—who was enjoying the view. That man was dressed in a dark pinstripe suit. His blue dress shirt was lightly splotched with sweat, his tie slightly askew, and his ruby bejeweled right hand stroked the Versace's upper thigh. To the older man's left sat another man, about the same age as the Versace, but smaller. Blond, with light-brown four-day stubble, he wore Dolce & Gabbana, revealing a smooth chest adorned with too much jewelry.

The two young men stood out, not so much for their youth or even looks, but for their aggressiveness. Even their clothes shouted above the din. The Versace and Dolce & Gabbana pressed against the older, balding, suited, slightly sweaty man in the center of the small couch like two sides of a panini press onto a caprese sandwich.

Other men crammed into the anteroom, either seated on the two remaining chairs or standing along a wall that led to a small hallway to Alan's left. The restrooms were there, and the men closest to the restroom doors appeared to be waiting for their turn—their turn for what Alan did not know, but he was no prude.

Boys will be boys. Men will be men. And gay men could be either, depending on what the situation demanded. There were pheromones in the Marlboro-infused air and God-knows-what on the carpet. Alan pressed further still into the back room, a middle-aged Alice going down the rabbit hole.

The back room was large, with walls papered in a deep red brocade that matched the flushed faces of the patrons. The crown moldings were gold, and the carpet, an explosion of floral design, likely brighter once but now showed the effects of time, feet, alcohol, and cigarettes. There was something about the décor of the backroom of The Edwardian that made Alan feel there should be a casket somewhere.

A bar to his right ran the length of the room and was as crowded as the one in front, but the vibe was different. The front room, by comparison, was subdued. The back room was more joyous. There was a good time to be had here, and it didn't depend on the transactional currency demanded by the Versace and Dolce & Gabbana. Alan studied the faces and shapes of men. If life was indeed a banquet, as Auntie Mame said, no gay man was starving to death at The Edwardian.

There was something for everyone at this buffet but think twice about anything that looked like it had been sitting out too long without proper refrigeration, Alan thought to himself, chuckling at his own cleverness. Alan clutched his cleverness like a string of pearls.

The bartenders were all busy, pouring drinks while chatting with the many regulars whom Alan quickly determined he would soon join. He could feel this was his place as clearly as he felt the occasional stray hand grab at his ass as he pushed into the center of the back room.

Sofas lined the wall opposite the long bar and filled with characters yet to be defined. Straight ahead was an ornate, three-drawer chest with a large floral display that didn't know quite where to go. Alan felt the flowers were a metaphor for himself. Where should he go? It didn't take him long to figure that out.

The pulse of the room was in the back left corner, coming from a large ebony grand piano. Around the piano, men stood and sang. A very old man who resembled a diminutive Adolf Hitler—if Hitler had worn short-sleeved shirts and suspenders—cradled a Bud Light. A wide, tall, 60-ish man in a blue suit tapped coins on the Lucite cover over the piano lid like Ann Miller dancing on a gigantic can of soup. An open-shirted man, about 48 in chest size and age, with a mustache big enough to have its own zip code, had his arm around a much smaller man who barely looked legal age as they sang "Hello Dolly." Three men in their 30s who screamed Fire Island house share belted, "I see the room swaying," as they sloshed cosmos, spilling them on each other without concern. A cute chorus-boy type, nearing 30, with rolled-up shirtsleeves exposing muscular forearms and flashing a youthful grin that was attracting the attention of the boys from The Pines and the ersatz führer, sang with confidence. In all, nine men had secured spots around the sides of the piano.

There was a second row behind them, which was notable because it included a man with a ventriloquist's dummy. Alan assumed at least one half of the duo was gay.

At the center of this eclectic group was Don at the piano. It was Thursday night at The Edwardian, but it was like Saturday night anywhere else in the world. Alan had never experienced anything like this. There was incredible energy in the room, and Don was the turbine generating the power. His hands moved rapidly on the keyboard as if it were all random, but there was nothing random about it. The notes were spot on as Don flayed his arms up and down in exaggerated fashion, while he crouched lower and lower until only his head almost touched the keyboard. He was Liberace, he was Chico Marx—he was 100 percent Don.

Of course, Alan didn't know any of that back then.

Don's face, while not exceptional, was expressive. It responded to both good and poor singers who took turns at an open microphone during Don's sets. Don wasn't rude to anyone that first night; honestly, he was never rude during the years Alan visited The Edwardian. But Alan could see what Don thought when someone sang terribly. His face would contort into exaggerated grimaces that could effortlessly transform into a grin before the singer was much the wiser.

And all would be forgiven if the offensive singer dropped a dollar or two into the tip bowl. It wasn't the size of the tip—it's not like his birthday cakes—that mattered to Don; a tip of any amount showed respect.

That was key to understanding Don and accepting him as a friend. You had to fully comprehend his endless need to feel respected and appreciated. He was complicated and often sad, but none of that was visible when he was behind the piano.

Don's face said, "Come on my ride. I'm not Mr. Toad, and this isn't Disneyland. It's something better. It's a ride that lasts as long as I play, and, on some nights, it will last longer when the guy who stood next to you at my piano, who loved the way you sang, 'Fifty Percent' from *Ballroom*, and began feeling you up by midnight, ended up in your bed. I can make that happen. I can make anything happen behind a piano."

And Don could, except perhaps for making lasting happiness for himself.

Alan watched Don from a distance that first night. Weeks passed before he moved through the ranks of the regulars and became a fixture himself, usually standing across from Hitler with the Bud Light and, if Alan was lucky, next to the 30-something guy with the great forearms whose name he would later learn was Sam. On that first night, Alan watched Don control the room.

Everyone in the back room seemed to be there for Don. That was the case 18 months ago when the virus came to The Edwardian. And now, Don was dead, and only his picture sat on the piano where the tip bowl should be.

Alan looked around the back room. It was starting to fill up. He didn't recognize most of the faces. Where were the other regulars? The "Donettes," the quartet of silver-haired men from somewhere deep in Jersey who harmonized backup to "Mr. Sandman"? Big Jim, who sang "Rose's Turn" like the second coming of Ethel Merman in the middle of the backroom without a microphone or a sense of pitch? Or Little Jim who couldn't sing his way out of a paper bag and was once banned from The Edwardian for three months after telling a reporter doing a feature on the bar that it was a place for hustlers, which was neither entirely true nor false—it just depended on your point of view on how many hustlers can fit on the head of a pin? And since Little Jim was not Jesuitical, Jellicle, or evangelical but rather just a little queer man with no talent, he found himself drinking at The Crow in the West Village from January through March of 2007.

And then there was the dummy with the ventriloquist. Where were they? Perhaps one of them had died?

That was the thing about now. Who died, who lived, and who got to take their spot around the piano? It wouldn't be the same without Don. It was hard to believe anything would be the same again. Alan remembered that was the way he thought back when AIDS was consuming his peers.

People either pass on or move on. If you did the latter, you could not look back.

The truth was that Alan hadn't been a regular at the piano for some time. He still came to The Edwardian and stopped in the back room to talk with Don, but the piano had lost its glow. It wasn't Don's fault. Don was still Don. The crowd was changing. He and Don were changing. They were getting older, and the crowd was getting younger—not young—but younger than them.

The Donettes hadn't been at the piano in years. They had a falling out with Don. And who hadn't at one time? Then they fell out with one another, and when one or two of them came in without the others, they were adrift in the room, no longer tethered to each other and no longer able to stay afloat in a gay bar where the tides had shifted.

The smoke inside The Edwardian cleared thanks to Mayor Mike Bloomberg, and when the haze lifted, the suits started disappearing as well. It wasn't closing time for The Edwardian; it was closing time for Alan's generation. They could still come to The Edwardian, maybe hook up every now and then, but they were now looking for something else—someone else—and they were old enough to know they wouldn't find it at The Edwardian.

Don and Alan talked about that a few months before the world ended. It was the Sunday after New Year's Day 2020, and the bar was quiet.

"I like it this way," Don said. "It's family night," he added, smiling as he played some Henry Mancini. Don liked to play Mancini when the room was not crowded.

"I guess," Alan answered. He was wistful. New Year's did that to Alan. It was a marker that another year had passed. "I guess it will be empty. People are still partied-out from Tuesday night. I stopped coming here on New Year's Eve at least a decade ago."

"I didn't have to play this year, because it was a Tuesday," Don said as he played "Moon River." "It's no fun. Amateur drinkers' night, and no one tips well because they have a cover at the door. Like that makes me money," Don added with that my-birthday-cake-wasn't-big-enough face. "Do you want to sing tonight?" he asked.

"Maybe. I don't enjoy singing that much anymore here. The crowd is different."

"I know, but you've got to get your Dolly Levi going before the parade passes you by." Don effortlessly switched to the song from *Hello Dolly!* "Ephrem, show him a sign," Don added in a bad imitation of Carol Channing. Or it might have been a good imitation of Carol Channing from when she had become a caricature of herself.

"Maybe someone will paint the shutters forest green," Alan replied.

"They don't paint anything here that isn't red. Red and gold. Red and gold." Don moved on to "It Only Takes a Moment," from the same show. "I hear you. Most of these guys don't know the lyrics to anything anymore. They look at the words on their phone. It's like I'm not even here. We're invisible to this new crowd."

"I am invisible," Alan said. "You make the party happen."

"Vodka and pharmaceuticals make the party happen," Don replied as he segued into "Put on Your Sunday Clothes." "I keep the rhythm. I'm like a metronome."

"No one here knows what that is."

"You're probably right, but whether they know it or not, someone is always marking the tempo."

"That's kind of existential for The Edwardian. I never took you for a philosopher. A Philistine, maybe, but not a philosopher."

"I'm a man of many talents. I am amphibious."

"Amphibious?"

"I was playing this audition once, and the casting director asked the singer auditioning if he could move to the left. The singer moved to the right so the director yelled out, 'Your other left,' to which the singer said, 'I get confused because I can use my right and left interchangeably. I am amphibious.'"

"You made that up. No one said that."

"If you have played for as many auditions as I have in New York City, you will have heard every variation of English imaginable and then some. It's the only thing that makes the process entertaining."

"You should have your own bar, a place where people come to just sit and listen to you."

"I used to, you know."

"When? Where?"

"Back in the early '80s. I was the star on a cruise ship. There was a cocktail room on the ship, and I played every evening. It was a very high-end, Cole Porter-like space. It was heaven."

"What happened?"

"HIV. They tested everyone. I found out that I was positive. They found out that I was positive. And they fired me."

"Was that legal?"

"Most cruise ships don't sail under US flags, and I don't think it would have mattered if it were a US ship. It was a tough time. I didn't know I had it...I didn't want to know if I had it because there was nothing to be done except to die. So, I found out I had it and got fired at the same time."

"That's just horrible."

"That was just how it was back then. You forget with time."

"Or with vodka and pharmaceuticals," Alan said, surveying the room as he stood at the piano.

"It was a bad time. I was a pariah." Don quickly shifted to playing the song, "They Call the Wind Maria," from *Paint Your Wagon*.

"That's a rather bitter musical switch," Alan said, noting the pun in titles.

"They call the infected 'pariah, pariah,'" Don sang off mic. "Anyway, I was out of a job, I cried for about a month, and then I pulled myself up by my jockstraps…"

"It's bootstraps," Alan corrected with a sour smile from the wordplay.

"I was never into cowboys and leather. It was jockstraps," Don added in a lighter tone. "I came to New York, and here I am the toast of Mayfair."

"You're going to switch to *Cabaret*, now, aren't you?"

"You know me too well."

"I don't know about that, Don. I don't think anyone really knows the real you. Maybe that is why we keep coming here. We want to figure it out."

"Now who is being existential?"

"Do you ever think the end of *Cabaret* applies to us?"

"What in the ending?" Don was now fully committed to the Kander and Ebb musical on the keyboard.

"At the end, Cliff says, 'There was a cabaret, and there was a master of ceremonies. And there was a city called Berlin, in a country called Germany. It was the end of the world, and I was dancing with Sally Bowles, and we were both fast asleep.' Maybe that's us here in our gay bars, dancing away the threats—the insanity outside these walls—believing that nothing can touch us here."

"Honey, I can touch you here and there," a stranger said who had walked up to the piano and grabbed Alan's ass.

"Excuse me?" Alan said, startled and annoyed. The stranger was unfazed.

"Showtime!" Don said loudly into the microphone and began playing the song "Cabaret." He winked at Alan, who moved away from the stranger, who immediately took his spot at the piano. The contemplative moment was over. Alan walked back to the front room.

Alan must have spoken to Don after that night, but he couldn't recall when or what they might have said. That was their last meaningful conversation before the lockdown, before the end of the world.

The back room was filling up now. It felt uncomfortably crowded, and Alan wondered if this would turn out to be a superspreader event—an ironic outcome for a memorial to someone whose death was caused by a superspreader event. But Alan wasn't leaving yet. He needed to hear the tributes. He needed to hear the songs.

Someone Alan did not recognize sat at the piano. He said he knew Don well, but Alan could not recall ever seeing him at The Edwardian. Maybe it was before his time, Alan thought. The pianist started playing, and in between songs, people Alan did not recognize—mostly younger men—took the microphone to say something neither meaningful nor insightful about Don. They had sung with him on some night or nights. They were the new generation. They were the generation that would grow old long after Alan had become cold, like Don was now.

Then he would be fast asleep, Alan thought. He wanted to leave, but he also wanted a sign. He wanted forest green shutters. "Ephraim, give me a sign," Alan said out loud.

"I always thought you were a closet Dolly," said a familiar voice behind Alan. It was Sam, a now-50-something younger man with still-great forearms.

"My God, I am so happy to see you," Alan said, giving Sam a big hug, which was out of character for Alan. He started to cry and was immediately embarrassed.

"It's OK," Sam said, patting Alan's back as he released him from the hug. "That's what this is all about, you know?"

"I never cry."

"You never hugged me before."

"I'm sorry, I'm a little emotional tonight. Are you here with someone? I haven't seen you in so long. I assumed you had a partner."

"I did. Not anymore. I used to be with Robert."

"Robert?"

"You know Robert." Sam mimicked the coins being tapped on the piano top.

"You were with that Robert?"

"Don't say it that way."

"It's just that…"

"Just that, what? You expected me to be with someone younger?"

"I don't know. Someone with less coinage."

They both laughed.

"He could do that with a credit card, as well."

"I don't have a response," Alan said.

"It was fucking annoying, let me tell you," Sam said, laughing, ensuring that the moment stayed light. "He was a man of many talents, but tap was not one."

"Sorry."

"Don't be. We broke up before the pandemic. He moved to Wilton Manors outside Fort Lauderdale."

"Never been."

"It's not for everybody."

"It's not for me. Don liked it, though. He had friends with a house down there and he would go down for a week in February. Some guys he met on a game night. *Settlers of Rattan.*"

"It's *Catan*."

"Are you sure?"

"Yes, I am sure," Sam said, laughing. "That was sacred to Don."

"I guess that is why he never asked me back to game night. I thought it was about the people who built those woven inserts in furniture that always break through."

"Hah, hah, hah," Sam replied with a wry smile. "You didn't say that to Don, did you?"

"No, I did not. I still wanted to be able to sing at the piano."

"Smart man."

"I try," Alan said, beginning to wonder if he and Sam were having a moment. He shrugged it off. "So, is this sad or what?" he said, gesturing around the room.

"I was thinking the same thing before I saw you," Sam said. "I know it's a memorial and it is supposed to be sad, but not this way. This is sad," he said, elongating the vowel clear down to 48th Street. "Don would not like this maudlin approach."

"And who are these people?"

"Exactly. I don't recognize most of them."

"They were latecomers to the party, I suppose."

"Or we left the party early."

"Maybe. Maybe. I didn't think I left the party, but I guess I have been pushed back from the action for some time. It took Don dying for me to notice that he might have been the only glue holding this place together for me."

"OK," Sam said firmly. "Now, you are sounding sad. None of that. We survived."

"Yes, we survived. I survived two plagues."

"I wasn't old enough to be affected by the first one. It must be strange to be on the other side twice."

"That sounds like a war."

"Wasn't it?"

"Not a war. The plagues were not wars—struggles, I think. Forces of nature battling people. Like a Greek myth without a lot of shirtless Athenians and Spartans."

"Speak for yourself. I live in Astoria."

"Hah, hah, hah," Alan responded, mimicking Sam's earlier laugh, acknowledging the large Greek population in that part of Queens. "Seriously, the only way to process what has happened now and then is to look to the Greeks. It's bigger than us. It's the gods versus mortals— something epic and tragic, and maybe sometime far away from now, it will have a dignity and a beauty."

"You're a romantic, Alan."

"Maybe. Don wasn't, though."

"No, he wasn't," Sam agreed. "He wanted romance, but he didn't buy into the magic of it. He was always too cynical. Tragic. Something else for the Greeks."

"Are you selling real estate in Astoria?" Alan asked, trying to sound playful.

"I do sell real estate."

"I was making a joke."

"I know," Sam said. "We have known each other for what? Decades? We have never talked about ourselves much."

"I guess not. You were 'All the Things You Are.'"

"And you were 'Trolley Song,'" Sam replied with a smile. "Don reduced us to our songs."

"He did," Alan said, also smiling. "Well, we were more than a signature song."

"We *are* more than our signature songs," Sam responded, putting an emphasis on the verb. "It was easier to know all of us by our songs—for him and for us."

"Easier, but maybe not smarter," Alan said. "Maybe there was something more to Little Jim than 'Send in the Clowns.'"

They looked at each other and burst out laughing.

"No, there wasn't," Sam said. "He was so bad." Sam stretched out the vowel like it was Gumby in the hands of an evil masseuse. "I wish this weren't so wrong. I don't recognize anyone here, except you."

"Where's the guy with the bitchy puppet? Remember him?"

"Do I ever. He used to think I was his dummy and try to put his hand up my ass."

"You're kidding?"

"You don't make that up. After the third time he tried, I turned to him and said, 'You do that one more time, and I will shove that puppet of yours so far up your butt it will be talking out of your ass for a week.'"

"What did he say to that?"

"Nothing," Sam replied and then paused with a broad smile and added, "but the puppet, lord what he said. What a mouth on him."

They both laughed loudly again. A stranger walked past them and said with concerted consternation, "It's a memorial. Show some respect."

Alan and Sam looked at each other and laughed again.

Alan glanced over at the offended stranger, now at the bar. "Talk about a puppet up your ass."

"You are evil," Sam said, squeezing Alan's arm.

"I don't know about that," he said, finding himself increasingly attracted to this middle-aged version of his long-ago bar crush. "Why didn't we ever talk?"

"It used to be different here. I was different. And there was so little oxygen in the room when Don was playing. He was the center of everything."

"And now, he is where the tip bowl should be," Alan said, pointing to Don's picture on the piano.

"That is so wrong. Not even a good picture of Don. He looks so introspective—like he knew he was dead."

They both fell silent.

Alan spoke first. "Do you think before the pandemic, we were all dancing with someone and yet we were fast asleep?"

"You mean like in *Cabaret*?" Sam asked. "Dancing with Sally Bowles while the world turned black and Don was our emcee."

"Exactly," Alan said, impressed that Sam got the reference. "I was thinking about that earlier. That was my last real conversation with Don before everything changed."

"Here we are, less than two years later, back in the same place," Sam said, looking around the back room. "I have spent so much time here. I met Robert here. I was young here."

"You're still young," Alan interrupted.

"Younger than you," Sam said, smiling as he squeezed Alan's arm to show he meant it in a caring way. "We both have grown older. To your point, we're always going to be dancing with someone while the world keeps moving forward, for better or worse. We can't see all the evil out there, and even if we did, there are forces you cannot escape."

"Forces of nature, yes. Forces of men, I'm not so sure."

"We're not talking about the plague and Don anymore."

"We are. Don stayed here, inside this red-and-gold funeral home, for about 30 years. He only left it because he died."

"A prisoner inside a funeral home freed by death. No wonder there is no cake," Sam added, making a joke about Don and his never-big-enough-birthday cakes that Alan didn't catch. "We do the best we can, Alan," Sam added, realizing Alan was lost and needed a guide. "It's like when we sing at the mic. We do our best in the moment. Sometimes, that's all it comes down to. Don could have been more, could have been a contender," Sam said with a slight Brando inflection, "but Don was Don and Jesus, Alan, he gave us a good time."

"Yes," Alan replied. They both fell silent again but were now standing closer to one another, neither dancing nor fast asleep.

More unfamiliar singers approached the microphone. Then a silver-haired man made his way past them toward the piano.

"I recognize him," Sam said. "What's his name?"

"I'm not sure," Alan said. "He looks familiar."

Another man of similar age soon followed, then another and another. At first, they did not hug or even touch, but they looked at each other with such intensity that both Alan and Sam were spellbound. The four silver-haired men stood silently by the piano, one next to the other for what seemed like an eternity, and then suddenly the great chunk of ice melted, leaving only tears.

"It's the Donettes," Alan said. "They came back. They came back for Don."

"They haven't been here together in maybe a decade," Sam replied. "I used to love their choreography to 'Mr. Sandman.'"

"So did I," Alan said. "Do you think they will sing?"

"Does it matter? We don't sound the way we did fifteen years ago. Better we hear them in memory."

"I am glad they are here," Alan replied. "I don't need the song."

"Don would be pleased."

"He would."

"But he would have liked them to have cake—a big cake," Sam added. This time, Alan got the reference.

"I was thinking just that when I came in tonight. Don was all about the big birthday cake."

"It was never big enough," Sam said, and they both laughed. Sam locked eyes with Alan. "Alan, or Mr. Trolley Song, do you want to go somewhere and have some cake?"

"Are you asking me out, Sam, or Mr. All The Things You Are?"

"Yes, I am. Let's get out of here. Don would approve."

"Maybe he would. But I feel we haven't said goodbye."

"To a picture, Alan? He's in this room for as long as there is red wallpaper. Time to stop dancing and wake up. Let's go." Sam put his broad arms around Alan, and they hugged.

The two left the backroom as someone began singing from *Hello Dolly!* A new group of men pushed against the piano; few probably knew who the man was in the picture atop the piano, where the tip bowl should have been. But these men sang. They sang.

Alan and Sam walked through the anteroom where three unfamiliar men sat on the two-seat sofa, then passed the bar in the front room, lined with men no longer fearful of the virus. The room was not smoke-filled as it had been decades ago when Alan first came to The Edwardian, so he could see clearly the faces of the men, all searching for something, and maybe some would find it. Maybe Don had been the magic, or maybe The Edwardian gave him the magic. Time would tell. Time always would tell. It was many things, but Time was never silent.

As the two men approached the foyer, Sam felt something grab his butt. He turned around, and it was the bitchy puppet. He hadn't aged, but the hand up his rear was different. It was a different man. The puppet winked at Sam knowingly.

"I guess nothing really changes inside The Edwardian," Sam said to Alan with a smile.

"Do you believe that?" Alan asked.

"I don't know," Sam said, squeezing Alan's arm as they moved outside. "It's time to see what's outside. That's our job. We're the survivors. Time to go outside. Let's get some cake."

"Yes," Alan said, looking back up the steps at the front entrance to The Edwardian with its familiar polished brass plate to the right of the door. As they brushed past two men smoking on the sidewalk, Alan said, "Let's get a really big cake."

The Younger Mr. Wilcox
(With great deference to E.M. Forster)

One may as well begin with Edward's conversation with Gordon.

Brooklyn Heights,
Thursday

"Clive. I always wanted to get it on with Clive." Gordon emphasized his point by waving the olive from his martini in the air, sprinkling tiny droplets of his namesake gin onto Edward's polished table.

"Clive? Get it in on? Are we back in the '80s?" Edward was more annoyed than amused. Gordon's views on literature were like his drinking: messy and all over the place. Edward waved a cocktail napkin at Gordon.

"Don't be such a snob," Gordon said, taking the napkin and wiping away the gin on the table. He crumpled the damp paper and tossed it on the table. "Sometimes you are just too gay for your own good."

"I'm too gay?" Edward asked as he took the moist napkin off the table, wiped the damp surface again with a fresh paper cocktail napkin, and then put both napkins on yet a third clean napkin. "This from a man who wants to get it on with Clive Durham. He's not worth the effort."

"He's hot. The most handsome man in the story." Gordon flashed that smile that said, but if Clive were in Edward's well-appointed living room right now, he, Gordon, would still be the hotter man. It infuriated Edward, who furrowed his brow.

"He's in the closet," Edward said, taking a larger-than-usual sip of his Macallan neat.

"They don't have closets in old English estate homes."

"OK. He's in the wardrobe. Clive is in the wardrobe." Edward's brow was now more creased than his pressed trousers, which could have cut a passerby like a sharpened Shun knife.

"That is not funny or even really coherent," Gordon replied.

"It is both, which is beside the point. Clive marries Anne. He walks away from Maurice, who is more interesting, but not my type."

"Who do you want? Alec Scudder?" Gordon asked.

Edward made a face. "Rough trade. I go to The Edwardian, not The Ballsack."

"La dee da," Gordon said mockingly. "Everybody goes to The Edwardian, now and then. Good drinks. Good piano. Don't knock The Ballsack, Eddie. It has a great backroom."

"Eddie? I will let that pass, Gordo." Edward hated nicknames, really any abbreviated form of anything, including his underwear. It was boxers only for Edward Forsythe. "Not my scene, and I still don't get why no one thinks Ballsack sounds like Balzac."

"Because no one knows who Balzac is except you, Edward," Gordon emphasized the second syllable of his friend's name as if it were a room in a psychiatric facility. "That is why you know nothing about Clive."

"I know he's fictional and he's in the metaphorical closet."

"Who would you have metaphorically, if we are going to be so la dee da?"

"Where does this 'la dee da' come from? Have you been listening to the cast album of *Oliver!* again?"

"That's Oom-Pah-Pah."

"Same thing."

"Not at all. And you're stalling. If it's not Alec Scudder, who?"

"Paul Wilcox."

"Who?"

"Paul Wilcox."

"He's not in *Maurice*."

"No, *Howards End*. He's the younger Wilcox."

"Younger than who?"

"Younger than you. There's Charles, and then there is Paul."

"I don't remember anyone named Paul."

"That's because you only see the movie versions. You should read the books."

"Nobody reads anymore."

"That is not my fault. If you read the book, you would know that Paul Wilcox, with Helen Schlegel, sets the train in motion, moves the whole plot of *Howards End*."

"The train is a nice metaphor—I think they used a train in the movie; I will give you that."

"How kind of you. 'Cake or bread and butter?'"

"What?"

"You're supposed to say, 'Cake is rarely seen at the best houses nowadays.'"

"Even for you, you are not making sense."

"It's dialogue from *The Importance of Being Earnest*—between Cecily and Gwendolen. I was being deliberately obscure. It's Oscar Wilde."

"I know who Oscar Wilde is."

"He wasn't in the closet."

"It didn't do him any good."

"I will acknowledge that. I always thought of us as Jack and Algernon. I am Jack."

"As in jack off?"

"Don't be crude; it is not becoming." Edward had retreated into smugness, which felt as comfortable as the cashmere sweater he was wearing.

"This is infuriating." Gordon placed his now-empty martini glass on the table, deliberately avoiding the coaster just as Cecily had deliberately ignored Gwendolen's food requests. "I don't care about cake or bread and butter. I don't care about Cecily and Gwendolen. Explain Paul Cock."

"It is not Paul Cock." Edward repeated the cocktail napkin ritual and placed Gordon's glass on the coaster. "It is Paul Wilcox. You've seen *Howards End*."

"I don't recall Paul. Ooh, I rhymed."

"La dee da—Christ, you've got me doing it now," Edward said, brow furrowing again. If this continued, he will need to call Dr. Traynor tomorrow to schedule a Botox appointment. "Paul is in the beginning and the ending of the book. He kisses Helen in a flight of passion, regrets it the next day, and goes off to Nigeria."

"That's a little extreme. I would have gone to Sussex."

"You don't even know where Sussex is."

"It doesn't matter. It has handsome men. Prince Harry is the duke of it."

"You are driving me to drink." Edward stood up and poured himself another Scotch. Gordon waved his empty glass. Edward ignored him.

"If you drink, eat something—maybe some cake or bread and butter."

"Why am I friends with you?"

"Because I am cuter than you and I attract men we both want to sleep with when we go out."

Edward relented and began mixing another gin martini for Gordon, which was rather simple to do: pour a generous amount of gin into a pitcher with ice, stir, and then empty it into a glass. Finally, spear an olive on a fancy toothpick and serve. Gordon had a rule when drinking martinis: vermouth would never touch his lips.

"I knew there was a reason," Edward said, handing Gordon the drink. "You have been helpful in that area. Thank you." Edward sat back down in the wing chair opposite Gordon, who was on the sofa. "Paul Wilcox is described as more handsome than Charles Wilcox by E.M. Forster. Charles in the film version of *Howards End* was played by the same actor who portrayed Maurice Hall in the film version of *Maurice*."

"I remember him. Clive was hotter."

"Paul, in the film version, is dreamy."

"Dreamy? Dreamy? Do they live in Howards End or Malibu Barbie's Dream House?"

"Don't make fun of me. I have a Master's in Literature."

"La dee..."

"Stop it right there."

"It is so easy to rattle you." It really was. Gordon had the gift.

"I always thought Paul was secretly gay. He can't go through with an engagement to Helen because he wants a man. If he had met Leonard Bast, things would have ended differently."

"I guess the book would have been *Howards Different End*," Gordon said with a smile, adding, "I could not resist."

"Try. Please try, Edward said dismissively. "*Howards End* has more gay people than *Maurice* does. Tibby is gay—that's Helen and Margaret Schlegel's fey brother."

"Which is better than their brother Fay."

"I will ignore you."

"Cannot be done." It could not. Edward had tried for some eight years now with no success. His best option was to press forward with his point.

"And Leonard Bast probably was hotter than Forster describes. Bast is broken down by failure, but he must have had something that made him attractive to Helen beyond his umbrella."

"Is that a metaphor—umbrella?"

"It's an umbrella, Gordon. That is how they get to know one another. Helen grabs Leonard's umbrella at a concert."

"That sounds like a metaphor—a little bent, but a metaphor."

"Your mind is in the gutter."

"Good things happen in the gutter."

"I don't need to hear about last night's adventure."

"He was hot. Just like Clive."

"You can have Clive. I would rather have Paul Wilcox. He's a blank canvas. He disappears at the beginning of the novel and resurfaces at the end, cranky and miserable because he is forced to run the family business after his older brother is found legally responsible for Leonard Bast's death. Paul is cranky because he probably had a boyfriend in Nigeria."

"That means he was out in Africa."

"Jesus!"

"That was funny. Admit it."

"It was clever."

"Thank you, Mr. Oscar Wilde."

"All I am saying is Paul is underdeveloped, as a character, so leave his privates alone."

"I don't want his privates. I don't want his generals. I want Clive."

"You've said that many times. I am getting tired of this."

"Is that a signal for me to leave?"

"Yes."

"I can take a hint. I can also take the bottle of gin. I'm all out at home, and it would go well with either cake or bread and butter, if you have them?" Gordon added for effect. Edward's face contorted. He would have to call Dr. Traynor tomorrow.

"Go home. Go now."

Edward handed Gordon the bottle of gin and saw him out. It had been a very pleasant evening. Edward and Gordon's friendship had evolved over time into a relaxed back-and-forth. Edward acknowledged Gordon was more than just a handsome face who could be a great wing man, and Gordon knew Edward's affections were more for show; it was Edward's way of getting people to notice him.

Of course, Clive was hot, but Forster chose to keep him in the closet while allowing Maurice to find love. Edward didn't want a man—even a fictional man—who was content being repressed. Paul Wilcox, he was sure, was hotter than Clive. Did not Helen Schlegel lament that Paul was broad-shouldered when she recounts to her sister that Paul looked frightened by his overbearing brother Charles the day after the infamous kiss with Helen? Our dear Edward should probably have realized that broad shoulders, without equally strong convictions, is not a sign of strength. Impetuous Helen figured that out quite quickly.

Helen Schlegel, though, as the construct of a closeted (or shall we indulge our two new friends and say "wardrobed") author, was not so smart with men later in the story. But Leonard Bast is not our concern, although—and this is a spoiler alert for those of you who have never read *Howards End* or seen the film or spent time with Edward at the bar inside Bergdorf Goodman—it would have been more poetic and ironic if Leonard Bast had been killed not by a falling bookcase but by a falling wardrobe. That is the difference between Forster and, say, Wilde. Oscar Wilde went for broke—he gave us our cake and our bread and butter, too.

Edward was tired. He picked up the glass on the cocktail table, the wad of used cocktail napkins, and headed into the kitchen. He washed the glasses, which were too delicate for the dishwasher, and put them back into the appropriate cabinet. He turned off the lights in the kitchen and the living room. While brushing his teeth, he surveyed the creases in his forehead. Perhaps a good rest would eliminate the need for Dr. Traynor. He would have to wait and see.

Finally, he undressed, put on a pair of sleep pants, and climbed into bed. He thought about his conversation with Gordon that evening. Paul Wilcox was a blank canvas. Clive was hot; Gordon was not wrong there. And Edward was sure the Schlegel sisters would have annoyed him because they were more opinionated than he was, but perhaps Tibby had possibilities. Yes, Tibby had possibilities, but Paul, with his broad shoulders, was dreamy. And dreamy was just fine for Edward Forsythe.

✳✳✳

London
Friday

Edward was confused. A dense fog descended on the rail platform. It emanated from the massive locomotive, its boiler fueling the noxious steam that obscured the faces of people coming off the train. He knew he was there to meet someone, but who? That was not yet clear, like the platform itself. Men dashed past him. Women strolled by, as if unaffected by the smoke and noise. It was all vaguely familiar to Edward, but at the same time, something was off. He checked his watch, and it wasn't there, which triggered panic that he had been robbed. He patted his pockets, and there was no smartphone. The panic grew until he looked over the trousers and jacket he was wearing and said to himself, "Yes, this is all correct. I understand." He pulled out the gold watch from his waistcoat. It was 11:15 a.m. The train was on time.

He caught his man ahead, seeing him tower above the other men who were not as handsome and—most definitely—not as broad-shouldered. Paul Wilcox proceeded along the platform oblivious to the crowds. He stopped at a porter, said something Edward could not hear, and then pressed on toward Edward.

"Hello," Paul said.

"Hello." Edward extended his right hand. "I'm Edward Forsythe."

"Paul Wilcox." His grip was firm, and his shoulders up close were like the arch in Washington Square. Edward practically swooned.

"I'm not sure why you're here," Paul said, "but I believe I am supposed to meet you. Does that sound odd to you?"

"No, not at all. I am not sure why I am here, either. I'm from New York."

"New York? I would rather be going there than to Nigeria. It is hot in Nigeria."

"It is hot now in New York, as well. But with air-conditioning, not so bad."

Paul looked perplexed. "Air conditioning?"

"Just something Americans use that cools the temperature inside. It's bad for the environment."

"The environment? I don't follow."

"It doesn't signify." Edward always wanted to say that, but it sounded too stilted until now. "You have luggage, yes?"

"The porter is taking care of it. I am spending the night in town and then I will have to go to the ship tomorrow."

"Do you have friends in town?"

"No. A girl staying at my family's house is from London. Her younger brother is at Oxford. We have classmates in common—but no real friends. He is slightly younger than I."

"And smaller." Edward could not be reticent if he tried.

"You know Tibby?"

"By reputation. He is prone to hay fever."

"Yes, hay fever. You can't let that control you. Life is to be lived to the fullest. I say, would you like to have lunch with me? I know that is presumptuous, but I have no friends in town, and you're an American, and I don't meet many Americans. I don't meet many people—it's as if I was born to interact with my family occasionally and then just disappear."

"I understand completely." Edward did while inwardly cursing E.M. Forster for his heartless omissions. "Perhaps I can add some exposition to your story, so to speak."

"I would like that. I am staying at my father's club, which I have never liked."

"I'm at The Savoy. I love The Savoy." Edward did. What American did not? Built by the impresario Richard D'Oyle Carte of Gilbert and Sullivan fame, it was both new and old-school English from its inception. Edward could not recall booking a room, but nothing quite made sense, and yet it did, like a memory that changes for the better the further it is removed from the actual event. "Why not tell the porter your luggage is coming with us to The Savoy. We can have lunch there, and then you can sort out your plans for the evening."

"I like that idea, Forsythe. May I call you by your surname? I call my good friends by their surnames."

"I thought you did not have many good friends."

"Yes, that is right, but I would like to call you Forsythe."

"Forsythe, it is. To The Savoy, then?"

"Yes."

The two men walked past the ticket inspector, found Paul's porter, and gave him the necessary instructions. Paul tipped the porter, and they were off. They took a taxi to The Savoy. The route was familiar to Edward, but not the conveyance. The motor was unfamiliar. Edward knew he was out of step with his time, but he felt in perfect rhythm with this new clock. Normally, he would have looked out the window at the unfamiliar sights on familiar streets. Edward knew London well, but not this London. It felt good to be inside the cab with Paul's broad shoulders rubbing against his—Miss Lucy Honeychurch had once longed for a room with a view because she did not have Paul Wilcox next to her in a taxi.

When the taxi pulled into the forecourt of The Savoy, Edward reached into his jacket and was surprised to find money. A good deal of money. He paid for the taxi, and they proceeded into the lobby.

"Mr. Forsythe, how was your morning, sir?" a man inside the door said. Edward was apparently known here.

"It was good, Soames, yes?"

"Good to hear that, sir."

Edward was unsure whether the hotel employee was called Soames or had been instructed to respond to whatever name a guest devised, but Soames was what he called the man. None of the rules that Edward knew seemed applicable anymore. It didn't matter. He was at The Savoy. He had money. And he was with Paul.

"Would you like to wash up before we have lunch?" Edward asked. "We could go up to my suite."

"I would like that," Paul said. "I feel a bit dusty. Can we have my bags sent up there, as well? I would like to put on a fresh shirt." Edward could barely contain himself. He told Soames that Mr. Wilcox's luggage, which a hotel porter had taken from the taxi, should be brought up to his suite so Mr. Wilcox could freshen up before luncheon, and could Soames also book them a table in The Grill for 2 p.m.?

Soames smiled a knowing smile that transcended time or whatever force had placed Edward into The Savoy in the summer of 1910. The two men headed toward the lift, where the lift operator also greeted Edward with a "good afternoon, Mr. Forsythe."

Edward knew the way to his suite as if two ominous twins from a deserted mountain hotel were standing in the hallway saying, "red room." This wasn't as frightening as that would have been. Paul walked close to Edward, so close that Edward could smell Paul's scent, slightly musky, which aroused Edward.

They walked inside the suite. It was large, with a front sitting room that opened onto a bedroom and an en suite bathroom. The windows looked out on the Thames. Edward admired the view and wanted to point out the London Eye, the enormous Ferris wheel, but there was no Ferris wheel in the summer of 1910.

"The river looks peaceful," Edward said.

"It is an illusion," Paul replied. "From up here, you can't hear or smell the activity. I must say, I like the distance."

"From the river?" Edward asked, standing as close as he dared to Paul.

"From everything," Paul replied. "Did you ever feel quite not like yourself? Like you are being invented as you go along?"

"Yes," Edward said. "I feel that way right now."

"I am glad it is not just me."

Edward looked at Paul standing near him by the window in a suite at The Savoy and understood that feeling completely. There was a knock on the door. The porter brought Paul's luggage. Edward handed the bellhop a generous tip. The bellhop gave him the same satisfied look as Soames did.

"Well, let me clean up a bit. The bath is in there, yes?"

"Yes. Do you need help with a bag?"

"If you wouldn't mind, Forsythe, could you bring me that small case?" There were four bags in all since Paul was headed to Nigeria for a time undetermined by anyone, including Mr. E.M. Forster. Paul and Edward were flying blind.

As Edward carried the smallest of the four cases into the bedroom, he could hear water running. Paul had drawn a bath and had also taken off most of his clothes.

"I didn't mean to interrupt," Edward said, unsure what to say when you walk in on an almost naked man in your hotel room at The Savoy in 1910.

"Not at all, Forsythe. Nothing you haven't seen before. At school, boys were naked all the time."

"That is not the case in America. We are still too connected to our Puritanical roots."

"You're not in America, Forsythe."

"No, I am not, Paul. Do you mind if I call you Paul and not Wilcox?"

"I prefer Paul. Wilcox sounds like my father or my intolerable brother."

"That may catch up with him."

"I would like to see that."

"You might not when it happens, but let's not talk about your brother Charles or your father."

"Come over here, then," Paul Wilcox said to our American friend Edward Forsythe. Edward wasn't sure what was about to happen. Men could not be so bold in Edwardian London, could they? Yet Edward knew they must have been, or there wouldn't have been the Oscar Wilde scandal, or Forster would never have written *Maurice*. In any event, he didn't really belong here, so whatever happened was not really happening. This was a dream or a memory; Edward could no longer distinguish between the two.

Edward kissed Paul Wilcox in his suite in The Savoy. He allowed himself to be enfolded completely by the broad-shouldered younger brother of the obstreperous Charles. The two men kissed wildly, as only men in memory can kiss. Then Edward found himself being lowered into the bath, and soon he and Paul were rhythmically sending waves of warm, soapy water onto the white tile floor.

Edward was literally awash in emotions. Was this real? Was this Forster? As he was about to climax, Edward wondered if this could be D.H. Lawrence?

After an hour or so, the two men dressed and descended to The Grill on the ground floor, where Soames greeted them near the entrance.

"We have your usual table ready, Mr. Forsythe."

"Thank you, Soames." Edward tipped again. He had no clue where the money was coming from, but it appeared limitless. The two men dined well and then retired to leather club chairs in a different public space.

"I don't want to go to Nigeria," Paul said after some time. The two men had been sitting quietly, both with a whiskey.

"Then don't go. You broke up with Helen Schlegel. You can choose not to go to Nigeria."

"Can I?" Paul asked. "I don't know what I can or cannot do. As I said earlier, I feel completely undefined. I only know that at some point I need to have come back from Nigeria."

"At some point, you need everyone to believe you have come back from Nigeria. I doubt anyone will check. The rubber business will continue with or without you." Edward knew the Wilcoxes had made a fortune in rubber.

"What should I do then?" Paul asked. He truly did not know, and Edward glimpsed what Helen Schlegel had seen—a strong, attractive man without a strong, moral center. But Helen was a woman, a fictional woman at that, and Edward was a gay man, a real man. Broad shoulders are broad shoulders.

"Stay with me," Edward said. "Stay with me at The Savoy."

"For how long?"

"As long as it lasts," Edward said, knowing he had no clue how long any of this would last. Do memories fade? Do dreams end? He was swimming in uncharted waters, and like the water in the bath in his suite many floors above, it felt wonderful.

Days went by. Weeks. The two men went everywhere. Museums. Theater. Opera. Helen Schlegel's opinions had been restricted by the parameters of Forster's closet, so she had determined that all Wilcoxes were the same. But Paul was his mother's son, the beautiful Ruth Wilcox. Paul had the physical strength of a Wilcox, but he had his mother's sensitivity; it just needed to be brought out. Paul Wilcox was a blank canvas, and Edward Forsythe always wanted to learn how to paint.

After many weeks, Paul suggested they assemble a luncheon, a small gathering of men with whom he had some limited connections. They would go to Simpson's on the Strand and consume mountainous piles of beef and mutton. The thought of mutton made Edward ill, but for Paul, he would eat mutton.

There were to be six in total. When Edward and Paul arrived, the other four were already seated. The bath inside Edward's suite was truly the couple's downfall when it came to timeliness. If either man had been prone to puns or irony, they would have called it their private Waterloo, but such humor eluded our young lovers.

At the table were none other than Tibby Schlegel, Maurice Hall, Alec Scudder—whom Edward noted privately had cleaned up quite well—and Freddy Honeychurch. Tibby and Freddy were classmates at Oxford, something Edward hadn't known—another unfortunate omission by Forster that was somehow being filled in before Edward's eyes. Maurice Hall was in finance and had some vague business connection with the Wilcoxes. Maurice and Paul had met through a mutual friend, who also knew Tibby, who, alas, was still suffering from hay fever.

"This is a gay group," Maurice said as they settled into their first course. Edward laughed.

"Did I say something funny?" Maurice asked.

"Well, gay," Edward said. "I would not expect you to be so open about being gay."

"We're happy. I don't understand," Maurice said.

"Neither do I," Paul added.

"I am drawing a blank," Freddy said unconvincingly to the group.

Ah, thought Edward, Freddy Honeychurch was yet another canvas left blank by Mr. E.M. Forster. But Freddy was not Edward's type—he was too young and too narrow in the chest.

Tibby sneezed. Alec Scudder said in a working-class accent, "I was told to only talk about the weather and people's health."

Edward realized his error. He had forgotten where he was—and when. "Gay is American slang for the secret that dare not speak its name," he said.

The five other men exchanged uncomfortable looks and then burst into laughter.

"Then we are gay," Maurice said.

"The gayest," Paul rejoined.

"Absolutely," Freddy added.

"To your health," Alec said.

"Ah-choo." Tibby sneezed again. He was likely going to be tiresome, and perhaps contagious, because how does someone get hay fever in London unless, perhaps, they have been frequenting a hayloft in a stable? As Edward considered that possibility, Tibby became slightly more attractive.

The men talked about many things. The latest shows in the West End, exhibitions, and what was performed at the Royal Opera House in Covent Garden. Last season, Freddy attended the London premiere of the fully staged production of Saint-Saëns' *Samson et Dalila*. It was the kind of conversation that Edward had hungered for all his life. There was not a speared olive dripping gin in sight.

Everything was going well at the luncheon at Simpsons-on-the Strand, but Edward should have known what was to come. It was right there in the novel. But Edward had lost all sense of time and place. Henry Wilcox had taken Margaret Schlegel for a meal, and with them were Paul's sister Evie and her fiancée, Percy Cahill.

It was Maurice Hall who noticed them first.

"Isn't that your father way over there?" he said, waving his fork in their direction.

Paul went ashen. Without being told, Paul knew his mother had passed sometime between when he met Edward at King's Cross Rail Station and that day. It was another memory that formed from nothing, which is often the case with memories. Paul was not sad that his mother had passed because it had happened a while back; he was sure of that, and he was sure that he must have mourned once and just forgotten it. No, Paul Wilcox was not sad or even bothered that his father was obviously courting Miss Margaret Schlegel. But he was frightened that his father would see him in London, not in Nigeria, as they thought, and with an American man.

Before Edward could say anything, Freddy Honeychurch concocted a scheme.

"I say we tip our waiter to go talk to the one attending on old Mr. Wilcox and tell him that Simpson's is out of mutton and beef and that all they have is fish pie."

"You cannot ask them to do that," Maurice said. "No one would believe that. Simpson's is out of mutton. It's quite ridiculous."

"Men like Wilcox will believe anything underlings tell them because they cannot imagine anyone below them ever trying to deceive them," Freddy said. "They are so content that they are the center of the universe, they do not think it possible that another star has claimed the Earth's orbit."

"The waiter will get sacked," Paul said in a panic.

"I agree," Edward said, knowing he had to protect Paul at all costs.

"We can take care of him," Freddy said. "We could tell him to tell Wilcox that there appears to be a miscalculation in the kitchen, and there is no more mutton or beef. After we see Wilcox's shock and agitation, we can send our waiter over and explain that it was a grave error. That their waiter had suffered an injury serving our nation in the Boer War that affected his hearing, and that he had misheard the conversation in the kitchen. There were indeed plentiful supplies of mutton and beef, and Simpson's would gladly pay for their luncheon because of the momentary inconvenience."

Edward was amazed by Freddy Honeychurch's scheme. The young man had a talent, if only he had a larger chest. Tibby agreed that while it was an expensive proposition because they would need to pay for the Wilcox party's luncheon, it would be good fun to see Wilcox's reaction.

Paul looked panicked, but Edward told him it would all come out all right. It would be like theater. Given the limitless amounts of cash that kept appearing in his clothing, Edward handed a large sum to their waiter as Freddy detailed the plan to him. The waiter would tell his comrade on the floor what to do, and Edward's pile of cash ensured all would be well compensated.

The six men looked on from a distance as the play unfolded. They were seated far from Paul's father's party, so there was little chance of being spotted. They could see Wilcox hear the news. At first, he looked perplexed, like he could not grasp the gravity of the situation—nothing but fish pie at Simpson's on the Strand! Then it sank in, and his face turned the color of a roasted beet, which prompted Alec Scudder to inquire after Paul's father's health.

All in all, though, the six men thought their prank extremely jolly because six young men need little more to amuse themselves than causing an older, rich man discomfort.

When it looked like Wilcox might explode, the young men's waiter appeared and saved the day. He was so convincing with his story of the wounded soldier about the other waiter that Wilcox gave both men a tip, in addition to tipping the carver who soon appeared with the mutton.

The young men finished their luncheon quite delighted. Edward had enjoyed meeting them all and hoped they would see one another soon. They all shook hands except Tibby, who was otherwise engaged with a linen handkerchief. Edward paid their luncheon bill as well—the money kept flowing—and he and Paul left through a side door that led through the kitchens. Paul was concerned that if they left through the dining room, his father would most certainly see them, so they went through the kitchens instead. It felt forbidden, and that excited them both. It had been a most successful afternoon.

When they returned to The Savoy, Edward and Paul made passionate love, as if it was their first time learning each other's bodies. Afterward, they lay on the bed naked atop the covers. Edward was on his side, his fingers stroking Paul's chest. He nuzzled his face into the crook of Paul's arm.

"This is nice," Edward said.

"It is nice, but I must go to Nigeria."

"Why? Aren't you happy here?"

"I am happy, but I am supposed to go to Nigeria. Seeing my father today, I know that. That is the only thing I am sure of. These last few weeks or has it been months?" He paused, unsure of the passage of time, "They have been revelatory, as if I learned I could be someone different than my destiny."

"You can," Edward said.

"You can," Paul replied. "I cannot. We are bound by different natures, you and me. My story has an ending...yours does not."

"Nonsense. And if that is true, I will write your ending for you."

"I would like that," Paul said, turning to face Edward. "But that is not how it works. Father and Charles would not allow it."

"Does that matter?"

"Not to you, Forsythe, but to me it matters."

And there was that look again. That Helen Schlegel revelation that some men are willing to write their own narratives, and some men are content to remain unfinished solely because someone else could not be bothered to make them a main character. It was unfair and wrong. Margaret Schlegel would say that "life is sometimes life and sometimes only in a drama, and one must learn to distinguish t'other which." Our dear friend Edward Forsythe finally distinguished the difference. This was not life. As much as he wanted it to be, it was not life.

"We will talk about this in the morning, Paul," he said, turning onto his back.

Paul Wilcox moved closer to Edward and put his hand on Edward's chest. "We will talk about this in the morning, Forsythe."

The two men lay like that for some time. Maybe Paul fell asleep first, maybe it was Edward. The room was warm, and a slight breeze blew in through the open windows overlooking the Thames. The noises of the water were faint, like a dream or a memory.

⁂

Brooklyn Heights,
Friday

Edward stirred in bed. The breeze felt good as it came through the open windows to the river. He kept his eyes shut, content to hear the breathing of the man to his side. It was a peaceful rhythm, the sound of someone next to you in bed. Who among us could deny anyone such a basic pleasure? To love is the most natural of things. Even Gordon knew that despite his whoring around. Gordon would never disturb the gentle rhythm of a man's sleeping breath after a night of glorious lovemaking. This was the dream that made the memories, or was it the other way around? Edward Forsythe was still not sure.

Gordon seemed so far away. Edward wondered what his friend had been up to these many months. Had he missed Edward? Gordon probably found a way into my apartment and raided my liquor cabinet, Edward thought. He turned to his side and saw it was past 9 a.m. on his watch. He thought nothing of sleeping late since he hadn't had a nine-to-five job in decades, and the unlimited pile of money did not appear dependent on employment, but it suddenly dawned on him that he was looking at his watch. Not the gold pocket watch, but his watch.

Startled, Edward sat up in bed and looked around. It was all familiar. His smartphone was on the nightstand. There was a snarky message from Gordon. Edward was confused. He got out of bed and went into the bathroom. He looked the same. He walked into his living room; everything was in its place. He looked into the cabinets, and the glasses he and Gordon used were where he had left them long ago; the bottle of gin Gordon took from the cart was still missing.

The whole adventure with Paul Wilcox must have been a dream. It had all been a dream. A glorious dream, but a dream. He walked back into his bedroom and looked at the bed. There was a man in the bed. This was no dream. It was a man.

Maybe it was Paul Wilcox. Maybe that was how this thing worked? He spent time in Paul's world, and now Paul would spend time with him.

The man stirred and sat up in bed, not the least surprised by where he was. He was naked and ran his fingers across his bare chest, which had not seen much sun.

"I am so hungry, Forsythe," the man said. "Maybe you could get me some bread and butter?" He grinned widely.

Edward looked at this naked, untanned man in his bed, who was immediately familiar to him. It was Clive Durham. And Gordon was right. Clive was hot.

Axel Rod and The Wizard

It was the kind of February New Yorkers had forgotten. It had been below 20 degrees for six straight days, and heavy snow still covered the city. The snow had nowhere to go—even Jersey wouldn't accept it, having 16 inches of the white stuff, as well.

New York's snow wasn't so much white anymore. Snow in New York stays pretty in parts of Central Park for days if it stays cold enough, but in the grittier parts of Manhattan, the city goes from white to grey fast, with streaks of yellow, thanks to all the would-be Jackson Pollock canines and drunk men. In the past, it was pampered dogs that dotted the landscape with urine, but now, feral men, careless, sloppy, and without concern for others, gave the hounds competition. Across this landscape, John made his way to The Crow, his bar in the West Village. He arrived by 2 p.m. to begin deicing the sidewalk around his corner establishment. Over a week ago, he had shoveled all the snow into piles nearly two feet high against the scraggly trees that dotted the sidewalk, but somehow, even in the extreme cold, some snow would melt just enough to cover parts of the sidewalk.

The last thing John wanted was some litigious passerby to slide on their ass in front of his bar. He chopped at the ice like he was on a frozen lake looking for a fish. Then he shoveled up the shards of ice and tossed them onto the grey-and-yellow piles of frozen snow. Finally, he threw enough salt to brine at least twenty briskets onto the cleared cement. This routine required a lot of muscle, and by the time John was finished, walked into his bar, turned on the lights, pulled off his coat, ski hat, gloves, and sweatshirt, his T-shirt was soaked in sweat.

He kept a fresh T-shirt on a shelf under the bar, pulled off the wet one, and started wiping his chest with it when the door to the bar opened.

"I'm sorry," the man said. "I wasn't sure you were open. Didn't mean to interrupt, but to be honest, I am glad I did," he added with an appreciative grin.

"We don't open for another half hour," John said, not the least bit embarrassed. He liked showing off and continued wiping his chest as he talked. "Normally, I would say come back, but it's so cold outside, you're welcome to sit at the bar. I just can't serve you any alcohol for another thirty minutes. But I will make some coffee. Usually, it's just for me, but you're welcome to join me," he said, finishing his après-deicing ablutions before putting on a worn, but clean, T-shirt. "I'm John," he said. "Take a seat."

"Thank you," the man replied in a voice John found seductive and as soothing as a hot toddy on a day like this in February. The man took off his hat, a classic red-and-black plaid hunter with ear flaps, revealing a lush head of jet-black hair that was a bit tousled from the headgear. His face was handsome, tanned, and with some lines of age. John guessed the stranger was in his early to mid-sixties. The man removed his puffer coat, which had concealed a muscular frame accentuated by a form-fitting charcoal grey sweater with a wide indigo-blue horizontal stripe just about chest level that continued across the top of the sleeves. The result, in John's eyes, was that the handsome stranger's torso had become the incarnation of a Rothko painting.

As the man sat down, John was more intrigued—besides always liking 20th-century modern art, the stranger looked vaguely familiar. Perhaps, John thought, they had hooked-up once long ago. Maybe it was in the bathroom of MoMA, the Museum of Modern Art. John walked over to his lone customer.

"Before you get too comfortable," John said, focusing his hypnotic green eyes on the attractive man. "I should warn you that you are in Tommy's seat."

"There's assigned seating?" the man asked, looking straight at John. The stranger had brown eyes that gave John's green a run for their money. The stranger didn't look angry, just amused. "Is there an app I should have gone on?" he chuckled.

"For seating or something else?" John replied with a wide grin.

"Too early for something else," the man replied. "I'm Ryan." He extended his right hand.

The two big men shook hands. The grips were unnecessarily firm, which is to say that both gay men were trying to impress the other with their physical prowess. When they released hands, it was a tie, which impressed John. His green peepers were now in overdrive.

"I know there's no one here, but that's Tommy's seat. He's more than a regular: he's a fixture at The Crow. He came with the bar."

"You're kidding," Ryan said, moving over three stools.

"Not really. He was here from day one, and I think he was here before that. I can't imagine this place without him sitting over there drinking Jack Daniels after Jack Daniels."

"That sounds sad," Ryan said, still focused on John's eyes.

"It is and isn't," John said, leaning in slightly over the bar. "What would be sadder is if he didn't have anywhere to go that was safe. He doesn't create a problem. He drinks and drinks until I decide it's time to cut him off, and then I let him stay there until he's ready to go home."

"That still sounds sad," Ryan said.

"From our perspective, yes. But not from his. He has a good time being among other gay men. For some people, it isn't about the conversations with you, it's about the conversations around you. I think Tommy likes the sounds of gay men more than the actual words they say."

"That is intense," Ryan said. "You should have been a therapist."

"I'm a barkeep. That's better. I don't have to deal with health insurance companies."

"You got me there," Ryan said.

"I have you here," John said with a twinkle as his big right hand pounded the bar. "I will put some coffee on." He turned and went to the end of the bar furthest from the entrance and began making a pot of coffee. He continued to talk, but in a louder voice. "Not many of my customers look for coffee. Occasionally, I get someone who is clearly in the wrong bar wanting an espresso martini, and I always tell them, 'So do I.'"

"That's wicked," Ryan said, "but also funny. How do they react?"

"Usually, they are confused because they assume that because I'm working behind a bar, I must be dim."

"The bartenders I have known have been smarter than most of the customers. They are exposed to so many different kinds of people and cultures. They are more interesting."

"Smart man, yourself," John said as he grabbed two mugs for the coffee. "Are you a bartender?"

"No, no," Ryan said. "Let's just say people used to think I had no brain. I'm retired now."

"If you're retired, you must have done something right. Most gay men I know can't retire until they are past retirement. You must not have spent your youth lying down."

Ryan chuckled.

"What's so funny?" John said, bringing the two coffees.

"Nothing, really," Ryan said, taking a mug.

"Do you want any milk?" John asked.

"Sure. You can pour some in," Ryan added flirtatiously. The two alpha men were trying to figure out the other. John poured some milk into Ryan's coffee and then into his.

"Cheers," John said. They both sipped. "This could be better," John added, making a face.

"It's fine," Ryan replied.

"Let me add something extra." John walked over to the whiskeys, grabbed the bottle of Jameson, and poured a small amount into both mugs. "I can't sell it at this hour, but we can drink it for free. Cheers."

They sipped.

"Much better," Ryan said. "You have the magic touch."

"I do," John replied. "I could be modest, but why?" he added with a grin.

"Considering the show that I got when I walked in, I did not expect modesty from you."

John laughed loudly. "You know how many regulars who come in here would have loved to have seen me pull off my shirt? You walked in for the first time and boom!"

"I feel lucky," Ryan said. He was going to say something more suggestive when the door opened. It was Tommy.

The older man walked in, stuffed his hat and gloves into the pockets of his winter jacket, hung it on a hook, and sat down on his stool. His silver hair was thinning, and his skin was spotted from the effects of too much sun long ago. Tommy was also too small for his clothes, something rarely seen in a gay man. John used to tell customers who were trying to figure out if a new guy in the bar was straight or gay, "Look at his shirt. If his shirt is too big, he's straight. If it's too tight, saddle up, boys, and go for a ride." Tommy was gay. Tommy drank too much. And Tommy, like every person in every bar—gay or straight—was so much more than he appeared. But Ryan was correct: Tommy looked sad.

Tommy pulled out a crumpled wad of dollar bills and placed them on the bar. John immediately went to the Jack Daniel's, got a glass, filled it with ice, brought the bottle and glass over to Tommy, and poured him a drink.

"Cold out, today, Tommy," John said.

"I didn't notice it," Tommy replied. "The seasons are all the same to me. Winter. Summer. All the same."

Tommy drank the first Jack quickly, and John refilled the glass.

"Take this one slow, Tommy," John said. "It's early."

Tommy, who was not yet in his Jack Daniel's comfort zone, replied, "Maybe it is for you." He looked down at his fresh drink, saying nothing more. John knew that was his cue to move on.

"Where were we?" John asked as he stood before Ryan.

"Something about your lack of modesty," Ryan said. "I feel sad," he added, indicating he was referring to Tommy.

"You can't. Bars are full of many kinds of people, and most of them are looking for something that just isn't here. Tommy's one of the few who have no illusions about The Crow, about any bar. We offer drinks. We offer absolution for whatever you have done, or you may do here or elsewhere. We offer a few hours of companionship if you want it, and privacy if you want that. But we can't fix you. We can't make whatever is wrong outside these walls right. Whatever magic spell a bar offers, it only works within the bar."

"Jesus," Ryan said, leaning forward on his stool, "all that and a fabulous chest. I should have come in here years ago."

"Where have you been?"

"Los Angeles."

"Sorry."

"Ah, the New Yorker's reply to LA," Ryan said, leaning back a bit now. "LA is so much more than New Yorkers think it is."

"More traffic," John said.

"Different traffic," Ryan said. "It's not New York. It's Los Angeles. It has everything you can imagine and things you cannot. It is exactly like New York, and it is exactly not like New York. It's a great place."

"So why are you here in winter?"

"Because it was time for another great place. It isn't about which city is greater. Both can be great. Both can offer more than any single person could possibly experience in a lifetime. I was ready for a new experience in a new place."

"You're in the witness protection program," John said with a laugh.

"Busted," Ryan answered. "It was time to be in New York. I like sweaters," he added, gesturing to the one he was wearing.

"And sweaters like you," John replied. "You may have seen me without a shirt, but I am getting a good idea of what your chest is like from that sweater."

"It doesn't show you everything," Ryan said, leaning forward again. If his brown eyes were lasers, John would have burn marks all over his chest.

"Tell me you have a hairy chest," John said. "I like furry men like me."

"I do now," Ryan said. "For years, I waxed. It was an LA thing," he added.

"You see," John said, "another reason why I should not like Los Angeles."

"Men wax in New York," Ryan replied.

"Not the ones who come in here. We have a sign on the door: "Wax On, Get Out.""

Ryan turned toward the door.

"Made you look," John said, laughing.

"I walked right into that," Ryan said, also laughing. "Good for you. No one gets me to do that. I'm impressed, Mr. Barkeep John."

"That was the plan," John said. "Look, I want to see you."

"That was fast," Ryan said, smiling. He leaned further into the bar, nearer to John, brown lasers fully fired up. "I'm not going anywhere. This is my stool," he added, putting an emphasis on the "my."

"Yes, but I am going to be busy in about…now," John said as he saw the door open. A couple of men wandered in and sat at the far end of the bar, across from the coffee machine. "There will be a steady stream of guys from now on, and I still have to do some prepping of the fruits."

"That sounds a little kinky," Ryan said.

"You have a dirty mind," John said. "I like that."

John turned to the new customers at the far end of the bar and got their drinks. He chatted with them as he cut up lemons and limes, while still smiling at Ryan. The bar continued to fill up. Jody came in and sat next to Ryan.

Jody was a regular at The Crow, a high school science teacher with a heart of gold. Usually, one of the shyest men in the bar, but always lovable to his core. He was not an unattractive man, but not in the same league as Ryan or John—not even in the same stadium on an off night. There was nothing memorable about Jody on the surface. But if you spent time with him, you would discover he loved teaching. But even more than teaching, he loved the possibility of being loved. And he still believed at his age that love—great love—was still possible.

That is why he came to The Crow. He might fare better at a men's meet-up group his age, but he never felt comfortable in those situations. Putting on a nametag or having to mingle his way through a strange bar looking for a like-minded person was too daunting. At The Crow, he just had to sit down. Sometimes, he had good conversations with other regulars, but the conversations rarely went anywhere, meaning they rarely went anywhere outside the bar.

Jody hooked-up occasionally. Every gay man hooks up occasionally— except Tommy, perhaps, but that was because Tommy had married Mr. Jack Daniels back when Bill Clinton was still anguishing over "don't ask, don't tell." Jody didn't drink much because he was a lightweight when it came to spirits. The last thing Jody wanted was to draw attention to himself as the drunk guy in the bar. That was the Catch-22 for him: he didn't want to be anonymous, and he didn't want to draw attention to himself. So, he came to The Crow most nights, familiar and still unknown.

He didn't advertise himself as Tommy did, but Jody was, in fact, the saddest man inside The Crow. When he sat down on the stool next to Ryan, he didn't really focus on him at first. He could see Ryan was handsome, which subconsciously could have drawn him to that stool, but Jody wasn't expecting a hook-up—and certainly not with a man as attractive as Ryan. Still, Ryan looked familiar to him, but he couldn't place why. He assumed their paths must have crossed in some bar over the past thirty years.

John approached Jody and asked, "What are you having? Usually, it's white wine."

"I don't know. It's so cold out. I should have something that isn't chilled."

"Give him a Glenlivet, with just a little ice," Ryan said.

"I don't know about that," Jody said, looking at Ryan, surprised that he suggested something. "That's Scotch. I can't handle Scotch."

Ryan smiled broadly and flashed his brown lasers at Jody, who was a deer in the headlights. "You look like a man who needs a Scotch. I will have the same." Ryan placed two twenties on the bar. "This is on me," he said to Jody and then smiled at John.

"You're the man," John said. "Two Glenlivet's with a little ice." John pulled the bottle from the top shelf and poured the drinks. He also gave both men glasses of water on the side. "I think you might need a water back," John said to Jody.

"I think you are right," Jody replied hesitantly, holding the glass.

"You'll do fine," Ryan said. "Cheers." He toasted Jody. "Look at me," he said before either of them had sipped. "It's bad luck not to look at the man who is toasting you. It means seven years of bad sex."

"That would be better than seven years of no sex," Jody replied innocently. "Cheers." He stared into the light like a moth going into a pest strip. He sipped and reacted to the hard liquor.

"It gets easier. I'm Ryan," Ryan said, extending his hand.

"I'm Jody." The two men shook hands, not as Ryan and John had earlier. Ryan's grip was firm—firmer than Jody's, but he wasn't trying to assert who was the alpha dog in the yard with Jody. It was as clear as day.

"I take it you come here often," Ryan said.

"Yes, I do come here a lot. Probably more than I should," Jody added, a little embarrassed.

"My first time here," Ryan said. "Just moved to New York from Los Angeles."

"Really?" Jody said. "I always wanted to go to LA. It sounds cheesy, but I also wanted to see the Hollywood Walk of Fame, the Hollywood sign, the Santa Monica Pier—all the tourist spots."

"Nothing wrong with that. Los Angeles has many sides—the tourist part is only one of them."

"Just like people," Jody said with surprise. It is not that he hadn't thought that before, but he had never said it aloud. The single malt Scotch was working its magic.

"Very smart perspective," Ryan replied, turning directly toward Jody, who clearly should have been wearing protective glasses to shield himself from the nuclear power of Ryan's piercing gaze. "You're a man of many sides."

"Thank you, but most people would say I have many sides, and they all look the same."

"Most people are fools," Ryan said, raising his glass towards Jody and downing his drink. Jody did the same. The Scotch was hot and unfamiliar, just like Ryan.

"Let's have another round," Ryan said. It was a statement, not a question, and he signaled to John, who looked surprised and amused by what he was watching. He poured them another round.

"I see you have met Jody," John said.

"Yes," Ryan answered. "He wants to go to Los Angeles, unlike some people here," he added with a smile.

"I didn't say I wouldn't go to LA," John protested.

"You sort of did, but that is OK," Ryan said. "I will show Jody the sights when he goes," he added, tapping Jody on his arm. Jody was so beside himself, he was sure he was having an out-of-body experience. "What do you do?" Ryan asked.

"I teach high school science," Jody answered. "I know—total geek."

"Not at all. I have great appreciation for science teachers. STEM is the future."

"Thank you," Jody said. He had turned scarlet. Compliments were rare. "I love teaching high school. I teach chemistry."

"Chemistry?" Ryan said truly interested. "You're a regular Mr. Wizard, I bet. I could see you with your own show—something on social media that would go viral."

"Me? With a show? I'd be petrified."

"Are you petrified teaching a group of high schoolers?"

"No, but that is different. No one expects me to be charismatic. They just want to get a passing grade. Occasionally, I get a student who loves science, and it's very rewarding."

"There's your problem," Ryan said. "You're a scientist. You understand chemistry, but you don't understand charisma. Charisma is more about internal confidence than anything else. I bet you would be adorable in a lab coat."

Jody nearly fell off his stool. No one had ever called him adorable. Even his mother. The closest he came to looking adorable was in a photograph of himself with his childhood golden retriever. The dog was more photogenic.

"You're being modest," Ryan said. "I know something about cameras, and the camera would love you because you won't try to make love to it. You'll respect it and it will respect you."

Jody was speechless. No one had ever tried to bolster his ego. He took a deep sip of his second Scotch. "I always wanted to do a science show...not just chemistry, but maybe geology."

John, who was half listening, couldn't resist saying, "Gay men would love to know how to get their rocks off."

"Ignore him," Ryan said, clearly amused. "I know it's hard to ignore him...he's so big and he controls the bottles, but trust me, this could be your moment. You should try something with a smartphone video. Put on a lab coat. Work up some ideas. You could be the next thing. Start small and then grow. And," Ryan added, looking directly at John, "not a word from you."

"Yes, sir," John said, surprised at his willingness to be subservient to this handsome stranger. "Let me refill Tommy. *He* still needs me." Indeed, Tommy did. He was in his comfortable drunk state, making a slight "wee" sound every few minutes as he waved his right hand as if he were the Queen Consort reviewing a parade.

"What do you do?" Jody asked Ryan. "Are you in the film industry?"

"Let's say I am retired, but I know my way around cameras."

"You're an actor. I knew it."

"I did not say that."

"A director?"

"Does it matter that much?"

"No, I guess not. I was just curious. I don't usually have conversations like this."

"Like what?"

"Like this with a stranger. You are very handsome, you know?" The second Scotch had fully kicked in.

"Then you should. You waste too much energy on looks. You are very adorable."

Two "adorables" and two Scotches—Jody wondered whether he should dare for three.

"Let's have another round," Jody said, surprising himself. "I may not be able to walk out of here, but let's have another round." Jody signaled to John, who was taking some rumpled dollar bills from the pile Tommy placed on the bar. John came over to Jody and Ryan.

"You waved?" John asked Jody wryly.

"I wasn't rude, was I?" Jody responded, fearful he had offended John.

"You couldn't be rude if you passed gas," John said. "I'm just messing with you. You should drink Scotch more often. This round is on me."

John poured out two more drinks.

"I think I need a pit stop," Ryan said to Jody. "Where's the restroom?"

"Straight to the back on the left," Jody said, turning to face the bar. His flushed face looked back at him from the mirror that stretched across the length of the bar behind the rows of bottles. Jody barely recognized the face staring back.

John was intrigued by Ryan. There was something about him, something familiar that he could not place, that nagged at his memory. He headed back to the restroom, hoping to have a private word with Ryan. As he walked into the bathroom, Ryan was turning slightly from the urinal.

John gasped. "Axel Rod! Fuck! You're Axel Rod."

"It happens every time. I think no one recognizes me anymore, and then I go to the restroom and wham!"

"Wham, indeed. Wow!"

"Thank you."

"No, thank you! *Rod and Reeling. Axel Greased. Axel's Lube Job.* You got me through my twenties, my thirties...if I had them on DVD, I would still watch them. I knew you looked familiar, but I couldn't place the face, but that...well, that is unforgettable."

"If you start singing Nat King Cole, I may need to hurt you," Ryan said. "No one can place the face, but when it comes to my dick, well..."

"You were big in the '80s and '90s."

"I am big. It's the pictures that got small," Ryan said, unable to resist the film prompt. "I always wanted to say that."

"Can't see you as Norma Desmond. That story would have been great, though, as a porn film with all men...aging male star looking for young, hot screenwriter."

"It's been done a thousand times. It's called Palm Springs."

"You are so much more than just your famous dick," John said without thinking. "God, that sounded like a backhanded compliment...Jesus, I did it again," he added, realizing the backhand could be construed sexually. "I'm not usually this awkward."

"It's the dick. I should put it away." John hadn't realized that Ryan had let it all hang out while they were speaking. Ryan returned his sizable package to his briefs and zipped them up. "Don't tell Jody, OK?"

"Why not? You can't be embarrassed. You were big...I mean, you are big."

"I came here as Ryan, not Axel Rod. I left that part of my life a long time ago. Don't get me wrong...I am not ashamed of working in gay porn. It was fun. I was safe and lucky. And I invested a lot of what I made into real estate, so I am comfortable now."

"That all sounds great. Why not own up to being Axel Rod?"

"Because Axel Rod doesn't own me. I am not defined by him. I defined him. He was my creation, and now I want to be...my authentic self. Jody would be overwhelmed by Axel Rod, and I like Jody. I don't want to be his lover," Ryan added with a little too much emphasis.

"Good to know," John said, interrupting.

"Good to tell you," Ryan quickly answered, "but I want to be Jody's friend. I want a regular friend...a nice gay guy who just wants a friend. At some point, I will tell him. We'll be hanging out on the couch with a pizza, and I will just bring it up...metaphorically speaking."

"Look, I tell people all the time, bartenders are like priests in the confessional...people tell us their darkest, deepest secrets and we keep them. I can keep this one."

"Good," Ryan said. "Now come over here." Ryan pulled John in close, and they kissed deeply. John was unaccustomed to being with a man equal in height and build. He was excited about the possibilities.

"You are big," John replied, putting pressure on Ryan's fly.

"So are you," Ryan said, reciprocating the gesture. "Now, go back to your bar. We shouldn't come out of here at the same time. People will talk."

"You are so provincial for a porn star."

"I told you, I'm Ryan, not Axel Rod. Now go."

John left the restroom, returned to the bar, and chatted with the regulars. He could see Tommy waving his hand in the air, making his "wee" sound. He would need to keep an eye on him today. Perhaps, he should keep an eye on Tommy more often, John thought. People are more than they appear—even Tommy.

Ryan came back from the restroom and put his hand on Jody's shoulder as he sat down. "How are you holding up, Mr. Wizard?" he asked.

"I'm drunk," Jody said. "I can't feel my feet."

"Yeah, you're drunk, alright. That's OK. Pace yourself now," Ryan said and signaled to John. "Can we have some more water here. The Wizard and I need to sober up a bit."

"I like that," John said. "The Wizard. You need a nickname, Jody. That's it. 'The Wizard.' It will give you caché."

"I thought all I needed here was cash," Jody said, turning to Ryan. "The Crow doesn't accept credit cards."

"Troglodyte," Ryan said to John.

"Do you know how many times people have called me that in this bar?" John said, laughing.

"I'm sure," Ryan replied, also laughing.

"I'm having a good time," Jody, aka, "The Wizard," said. "I am having a really good time."

"I'm glad," Ryan said.

"So am I," John added.

"I think I need to go to the restroom," Jody said, getting up. He was a little unsteady. "I feel like Tommy," he added.

"Wee," came from across the bar, as if on cue.

"You have a way to go before that," John said. "Walk deliberately and slowly one step at a time. If you think you are going to fall, shout out, 'Timber!'"

"I always said, 'hands,'" Ryan added.

"I am not surprised," John said as he and Ryan watched Jody walk toward the restroom like John Wayne wearing 4-inch pumps. He swaggered and swished, swaggered and swished. John and Ryan smiled broadly.

"I am going to help him find himself," Ryan said. "The Wizard could do well on social media. I can bring him out of his shell. He has a kind face...people will relate to that."

"He's not the only one with a kind face," John said. "I can't believe all those years I watched you in videos, I never saw what a great face...what a kind face you have."

"That wasn't the purpose of the films. They were about fantasy and pleasure, and let's be honest, particularly back in the '80s and '90s, gay men didn't watch porn for kindness."

"Thank you. It makes me feel less like an aging whore."

"I have a fondness for aging whores," Ryan said, touching John's hand. Their respective lasers focused on each other's faces. "Here's the deal," Ryan said without moving his hand. "I am going to stay here with The Wizard and sober him up enough to safely walk. I will get him home. Then I will come back here and drink water the rest of the night—or at least until I have sobered up enough—and wait for you to close this place."

"Are you expecting me to go home with you?" John asked in a mock demure way.

"No," Ryan said emphatically. John looked a little disappointed. "I expect to come home with you," Ryan added. "My apartment is still a mess, and I want to see you in your natural habitat."

"This is my natural habitat," John said, regaining his mojo. "My apartment looks exactly like this down to the stools."

"I'm sure," Ryan said, not convinced. "I bet you have bookcases all over the place with big, thick books," Ryan added, putting the emphasis on the words big and thick. "I don't think you're what you appear to be either. We all put on costumes. Although, in my case, my costume was no costume."

"You're going to come home with me?"

"That's what I said," Ryan replied. "It's an order. Like in my classic film..."

"*Axel's Lube Job*," John said, completing the sentence. "I thought you were more than Axel Rod?"

"I am more. But he comes with the package." They both laughed at the double entendre. Ryan turned toward the restroom and shouted, "Here comes The Wizard." He said it loudly, so other men could hear, and some of the regulars picked up the moniker immediately. For all the years Jody had been coming to The Crow, he was Jody, a high school science teacher whom people looked at and talked to but never saw or heard. For the first time, the regulars at The Crow saw and heard The Wizard. Jody felt better than a million dollars; he felt like himself—and for the first time, he felt comfortable being himself in a public place.

Maybe it was the Scotch. Maybe it was Ryan. Maybe it was something in the cold air outside. Jody didn't know, and neither Jody nor The Wizard cared. It felt good.

He sat down next to Ryan, but instead of just talking with him, other regulars began approaching to talk, attracted to Ryan, who was incredibly handsome and strangely familiar to every man over 55 in the bar—and that was almost every man inside The Crow. They were also attracted to The Wizard, another strangely familiar but unknown man at the bar.

It was a loud, raucous afternoon that turned into a loud evening. Around 7 p.m., Ryan helped Jody up and took him back to his apartment. Jody invited him in, and Ryan accepted. Ryan helped Jody make himself a sandwich and then got him to lie down on the couch. It didn't take long for Jody to pass out.

Ryan left his phone number on Jody's coffee table with a message: "Call me tomorrow. You may know chemistry, but I know hangovers. Talk tomorrow, Wizard. Best, Ryan."

Ryan left Jody's apartment and headed back to The Crow. The next day, around 2 p.m., John was back in front of his bar, looking at the thin sheet of melted ice coating the sidewalk. It was still freezing outside, and he marveled at how any of the snow piles could melt enough to cover his sidewalk every day. John started to hack at the ice with the blade of his shovel.

"Don't be such a showoff," Ryan said, carrying John's spare shovel. "It will go faster with two."

"I hope not," John said, smiling. "I hope not."

The Boxer

The original Madison Square Garden, as its name suggests, was adjacent to Madison Square Park. Opening in 1879, it was demolished in 1890. The second Madison Square Garden was the thing of legends, with minarets, a bell tower, and a rooftop restaurant-cabaret. Designed by Stanford White, that Garden iteration lasted from 1890 to 1925. Not a long run for a building of grand ambitions, but its famed architect, White, did not fare much better. He was shot dead by the husband of an ex-lover inside The Garden in 1906 in what was known at the time as "the crime of the century."

The next incarnation of Madison Square Garden was built on Eighth Avenue in the theater district. To say it was near Madison Square would be like saying that Hoboken, New Jersey, is near the Chrysler Building. By this time, America's love of professional boxing had blossomed like cherry trees along the Potomac, and the third iteration of Madison Square Garden was the site of many a famed match. Nothing lasts in Manhattan, and this third Garden would be razed when a new, circular one was created atop Pennsylvania Station in 1968.

The outcry over the demolition of the original Pennsylvania Station is also part of New York City lore, but most contemporary New Yorkers have no memory of that glorious temple of the Gilded Age, so the Madison Square Garden as it exists today is The Garden they believe has always existed. It is a rare moment when anyone asks, "Why is it called Madison Square Garden?"

If a building could attain personhood, this one would proclaim, "Because I identify as a Madison Square adjacent building." But if the powers that be or not to be at present debate whether an actual person can transition into who they authentically are, there is little hope for a building, so it is best for this fourth version of The Garden to keep silent and let its walls do the talking. Which they did.

The bright signage around The Garden, in a testosterone-pumped roar, advertised a celebrity boxing match: A long-retired heavyweight champion was fighting a social influencer with boxing ambitions. This was not Max Schmeling versus Joe Louis; it did not matter which man won. Both men would receive large sums of money, and that was pretty much the whole point of the match—that and lots of publicity. The whole commercial affair screamed of metaphor, but Brett could not figure out what that metaphor was.

Little made sense to Brett. Everything had become, in the words of the great Yogi Berra, "déjà vu all over again." The early 21st century was a repeat of the early 20th century with the addition of smartphones, laptops, and expensive Japanese toilets. The global pandemic was a replay of the influenza pandemic of 1918 and 1919. Although, this virus had not slandered the Spanish, but instead the Chinese. For the dead, who were slandered mattered little—ah, but for the living! To them, it mattered greatly. Who to blame mattered very much to them.

Speech, like viruses, is airborne. While COVID was no longer a societal threat, a different virus was spreading, just as one had spread following the influenza epidemic of 1918 and 1919. Brett feared this virus more than he had COVID, because he had believed science and good genes would carry him through the recent pandemic. But this new airborne virus scared him to his core.

The years after the influenza pandemic of the early twentieth century were a time of great push and pull, between extraordinary freedoms of expression and equally extraordinary acts of repression. Strong men, literal and metaphorical (ah, the damned metaphor, again!), amassed great power.

The 1910 "fight of the century" between black heavyweight champion Jack Johnson and white boxer James J. Jeffries was already one for the history books, as were the race riots that followed Johnson's July 4th victory. By the 1930s, the new "Great White Hope" was German-born Max Schmeling, and his two fights with black boxing champ Joe Louis—winning in 1936 and losing in 1938 —were more inscrutable metaphors for the battles to come between equality and Aryan hatred.

Just one year after the second Schmeling-Louis fight, on February 20, 1939, the German American Bund held an infamous Nazi rally attended by 20,000 people inside Madison Square Garden, replete with a large portrait of George Washington flanked by swastikas. It was technically a birthday celebration for the nation's first president and, pardon the pun, the Yankee-Doodle-Do-Nazis baked a bund(t).

The German American Bund didn't last much longer in America, but that was more due to their leader being charged with embezzlement than their ideology. But the hatred spewed by the Nazis did not go away any more than any virus goes away. It mutated, and if you had good genes and luck, you were not seriously infected.

But the hate lives, the hate lives.

For Brett, a senior gay man living in an affluent Long Island suburb of New York City, hatred had not posed a serious civil-rights or health threat for generations. He was safe here, as others like him were safe in or near other big cities. It was what an ancestor of his might have said in 1925 Berlin.

Déjà vu all over again.

In America during the first quarter of the 21st century, antisemitism was on the rise; so was racism. Still, most gay men were reasonably safe, at least in the neighborhoods where Brett visited. Most homophobia targeted men who either did not look traditionally masculine or who transitioned to become women. Any cisgendered man who appeared less than a man or had transitioned was considered less than a person. This was not Dred Scott—not even close at this point—but things change.

The "guaranteed" freedoms Brett had grown comfortable with were only as good as the paper they were written upon. History offered hard lessons to anyone willing to read. But Brett was living in a paperless society.

Historians long ago wrote that within a month of Adolph Hitler's rise to chancellor in 1933 Germany, all civil liberties were under attack. Jews, intellectuals, and anyone who did not conform to the Aryan view of the world—and that included homosexuals—found themselves hunted. Brett did not believe it could happen here, in his beloved New York City or comfortable suburban enclave. And yet, as he held to that view, he knew history did not support it.

Brett was not by nature a fighter. He would neither be James Jeffries nor Max Schmeling. Brett was not "The Great White Hope." He stood on the sidelines during the AIDS epidemic; fearful of coming out, fearful of becoming infected, and most fearful of pushing back against what he saw as the guardrails protecting society.

It had taken years for Brett to distinguish between guardrails created for protection and iron gates erected for detention. Still, the knowledge did not put his mind at ease as he emerged from Penn Station and walked past the fourth Madison Square Garden with its signage advertising a publicity fight. This boxing match was all artifice, and yet in a society completely enthralled with artifice, non-conformist men had become something to rail against.

The masses who would follow this fight didn't care if it was genuine or staged—although the physical blows were real enough. That was a part of the appeal—two big men slugging it out, sweating, and hopefully bleeding just enough to prove they were men. The prize of the fight was not the winning of a title, but the gaining of publicity and the gaming of the system.

Pundits warned of a new age of fascism. Maybe it was a new age of fascism; it was most definitely the age of Darwinism. This weighed on Brett, a slight, upper-middle-class man nearing seventy. He had not stood his ground in his thirties—how would he do it now? Still, Brett knew that those who do not stand their ground are fated to be buried under it.

He continued walking east of The Garden toward Herald Square, which was nearby. There, he would take any of the yellow-colored subway lines north to The Edwardian, his usual bar on the East Side. The ride to The Edwardian was uneventful, and when he entered the bar, it was not crowded. Brett sat along the long side of the bar in the front room, ordered a glass of wine, and glanced around the room. No one caught his eye to his left or to his right until he saw the young man.

The young man sat in the far corner of the front room, the overhead lighting casting a slight shadow across his face, as if he were sitting for a Rembrandt portrait. He was beautiful; his expressive lips coated in a Pomegranate gloss. Brett, staring from slightly down the bar, wondered whether a taste of those lips would bind him to this beautiful young man like Persephone to Hades. Try as he might, Brett could not look away from the beautiful young man's face, regardless of the price that might be exacted in the future.

Brett was not thunderstruck—no bolt of lightning had blinded him. It was enchantment, which was more the work of The Fairies than of Zeus. The obvious double-entendre amused Brett, who easily amused himself; he was that kind of aging gay man or gay man of a certain age. Brett would ponder the word order of that concept too often, as well.

Enchantment was a rare experience for Brett, or really for most of us. We can easily be enthralled by the possibility of the chase, the hunt, or if we are slightly less refined and honest, by the physical back-and-forth of torrid passion, but enchantment? Gay bars are filled with mortal men searching for mortal men, but The Fairies with their powers of enchantment lived in poetry or occasionally a forest on a midsummer's night. There was nothing poetic about The Edwardian at 6 p.m. on a Saturday in February.

The beautiful young man was enchanting. His lips were but one feature of a flawless face dusted in a pale powder with faint traces of blush on his cheekbones. The luminous eyes, while clearly enhanced by liner and mascara, were the real thing. Brett searched for a color. Emerald was too deep a shade and so clichéd that Brett frowned at the very thought of emerald. No, the eyes were not emerald, but a shade of green that reminded Brett of the ocean. To be lost in that sea, Brett pondered, might not be a bad thing. Once again, that was the enchantment at work. He would be, Brett thought, as a young sailor pulled into the watery depths by an alluring nymph to never be seen again. Was the fire in those green eyes the flames of all the young sailors who had come before? Yes, Brett was under the spell.

He could not look away. He was staring, not cruising in a casual way, but staring. The beautiful young man was not Brett's type. Brett's fantasies centered on meeting a slightly dangerous stranger akin to the eponymous lodger in James Baldwin's *Giovanni's Room*. The beautiful man with the Pomegranate lips and Rembrandt shadows was no Giovanni. Yet, there was a masculinity to him.

The sandy blonde hair was tightly cropped, not hidden by a wig. And while he appeared slight in build, he was sturdy enough. He had shed his navy zip-up hoodie, and his T-shirt revealed slightly muscled biceps as he lifted his cocktail to his Persephone lips.

Brett made eye contact with the young man, who smiled and lifted his glass as in a toast. Brett raised his wine and smiled back. He was enchanted, but he was not inclined to make a move. That would take Zeus, so Brett sat with his wine waiting, like a well-groomed Estragon or Vladimir on the side of a road, for Giovanni to enter The Edwardian and sit next to him.

The Edwardian was not crowded at 6 p.m. on a Saturday. A few men were already sitting in the front room when Brett arrived. Shoppers or tourists were common at this hour. The Edwardian was too far from the theater district to get men this early after a matinee or before an evening performance. The crowds would come a little later, but not now.

Still, a few men ambled in as Brett sipped at his wine and occasionally glanced over at the young man in the corner. These were regulars like Brett, men he knew, but not well. The Edwardian was not like The Crow in the West Village.

The Crow, due to its owner and main bartender, John, had a close family feel to it—people were in each other's business, like brothers and uncles gathering at a large party. At The Edwardian, people knew each other's business, but few became that close. Brett, who occasionally visited The Crow, attributed it to the lack of a John figure. Don, the late pianist at The Edwardian, drew a particular crowd by the piano, but even those men didn't know much about the men around them beyond their favorite songs, vocal ranges, and public eccentricities.

Brett preferred The Edwardian over The Crow. Like the beautiful young man, a little artifice was appealing. At The Crow, the men were real. At The Edwardian, they were real enough.

Two newcomers to the bar approached the young man and started talking. They did not appear to Brett's eye as having known each other before. But unlike Brett, who was disinclined to make a first move, they immediately sparked up a conversation. Brett ordered another glass of wine, trying not to look too often at the far corner of the front bar. He was only minimally successful.

A draft swept behind him—someone was entering the bar, but taking their time about it. Brett saw the man as he emerged from the vestibule.

He was massive, at least six feet three, and wore an enormous fur coat that looked like the real thing. How many little furry critters had been sacrificed for this very large one, Brett wondered. To be clear, Brett secretly wanted a coat with a mink lining, but economics, more than morality, had to date prevented such a purchase.

This beast's coat was excessive, and rather than augmenting the beast's ferocity, it had the reverse effect. Brett named the man "The Beaver." He liked that because it was both a diminutive animal and a crude term for female genitalia. Emasculating the furry beast gave Brett pleasure.

The Beaver had been drinking. It was clear to everyone except the bartender on duty at 6 p.m., who made him a Long Island Iced Tea, a drink as ridiculous as The Beaver's coat. No man over the age of twenty-two should drink a Long Island Iced Tea, and even then, they should be near an ocean, a pool, or a hot tub filled with other twenty-two-year-old gay men. The closest The Edwardian came to any of those three was when the toilet in the private bathroom overflowed.

Brett looked at The Beaver with smug contempt but kept it all inside. The Beaver was big. His face was red from the booze and the cold outside. His thick black beard seemed to grow up from his neck, but his teeth, like those of all beavers, were large and brilliantly white. When he asked for a bowl of mixed nuts, Brett wanted to suggest that he ask for a log instead, but just as he hid his smug contempt, Brett kept that thought to himself.

"When do they open the downstairs?" the Beaver asked the bartender.

"At 10 p.m.," the bartender answered.

"10 p.m.?" The Beaver responded with aggravation. "What am I supposed to do until 10 p.m."

"There's a tree that needs trimming outside," Brett wanted to say aloud, but again, he kept it to himself. Brett sipped at his drink while The Beaver moved away from the bar to survey the room. He spotted the beautiful young man.

"Why are you wearing lipstick?" he shouted across the room. "You're a good-looking man. You don't need that shit."

The beautiful man did not respond. He just smiled at The Beaver. The atmosphere around the bar changed. While the men continued to talk, something unusual hung in the air, yet it wasn't entirely unfamiliar to the older gay crowd. Tennessee Williams wrote about the smell of mendacity. This was the smell of menace.

"Talk to me," The Beaver said, moving closer to the back corner. "You don't need that shit on your face."

"It's better than the shit out of your mouth," the beautiful young man said. He was nonplussed.

The Beaver, taken aback by the young man's courage, laughed. "You're alright," he said. "I don't mean no harm. You're just a good-looking man. You should look like a man."

"Thank you," the beautiful man said, trying to end the conversation.

The Beaver was not letting go. "Come over here and talk to me."

"I'm fine over here."

"What's your problem?" The Beaver shouted, his anger returning. Whether it was rising rage or the booze, his voice and body language were increasingly threatening.

"I have no problem," the young man said. "Have a good evening."

The Beaver retreated slightly and ordered another Long Island Iced Tea from the bartender, who now could see the danger ahead.

"I think one is enough," he said to The Beaver. "Why not a water?"

"I didn't come to a bar for water," he snapped.

"I can't serve you anymore," the bartender replied. "I think you have had enough. Why don't you sit down for a while?"

The Beaver took a moment to think. The bar patrons hoped he would just leave, but instead, he sat down on a sofa. He nursed his nearly finished drink. Brett stared at the beautiful young man with the Rembrandt lighting and could not remain silent. He leaned forward on his stool and said loudly to the young man, "You look stunning. You are stunning."

The young man's face lit up, adding to the glow of his flawless skin. "Thank you, honey. I respect you."

Brett blushed. He was embarrassed. The men nearby smiled at him, leaving Brett unsure whether they were mocking him or agreeing with him. He retreated to his safe spot on the bar stool, raised his glass to the young man, who nodded back, and then returned to his conversation with the two men who had joined him earlier.

"I used to wear eyeliner and that shit," boomed from the sofa. The Beaver was on the move. He was louder now. "I used to wear that shit. No more. You should look like a man." The Beaver stood almost directly behind Brett, which made Brett uncomfortable.

Brett signaled to the bartender, who could clearly see what was happening. The bartender texted another bartender in the back bar, which was not yet open. That bartender came out. He was not as big as The Beaver, but size doesn't matter if you have your wits about you.

"I think you need to leave," the second bartender told The Beaver.

"I need to leave?" The Beaver asked incredulously. "I'm just talking."

"You're talking a little too loud and you're making the other customers uncomfortable."

"I'm just talking."

"We need you to leave. Come on. You've had enough."

"You're throwing me out?"

"I'm asking you politely to leave."

"You can't force me to leave."

"I can call the police. Do you want me to call the police?"

The Beaver was drunk, but not that drunk. Hearing the loud conversation, another bartender from the lower level came up and joined the bartender by The Beaver. This new bartender was larger and furrier than The Beaver. Rock beats paper; bear beats beaver.

The Beaver weighed his options. "You're too good-looking to look like that," he shouted again at the beautiful young man who displayed no outward emotion. The Beaver's obsession with the young man's appearance and his comment that he used to wear makeup—whether real or imagined—revealed a self-loathing that made The Beaver truly dangerous in a gay bar. He was Roy Cohn, reduced to primate—self-loathing while also self-absorbed. The Beaver was attracted to the beautiful young man, and perhaps wanted to be the beautiful man, but at present, he was mainly a big, loud, menacing drunk.

The two bartenders guided The Beaver out of the bar, avoiding any physical contact, knowing from experience that men like The Beaver do not respond well to being touched. The bartenders got The Beaver outside and came back in. The cold wind blowing into the bar seemed to clear the air of the menace.

There was a loud noise outside, and one of the two bartenders quickly went to the front door to look out. The Beaver, now heading east on the street, had knocked over the two cement planters in front of the bar. That bartender waited until The Beaver turned the corner at the end of the street, then the two bartenders went outside to right the planters. When they returned inside, the men in The Edwardian were buzzing.

This was unusual behavior inside The Edwardian. Gay men are capable of being homophobic—they are more than capable of it. In fact, many had perfected the art form through passive-aggressive actions that separated members of their community by race, income, education, dress, and gender identity. But raw, aggressive actions unsettled even these men because they reminded them that if societal guardrails collapsed, they would all be the same to those who wanted to erase them, like a pencil notation of a letter in the alphabet. A single swipe of an eraser could reduce twenty-six letters to twenty-five, and no one would even blink.

Makeup, no makeup, White, Black, or Asian—male, female, or transitioning—none of that mattered to the aggressive. So, The Beaver, while most likely a self-loathing gay man, served as a reminder that the wolf at the door might already be inside the room.

Brett shivered, and he could not attribute it to the gust of cold wind from the closing of the front door. He had been sitting on his stool, seemingly unmoved by what had happened, when he was thunderstruck by the truth he had always known: Stand your ground or be buried beneath it.

Zeus finally awakened and threw his bolt. This was not enchantment.

Brett got up from his chair and walked behind the row of men toward the beautiful young man. "How do you deal with that?" Brett asked the man, who was now just inches away. The Rembrandt was authentic.

"How do I not deal with that?" the man said. "I choose to be who I am. I never expected it to be easy."

"It shouldn't be this hard," Brett said.

"That wasn't hard, honey. I could show you hard," he added, breaking the mood slightly. The light in his face faded, and the beautiful young man with the perfect makeup for a moment was just another gay man in a gay bar. While it startled Brett at first, he realized that this man was exactly who he was. This beautiful young man was no different than him, just better-looking and more courageous.

"I respect you," Brett said. "You are the fiercest man in this bar—and the best looking." Brett had no idea where the words were coming from, but he hoped he would find his way back to this spot again.

"You are so sweet, honey," the young man said. "Don't worry about me. I can take care of myself, even if the world goes crazy. I can take care of myself."

"I'm sure you can," Brett said. "I wish I could say the same about myself. I should have said something."

"Honey, don't sweat it. You are saying something to me, now. Not many men like you even do that. Most just sit around and judge like they were on the Supreme Court with a stick up their ass. I respect you, honey. Now, come and see my show. I headline at several clubs. If you really want to show me how brave you are, come and see my show."

The beautiful man handed Brett a business card. It read: Lavender Sashay. "That is my stage name." The man proceeded to tell Brett about the clubs he worked at, none of which were places Brett had ever been to. Brett smiled a smile that, had he been more self-aware, he would have realized was the smile of a very polite passive-aggressive man.

The beautiful young man was not so self-deluded. Drag changes how a man looks on the outside, but it can also reveal who that man is inside. "Don't be shy, honey. Come to my show sometime." And he added, "Be a real man, come to the show."

Brett blushed again. This time, not so much from embarrassment, but from shame. "I will. One night, you'll see me."

"Honey," the young man said, "I see you now. When you come to my show, you will see yourself, not me. Drag queens—we are the magic mirrors. Mirror, mirror on the wall, who is this man who has come to my ball? Look at us, and you will see all your possibilities, honey. I put on makeup. You put on a suit. It's all armor, honey. Underneath, we're the same."

Brett smiled that smile again. "Have a good night and be safe," he said before turning to leave. He looked back at the beautiful young man, and they made eye contact for the final time.

"I don't know your name," Brett said. "I'm Brett."

"Good to meet you, Brett. I'm Lavender."

"I meant your real name," Brett said.

"That is my real name," he said, and blew a kiss.

Brett smiled—and this time it was not the passive-aggressive smile, but a real smile. He stepped outside. Dirt was scattered on the pavement, the remains of The Beaver's rage. Brett headed to the subway, got out at Herald Square, and walked toward Penn Station to catch his train home to Long Island. The signage on Madison Square Garden still advertised the big publicity fight scheduled for later that evening. The faces of the two boxers—one young and one not-so-young—grimaced at one another on the LED display. The two men looked menacing enough to even scare The Beaver.

Brett stared for a good while, long enough to attract a stranger's interest. "Need a ticket to the fight? I have good seats," the man said.

"No, thanks," Brett replied. "I already saw the best boxer in New York. Here," Brett added, handing the man Lavender Sashay's business card. Every Saturday night at 11 p.m.," Brett said before naming the club. "And it's only a $20 cover," he added. The ticket hawker looked perplexed as Brett turned away.

He entered Penn Station and checked the train schedule. He could be home by 9 p.m. Brett smiled again, the real smile he was rediscovering. Enchantment lasts but a moment, a thunderbolt changes you forever—rock beats paper, bear beats beaver, and Zeus beats The Fairies every single time. Brett walked back up to the street.

At 11 p.m., he was upfront near the stage as Lavender Sashay came on. Now in full costume, she was not the shaded Rembrandt beautiful man of The Edwardian, but a dazzling mirror. Lavender Sashay spotted Brett right away.

And for the first time in his life, as Brett looked into the dazzling mirror before him, he saw himself clearly.

Angels on the A

"The first day is the hardest, Danny. Just follow my lead, and you'll be fine."

"Thanks. It's new territory for me to learn. I appreciate you riding with me. And if you don't mind, I prefer Daniel. I've never been much for nicknames."

"Sure. Sure, kid. Daniel, it is. But call me Gabe."

"Gabe, it is. Funny, how that goes—some people like nicknames and some people don't. I like the sound of Daniel."

"That will pass over time. After a while on this job, the sound of your name is the last thing you want to hear."

"What do you mean?"

"You'll understand when you need to. Everyone has that moment when it becomes clear. I can't tell you when it will happen, but you'll know. Trust me."

"Trust me. That's our business, right?"

"How long have you been on the job?"

"I sound that green?"

"Like that stuff they put on the bottom of Easter baskets."

"I hate that stuff. I hate that whole tradition—what does it have to do with Easter?"

"I agree. You'll learn to let that go, as well."

"Let go of what?"

"Judgement of other people's choices. Rule one..."

"I know. Rule one: Never judge." Gabe's slight grimace reminded Daniel of rule two. "Rule two: Never interrupt," Daniel added apologetically.

"That one's a bitch," Gabe said with a knowing smile. "Sometimes you just want to tell them to shut up already, but you have to hold your tongue."

"How do you do it?"

"*Glory Days*."

"Like *Gloria in excelsis Deo*?"

"Forget the rule book, Daniel. This isn't church. This is the real world. *Glory Days*, like in the Bruce Springsteen song. I sing it to myself. It keeps me centered when I listen to foolish people spout on and on." Gabe could see that Daniel was drawing a blank.

"Don't know it?" he asked his trainee. "Where have you been? Wait, don't tell me. It doesn't matter. Listen to The Boss. The song is about people who live in the past. They think their best moments were when they were young, and the truth is, if that's how they live their lives, their best moments are in the past because they're not focused on the present. It's a self-fulfilling prophecy."

"I'll listen to the song," Daniel said eagerly. He pulled his phone out of his pants pocket and made a note. "I'll download it tonight. *Glory Days*." As he put away the phone, he said to Gabe, "I hate Androids. I miss my iPhone."

"Get used to it. The Big Guy has a thing about apples."

Daniel chuckled, "So I've read." He looked at Gabe, who was scratching his dark, three-day stubble, and asked, "How much time do we have?"

"Is that an existential question, Daniel, or a practical one?"

"I sound uptight, sorry."

"You're stressed. I get it. I was the same way once. You know we don't get to choose the people. They choose us. We engage when they engage. That's rule three."

"Do we ignore the people who need us and don't engage?"

"No. We're here. We smile. We look friendly."

"You make us sound like hookers."

"Daniel, you're all right. Hookers. I never heard that one. Hookers! I wouldn't expose myself to get attention—that would have the opposite effect of what we are here to do."

"What about violence? Do we engage then?"

"This isn't your first job, right?"

"It's not, but my previous assignment was quieter. I was stationed for a few weeks inside the public library."

"Ah, yes. There was a lot of that back in the day. That German movie made it all the rage."

"*Wings of Desire.*"

"It messed up our cover. Everybody was looking for us at the main library building. I used to go there to read, and boom, it was like *Ghostbusters.*"

"The library is quieter now...nobody reads books."

"I still like to have something with me." Gabe pulled out a worn paperback from his backpack. "*The Adventures of Tom Sawyer*; it's a classic."

"Always like the part with the fence painting. Was the whitewash a metaphor?"

"You're deep, Daniel. I like that. Was the whitewash a metaphor? That's deep. Look sharp." Gabe pointed at a beautiful trans woman in her early thirties who just stepped onto the train. She sat across from Gabe and Daniel. "Remember, we cannot engage first."

"She looks sad."

"She is sad."

"Listen. Rule four: Listen to their soul. It speaks truth—not the words people speak, but their souls. Listen to their soul."

Gabe and Daniel focused on the beautiful, sad woman. They heard her soul.

She was leaving her apartment earlier that day when two men suddenly shouted out "freak," taunting her. It caught her by surprise, and she hurried to the subway station. She was in pain. Gabe and Daniel listened more intently:

"I wasn't doing anything. I was in a good mood. I'm wearing my favorite jacket. I wasn't looking for any trouble—I just want to be. I just want to be. Why do they have to target me? I wasn't doing anything. What is wrong with people? They don't have to understand me, just respect me. I am a person just like them."

The woman started to sob quietly. Her soul cried out in pain. Gabe and Daniel looked across at the beautiful woman. They both smiled at her, saying nothing. That was the rule.

"I must look a mess," the woman said to them, freeing Gabe and Daniel from their enforced silence.

"I think you look stunning," Daniel said reassuringly. "Doesn't she look stunning, Gabe?"

"Yes, she does, Daniel," Gabe replied, impressed by his new recruit's instincts. "Life is hard sometimes," Gabe said to the woman.

"It's hard all the time," she said. "I thought it would be better. That's what they say, 'it gets better.' But it doesn't."

"It gets different," Daniel said. "Sometimes better. Sometimes worse. But it changes all the time. You must move forward and trust that you can find solid ground ahead."

"Easy for you," she said. "You two are a couple."

"We're not a couple," Gabe said, taken aback. "Do we look like a couple?"

"Yes, you do," she said.

"We're friends," Daniel said. "New friends, but good friends. Sometimes a complete stranger can become a good friend."

"That's right," Gabe said, picking up on Daniel's rhythm. "A good friend doesn't have to be there in the future...sometimes just right now is all that's required."

"My name is Denise."

"Nice to meet you, Denise. I'm Gabe, and my friend—my good friend—is Daniel."

"Where are you going, looking so pretty?" Daniel asked.

"I was going to lunch. I treat myself sometimes to a fancy lunch."

"You will raise the bar wherever you are going," Gabe said.

"I completely agree," Daniel added.

"You have made me feel so much better," Denise said. "Thank you. I got rattled by these two assholes. They called me a freak."

"They were the freaks," Daniel said. "The world has gone crazy right now. Some sick people need to find something healthy to destroy so they can feel better about themselves. They want to blame someone vulnerable for their discontent. They're the freaks, Denise. Just remember, you are a beautiful woman—inside and out—a beautiful woman," Daniel emphasized the last words. He wanted Denise to believe in her beauty; he wanted her soul to feel peace.

Two young men—early twenties, Gabe assumed—entered the train at the next stop. They stood near the door and stared at Denise. Gabe felt Denise immediately tense up. Gabe could not engage with the young men, but he could keep talking to Denise.

"Where are you having lunch?" he asked her, trying to divert her gaze from the two young men.

"I am going to a place off Columbus Circle," Denise said. "It's too pricey for dinner, but for lunch it's a good splurge. I thought that after lunch I might stroll in the park. The weather is so fine today."

"That sounds wonderful," Daniel said. "I wish we could join you."

"You have plans?" she said, smiling and suggesting something intimate between Daniel and Gabe. Both men understood her and chuckled.

Gabe answered for both. "Work."

Denise smiled at them, finally relaxed. "I took the day off. It's my birthday."

"Happy birthday!" Gabe and Daniel said in unison.

"It's actually not my birthday in the traditional sense. I mark the day I told my parents I was trans as the day I was born."

"Then you get two birthdays a year. How lucky is that?" Daniel said.

"I don't know if it's lucky or not," Denise said. "But it's how I roll."

"Good for you," Gabe replied.

"Thank you—it's Gabe and Daniel, right? My stop is coming up," Denise said as she stood up. "Thank you so much," Denise reached out her hand to Daniel, who grasped it and gave it a squeeze. Denise reacted to the warmth.

"Is everything alright?" he asked her.

"Yes, it was something I felt. I can't explain it. Thank you so much, both of you—Gabe and Daniel. I'll remember that. I'll remember you."

"Happy birthday!" the two men repeated as Denise exited the train. She was smiling.

"You did very well," Gabe said. "I'm impressed."

"Thank you," Daniel replied, looking out the train window as it moved out of the station. "Will she be alright?"

"I don't know. That's the thing about free will. Everybody's got it, so anything can happen."

"I know," Daniel said. "But I don't like it—the randomness of the good and the bad."

"I understand. That's why we are here to help. Anyway, at least you and I can date?" Gabe added with a chuckle.

"We're not a couple," Daniel protested and then took a good look at Gabe, who was very attractive, especially when he was grinning— which he was. "Would you go out with me?"

"You're a little young," Gabe said, "but you are my type. I like the goatee."

"Thank you. You're very attractive, as well."

"I don't recall saying you were attractive—just my type. I may like someone who is less attractive than me," Gabe added with that grin that revealed he thought Daniel was indeed attractive.

"What's the rule on dating?" Daniel asked.

"There is no rule for that. We can do what we want. Free will."

"Even for us?"

"All creatures great and small, Daniel. Even for us. Look sharp, now. This one will not be so easy." Gabe nodded toward an older man who shuffled into the car. He was carrying a briefcase, which he kept on his lap.

"How do you know he needs us?" Daniel asked.

"Listen to their souls, Daniel. It precedes them."

"I don't understand."

"People tell you so much about themselves before they ever say a word. It's in the face, their gait, their mannerisms. Listen. Listen."

Daniel looked at the man seated across from them. He was approaching 60, Daniel thought. His clothes were old, but not shabby.

He looked down at his briefcase, avoiding eye contact. Daniel could hear the anguish. This man was lonely. Daniel wanted to say something but rule three forbade it. He stared intently at the man, trying to will him to look up and see a smile. Gabe touched Daniel's shoulder.

"In the library, you didn't see this much, did you? That's the hard part of the job. We can't engage with them unless they engage with us. It's the free will thing. They know we are here—deep down, they know we are here."

"Can he hear us?" Daniel asked.

"Not the way you think. He can hear us the way we hear his soul...we're in the same place inside him. But he must engage us first."

Daniel and Gabe sat across from the man, waiting for any sign of engagement. The sad man never looked up. Five stops later, he got up and slowly shuffled off the train.

"I wanted to help him," Daniel said.

"I know. I did, as well. Maybe he will reach out to another team."

"I hope so. Did you hear that?" Daniel asked, startled.

"Yes. You see, you are getting the feel of this. She is coming in now."

"She reminds me of my mom," Daniel said.

"I was going to say the same thing. People have an aura about them. I know that sounds New Age, and I hate that stuff. But they do. Good people at their core remind us of good people we knew. She is a very good person."

"She is dying."

"Yes, Daniel, she is."

"How can we help with that?"

"We help her believe that her pain will stop."

"But it won't for a long while. What's ahead is horrible. It's not fair."

"No, it's not fair. It just is."

"Excuse me," the woman they noticed said. "Would you mind moving over just a bit so I can squeeze in?"

"No problem, ma'am," Daniel said, as he moved closer to Gabe.

"You slid over to your right so she would have to ask you to move to your left. You forced her to engage," Gabe said to Daniel.

"You're angry?" Daniel asked.

"Impressed. That's not a rookie move." Gabe allowed Daniel to slide closer. Gabe appreciated the contact. "Well, now that you got her to engage, say something she can hear."

Daniel looked at the woman, smiling his warmest smile, and asked, "Is that enough room?"

"This is lovely, young man," she said. "I don't need much room. I'm a small woman."

"I'm sure you make up for that with the size of your smile," Daniel said. The woman immediately smiled broadly.

"I haven't done that in a long time," she said.

"What?" Daniel asked.

"Smiled. Thank you. You have a nice boyfriend," she added, looking at Gabe.

"I do," Daniel said, much to his and Gabe's surprise. "He sees what is in front of him and almost no one sees that."

"Then he sees an old woman."

"We all get old," Daniel replied, which of course neither Daniel nor Gabe did in the conventional way. "How is your day going?"

"Do you really want to know?" she asked. "I will tell you if you want to know."

"I want to know," Daniel said. "We want to know," he added, looking at Gabe.

"I'm Gabe." He smiled broadly toward the woman seated on the other side of Daniel.

"Like Gabriel, the archangel?" the woman asked.

"Yes, ma'am. But I'm not so fancy."

"Well, Gabriel, if I were a younger woman, I would ask to sit next to you—no offense, young man," she said, looking at Daniel. "I always liked a bigger man."

Daniel and Gabriel exchanged looks and blushed.

"I embarrassed you both," she said. "I've been doing that to people for more than sixty years. Not many more of those are left. I just saw my oncologist. The cancer is back. Stage four. I was in remission for more than a year."

"I'm sorry," Daniel said.

"Don't be. You didn't give it to me. I didn't give it to me. I lived a very healthy life. Never smoked. Walked four miles every day. My one vice is my evening whiskey sour. I love that whiskey sour."

"It's a great cocktail," Gabe said. "Very classy. Very classy, like you," he added.

"Now, young man, flattery will get you nowhere with me. I don't have the energy, and your boyfriend won't like that."

Gabe and Daniel chose not to argue that last point. Their job was to offer this woman comfort.

"Does the doctor want you to start treatment again?" Daniel asked.

"Yes," she said. "'Jenny, we want to start a new round of chemo,' my doc said."

"Jenny—may I call you Jenny?" Daniel asked, "Are you going to do it?"

"Please, call me Jenny. No point in formality. We're on the A train, right? Yes, she wants me to start treatment, and no, I am not going to do it."

"Don't you want to fight?" Gabe asked.

"Yes, I want to fight to enjoy what life I have left. I can't go through chemo again."

"Maybe you will change your mind," Daniel offered. "The news is still fresh."

"The doc saying it to me is fresh, but I knew. I knew."

"Give it time," Daniel continued.

"Easy for you to say. You are young. Time is what I don't have much of—with or without the cancer. I want to live in the present. I don't want to suffer for the possibility of a few more years. The math doesn't add up, young man."

"I never was good at math," Daniel said. "I rely on faith."

"If you hand me a flower, now, I will have to hurt you," Jenny said, giving a slight laugh. "I have faith. I have faith in him," Jenny added, looking upward.

"God?" Daniel said.

"The chairman of the MTA," Jenny replied, laughing. "God only goes so far. But the guy who runs this transit system is more important right now. When you're on the A train, heaven is not an authorized stop. I just want to get to Brooklyn."

"We're going that direction—to the Rockaways."

"The end of the line," Jenny said. "I will get there on my own schedule," she mused. "But for today," she continued in a more forceful tone and slapped her knees, "Jay Street in downtown Brooklyn is good enough." Jenny let out a sigh, as if the small effort of slapping her knees had sapped her energy. "I'm a little tired, young man," she added. "Would you mind if I just closed my eyes for a bit, and then could you keep an eye out for Jay Street for me in case I fall asleep?"

"We would be happy to," Gabe said.

Jenny closed her eyes and fell asleep quickly. Gabe and Daniel looked at her. Jenny's well-worn face looked beatific. She dreamed of a long-ago childhood swim off the Rockaways with her two sisters, older, and now deceased from the same cancer Jenny has.

"It's a pretty dream," Daniel said.

"Yes, it is." Gabe agreed. "We should do it sometime. The beaches at the Rockaways."

"You mean now, don't you?" Daniel asked, understanding Gabe's suggestion.

"Rule five: Bring them joy when you can."

Daniel and Gabe joined Jenny in her dream. They saw her as a young girl playing with her two sisters—Greta and Joanne—in the water. The five of them splashed each other with silly abandon. The lines on Jenny's face disappeared in the poor lighting of the A train, while Daniel and Gabe sat contentedly side by side, watching Jenny revel in a memory that was distorted just enough to bring her only joy. As the train neared Jay Street, Gabe tapped Daniel, signaling it was time to wake Jenny up.

"Jenny," Daniel said, lightly touching Jenny's shoulder. "It's time to wake up."

She stirred and opened her eyes. "I had a wonderful dream," Jenny said. "I was young again on the beach with my sisters, and you two were there. Lord, you are handsome without your shirts."

Daniel and Gabe blushed again.

"We're glad you had a good dream," Gabe said.

"It was a lovely dream. I must go. I feel better now."

"Good," Gabe and Daniel both said.

Jenny stood up and squeezed both their hands. "Thank you," she said before leaving the train.

"I feel good," Daniel said. "Bring them joy when you can. I like rule five."

"It's the best of the bunch."

Daniel and Gabe sat side by side until the end of the line. A few more people engaged with them, but several in crisis did not. Both men followed the rules, hard as it was to silently hope that the person in need would just ask for help.

The train had turned around and was heading back toward Manhattan when Gabe heard her call out his name. He looked over at Daniel, who looked ashen. He heard it too. "Gabe. Daniel." Their names shouted out into the silence of the train. There was no one in the car now.

"It's Denise," Daniel said.

"Yes, Daniel," Gabe said, concerned.

"She is calling out for us."

"Yes, Daniel. She is."

"We can't help her, can we?"

"Not now, we can't. In a little while, we can. That is why we stayed on the train. When we get to Columbus Circle, we will walk into the park. She will be there. We can help her then."

"This isn't fair. It's her birthday, for Christ's sake." Daniel was distraught.

"Watch your language," Gabe said kindly. "He's on our side."

"I'm sorry. I'm upset. It just isn't fair."

"No, it isn't fair. We can't change anything. That's not our job. He can't change anything," Gabe added with a slight nod upward. "That's not his job either. Free will."

"I want to be there now."

"I know. I know. We are not alone in this job. Denise is not alone right now. But we will get to her, and she will see familiar faces. Then, after we see her, she will be ready for the next part of her journey.

"She is in pain now. This is horrible. I can see what is happening to her. There are three or is it four men?"

"That didn't happen before?" Gabe asked. "I guess not in the library. But here, in the real world, it happens too often. We see it. We see the violence wrought on beautiful people, and we cannot stop it."

"It's because she called out our names—that's why we can see it, yes?"

"Yes, Daniel. I told you there's a moment when we don't want to hear our names. This is why. If we speak with someone like Denise, they come to realize who we are, and they call out to us in their most dire moment. We hear them and see it all. That's the good side to free will, Daniel. If someone chooses to believe, they will not be alone. They will not face their darkest moment alone. But we have to see and hear everything that is happening to them, so we can absorb some of their pain. We cannot absorb it all, but we can lessen Denise's pain, so she can bear it."

"I feel pain, right now. Physical pain. How is that possible, Gabe?"

"It is possible because it is. I feel it, too. It will pass. We will get through this together. That's why we work in teams. When we get to Denise, it will be good again. She will have peace. It will be good again. Trust me."

"Is that rule six, Gabe?"

"No, that is just my rule—Gabe's rule. Trust me."

Daniel felt as if his insides were bleeding. Every blow Denise received, he felt, as did Gabe. The two men sat close, side by side on the bench of the empty A train. Soon it would fill up with new passengers. Some would engage, and some would not. Some would find joy, and some would not. Some would sit in silence, and some would spout on and on.

And some, like Denise, would call out their names.

A Table for Four

Edith arrived early, as she intended. She loved Kathrine, Susan, and Maryann like sisters, but she relished her fifteen solo minutes at the bar.

It wasn't that she didn't have enough alone time since George went south seven years earlier; her husband had left her for a woman half his age with large breasts and little else to recommend her. The divorce had not upset Edith. Truth be told—and truth should always be told sitting solo in a bar—she and George hadn't been in sync for years, maybe never. No, that wasn't fair to either of them, but what irked Edith most was that George chose to leave her for a woman young enough to be his daughter. That was too much the cliché.

De trop. De trope. Definitely not, "de lovely." Edith loved Cole Porter and the days of Bobby Short at the Carlyle. That was never George's scene, but it was with Kenny, their son. That was their bond, even if he was too young for Café Society. But now, Kenny had also gone south, not metaphorically as his father, but to Atlanta, where he ran a theater company. Edith was concerned that her son was nearing 40 and still single.

She didn't understand the problem so many men, both straight and gay, had with commitment. Kenny was handsome and talented, had been out since middle school, and worked in the theater. Where was the cliché when Edith needed it? Kenny should be coupled. And she should order her martini before the girls arrived. There was no one sitting at the bar.

"Do you want to check your coat, Mrs. Henderson?" Paolo asked as he helped Edith with her tan cashmere coat.

"I don't think so. I like it near me. It allows for a fast getaway. You know the girls."

"You always have a lovely time. You're our favorites."

"You're just saying that. I see the fuss you make over that gay couple whenever they eat here."

"That describes many couples who eat here."

"You know the one...late middle-aged. One is tall and Black, while the other man is shorter and white. The short one is always in a suit."

"Ah, yes. They are not a couple."

"Of course they are."

"No, they are not."

"Men. You really don't see what is in front of you."

"Do you want to be seated, Mrs. Henderson, or wait at the bar?" Paolo said, not taking the bait.

"You know the answer to that."

"Hendrick's, up with olives?" Marina, the bartender, chimed in.

"That's my girl, yes. You see, Paolo, women are on top of everything. They see the world as it is. Men see the world the way they imagined it when they were thirteen. That's my theory."

"That explains their perpetual adolescence," Marina said as she pulled the Hendrick's from the shelf behind the bar. "Vermouth?" she asked, then, in unison with Edith, added, "in and out quickly."

"Just like my first husband," a female voice rejoined. It was Susan wearing an enormous coat.

"You are terribly politically incorrect," Edith said, taking a sip of her martini. "Definitely not 'woke.'"

"It's the Ambien. It keeps me in a constant state of ambivalence."

"I prefer gin," Edith said, taking another sip. "This is divine," she said to Marina.

"Thank you, Edith. And for you, Susan? A white wine?"

"Not tonight. I'm celebrating."

"What are we celebrating?" Marina asked.

"Yes, what are we celebrating, Susie?" added Edith.

"That is for later, when all the girls are here. I'll have what she's having, except I want Grey Goose vodka instead of gin. No vermouth. Not even a rinse. And a lemon twist."

"That is nothing like my drink, Susie. You just ordered a straight vodka."

"Don't be vulgar, dear. You see," Susan said, pointing to the chilled martini glass Marina placed before her. "Once it's in the glass, it looks the same. They both look the same."

"Just like men in the dark," a raspy-voiced woman said as she took off a well-tailored navy coat, revealing a houndstooth wool suit that showed off her toned 62-year-old figure.

Katherine McCormick was the most fashion-forward of the quartet. She refused to embrace her sixties as an entrance to the world of senior discounts and sensible shoes. Instead, she saw this period of her life as providing her access to a private Red Door, albeit in a world where no one under 60 had heard of Elizabeth Arden.

"Kate, I didn't see you come in," Edith said.

"Of course you didn't see me, Edith. You were focused on Mr. Hendricks."

"I like my martini," Edith replied.

"And don't we all? Martinis are dependable," Katherine added.

"Oh, dear," Susan said. "It's over between you and James."

"It never really began."

"She needs a drink," Edith said. "Another martini. Oh, hell, give her something straight but make it cold."

"That describes James."

All the women laughed.

"Let's get a table," Katherine said. "I want to get settled before I start to drink. Paolo?"

"Right this way, Mrs. McCormick. We have your usual table ready."

"You spoil us," Susan said, trying to pick up her glass, which was still almost full.

"I will bring the drinks to your table," Paolo said.

"No need for me. I can manage this," Edith said, downing most of her gin martini. "Amateurs," she said toward Susan and Katherine.

"I would rather carry myself well than a cocktail," Susan chided.

"This from someone wearing an endangered species."

"These sables were working for Putin. I did the world a favor," Susan said as she and her enormous coat maneuvered through the small maze of tables to their table for four against the wall near the windows.

"That coat is perfectly ridiculous," Katherine said. "But I quite like it, nonetheless."

"Thank you, Kate," Susan said. "And I really love your suit."

"St. John's," Katherine replied.

"My favorite apostle," Edith said, lifting her martini to the heavens.

The women settled in. Paolo brought Susan's drink to the table. Enrico, their favorite waiter, followed him.

The women loved flirting with Enrico. He was a native of Sicily. Uncommonly tall and sporting a well-trimmed, but very full black beard, Enrico spoke with a Sicilian accent that, given his deep baritone, made everything he said sound sensual. The pasta specials were a favorite of the women—not for ordering them, but for hearing Enrico pronounce them. *Tortellini. Fettuccine. Linguine. Orecchiette con Salsiccia e Cime di Rapa.* It was no-calorie foreplay.

Enrico was on to them, but the four women had no clue, which worked well for everyone involved. Enrico leaned slightly over the table and asked Katherine, "May I get you a drink?"

"Absolutely," Katherine said. "I need to break with the trend here. I want a whisky sour."

"A whisky sour?" Edith said. "My mother used to drink whisky sours."

"Everybody's mother drank whisky sours. It was quite the thing once," Susan said, sipping her vodka.

"Well, ladies, it is still quite the thing for me. Our mothers were on to something."

"One whisky sour coming up," Enrico said.

Before he could leave, Katherine asked, "When you come back, can you tell us the specials?"

"You don't want to wait for your friend?" Enrico asked, pointing toward the empty chair.

"She's always late, and you can always repeat them to all of us," Katherine replied.

"Of course," Enrico said as the three women smiled at each other knowingly. They didn't notice Enrico was similarly smiling once he turned toward the bar.

"Of course, Maryann is late," Katherine said. "She is never on time."

"Don't be unkind, Kate," Susan said over her martini. "She is coming from the west."

"You make it sound like Wyoming, Susie," Katherine replied. "Maryann lives just above 74th on Central Park West. She has lovely views."

"Yes, of the East Side. Listen, Kate, she should live here," Susan added for emphasis.

"That is very provincial," Katherine said as she adjusted the gold bracelet on her right wrist. "The world does not revolve around the East Side."

"And that is why we have global warming," Edith added.

"Oh, dear. Global warming on your first Hendrick's," Katherine admonished with a smile.

"You're just impatient because you don't have your mama's cocktail," Edith said after downing the last of her Hendrick's.

Before Katherine could reply, Enrico arrived with the whiskey sour. "Here you are," he said, leaning in with the drink between Katherine and Susan. The two women inhaled his scent. Katherine raised her glass to Susan and Edith. "To us."

"I'm dry," Edith said.

"Not even in January," Susan retorted.

"Thank you, Betty Ford," Edith replied. "I would like another and please do not take this glass. I like to let the olives soak."

"Soak in what, dear?" Katherine asked. "You've sucked it dry."

Edith turned to Susan and said, "Do not say anything."

"I wasn't going to say anything," Susan protested.

"I have known you for what? Twelve years? We were reading *Lady Chatterley's Lover*," Edith said to Susan.

"It's a book about sex. What was I supposed to talk about?"

"Now, ladies," Katherine interjected, "it's a classic, and it is how we all got to know one another. To Lady Chatterley."

"I'm still dry," Edith said.

"Not even in January," Maryann said, walking up to the table. "So sorry I am late. There was terrible traffic crosstown."

"If you lived on the East Side, there would be no traffic," Katherine said.

"And that, Kate, is because everyone lives on the Westside."

"Please, this should be neutral ground," Susan said. "We are only blocks from the UN."

"And I am still dry."

In unison now, the three other women said, "Not even in January." They all laughed, even Maryann. Good friends don't let cocktails or a "classic six" in the San Remo get in the way of friendship.

Enrico, who was still standing by the table, asked Edith, "Another Hendrick's?"

"Yes, Enrico. Marina knows how I like it."

Again, in unison, the three other women said, "Hendrick's. Vermouth in and out quickly. Lots of olives." They all laughed.

"I will have a Sancerre," Maryann said as she smoothed out a wrinkle in her black silk skirt. Of the four, she was the thinnest and youngest, having turned 59 a month earlier.

"You should have something stronger," Edith said.

"If I want something stronger, I will find a man."

"You're making Enrico blush," Katherine said. That was hard to tell with his olive skin and thick beard.

"I can help you with the wine," Enrico said with a smile as he headed to the bar.

"He has a nice ass," Edith said.

"Edith!" Maryann said. "We're in a restaurant."

"His ass is nice. It would be a nice ass in a restaurant or in Central Park. Since he and his ass are in this restaurant, it is an appropriate observation."

"Maybe you could say 'rear end' or 'tush,'" Maryann said.

"Tush? Did you come from the Westside or the 1950s?" Edith asked.

"I can't help it. I don't like saying 'ass' in public." Maryann quieted her voice on the "ass."

"That's quite all right, Maryann," Susan said. "You keep Enrico's ass to yourself." Edith and Katherine laughed. "So, I have news."

"That's right," Edith said. "You said when you came in, you had celebratory news."

"You dumped Brian," Katherine said.

"I thought you liked him," Susan said.

"No, I never liked him. He reminds me of my Uncle Steve."

"I have not left Brian," Susan said, shooting a look at Katherine. "In fact, things couldn't be better with Brian. That is not my news. I sold a painting."

"You sold a painting?" Maryann repeated. "That is fabulous. Which one?"

"It was the old woman sitting on a pier up on the Cape. Here, I can show you on my phone." Susan opened her phone, found the image, and shared it with the group. Everyone made approving comments.

"She has such a soulful expression. Did you know her, or was she a random subject?" Maryann asked.

"I knew her in a casual way. Her name was Grace, and I would see her whenever we went up to the Cape. She was always sitting in the same place, staring at the sea. At first, I thought maybe she had been the wife of a sailor or someone who worked on a boat and had died. But it wasn't that. She was a widow, but her husband had been something in insurance and died from natural causes at 60. She was near 80 when we started to chat. She said she liked looking at the ocean because they had always wanted to take a transatlantic cruise, but they never did. They always said they would do it when they retired, and then he died. She said she looked out on the Atlantic, imagining the crossing."

"She could have gone by herself," Edith said.

"I asked her about that, and she said it wasn't the same thing. It was a shared dream that they put off. So, she looked out at the sea, thinking about when they first talked about going. They were newlyweds, just starting out. She said she could see the two of them as they had been if she stared long enough at the water. It made her sad, but it also gave her some joy, remembering that moment when they were young enough to think that dreams could be put on hold. That's what I wanted to capture in the painting—the sadness mixed with a warm memory."

"Brava, Susan, it's powerful looking at it on the phone," Edith said. "It must be something magnificent in person."

"I'm proud of it. And I am proud of this." Susan pulled out a bank receipt and passed it around the table.

"My goodness," Maryann said. "Those are five figures."

"Five large figures," Susan added with pride.

"I guess you are buying," Edith said.

"Yes, I am buying, Edith. Olive up, ladies, it's going to be a bumpy night."

Enrico arrived with a Sancerre and Edith's Henrick's. Once the women all had drinks, Susan raised her glass and said, "To Grace."

"To Grace," the four women said.

"To us," Maryann added.

They all sipped at their drinks.

"Do you want to hear the specials now?" Enrico asked. We have pasta tonight."

"To the pasta specials."

They toasted again.

"Tonight, we have *linguine alle vongole*, *penne alla Norma*, and of course, *orecchiette con salsiccia e cime di rapa*," Enrico said in his deepest voice, accentuating each syllable.

"That sounds wonderful," Maryann said.

"Yes, it did," Susan rejoined. "We'll work on these drinks first."

"Certainly, ladies. Everyone good drink-wise?"

"I could use another Grey Goose," Susan said.

"I will have another whiskey sour," Kate said, holding up her nearly empty glass. "They put egg whites in their whiskey sours here. It's the best of both worlds...alcohol and protein."

"You know, Enrico, this Sancerre is very nice," Maryann said, looking at her half-empty glass. "By the time you come back with their drinks, I will be ready for another, so you might as well bring me a Sancerre."

"Don't look at me," Edith said to Enrico. "Even I need about 10 minutes to finish this martini."

"All right then. Another Grey Goose, whiskey sour, and Sancerre."

"Do you think they could bring us some bread, maybe?" Maryann asked.

"I will tell the kitchen," Enrico replied. He headed toward the kitchen.

"Amazing news about the painting, Susan," Maryann said. "That story about the woman on the pier was very moving. It makes me think about how I have put off my dreams."

"What dreams?" Edith asked.

"You'll laugh."

"Of course, we will laugh," Edith said. "We're your friends. That shouldn't stop you."

"I want to run a half-marathon."

No one laughed. They just stared.

"I think I would have preferred laughter."

"Maryann, we love you, and we will support you, but a half-marathon—what is that, like 10 miles or so...?" asked Susan.

"It's 13.1 miles," Maryann said.

"13.1 miles? Even worse," Edith said as she picked at an olive in the empty glass.

"You take an Uber to Lincoln Center, and you live on West 74th," added Katherine.

"You don't run a half-marathon in heels," Maryann replied. "I always wear heels to the Met."

"You're not a Rosie Ruiz," Edith said, stabbing an olive like it was Carmen at the end of Act IV.

"No, actually, she could be," Kate corrected. "Rosie Ruiz was the runner who took a cab and then jumped into the Boston Marathon right at the end. But you don't want to be her, Maryann."

"I don't want to be her. I'm not trying to win the race, just finish it. I just want to do something athletic before I become too feeble."

"Have you thought about having more sex?" Edith queried.

"I have enough sex."

"Here, here, Maryann," Susan added. "It's always the quiet ones with the pearls. And they are very nice pearls."

"Thank you," Maryann replied. "I always wanted to run a half-marathon. I ran track in college."

"I didn't know that," Susan said. If Dr. Elliot Garber on East 69th hadn't been so thorough last week, Susan's face would have registered surprise. "How many years have we known each other? And I never knew that about you?"

"There's a lot we don't know about one another, Susan," Maryann said. "We met in a book club. We talked about books. The book club disbanded, but we didn't."

"We talked about a lot of things other than books," Susan said. "Men. Husbands. Boyfriends. Children."

"We don't talk about dreams," Maryann said.

"Maybe we don't. Maybe we haven't," Susan added before pausing for a moment. "But I think it's a good dream, Maryann, and I, for one, will support you," she added, hoisting up her glass. "I will be at the finish line with a cold martini in a thermos, cheering you on."

"So will I," Edith said, downing her second gin martini.

"I will, as well," Katherine said. "I don't want to step on your dream, Maryann. Have you started training?"

"No, I said it's something I wanted to do, not that I was doing it."

"You have to do it now," Katherine said, leaning in towards Maryann. "Once you declare a dream in public, you are committed. Let's drink on it."

They all drank.

"Now that we have Maryann settled, and I told you the story behind my painting, what's an unfulfilled dream for you, Kate?" Susan asked.

"I want to write something."

"You do write, Kate," Susan replied. "I just finished your piece in *The New Yorker*. Very clever."

"I want to write a romance novel."

The women all laughed.

"That wasn't the reaction I expected. Shock, maybe. Laughter, no."

"It's just a strange dream, Kate," Maryann said. "You are successful as a serious journalist."

"I always wanted to write an over-the-top romance novel devoid of deep psychological characters—just overly written smut. The kind of novel you read on a rainy day on the couch with a bag of Milano cookies."

"I love Milanos," Maryann said.

"Then write it, cookie," Edith said with a twinkle.

"And use a pseudonym," Susan added.

"A *nom de plume*," Maryann said.

"Yes, Maryann, we know you went to Vassar," Edith said flatly.

"Eleanor Lavish," Susan said.

"From *A Room with a View*," Katherine replied. "I didn't go to Vassar, I went to Brown," she directed toward Edith. "Eleanor Lavish. I like that."

"It's very gay," Edith said.

"How do you mean?" asked Maryann.

"Gay men love all things E.M. Forster," Edith answered. "Why don't you write a gay romance novel?"

"I always wanted to write a women's romance novel," Kate said.

"It's really the same book," Edith said as she stabbed another olive. "One has a woman pining for a hot man who is objectified for about 180 pages. A gay romance novel has the same page count and same object, just the woman is a man. Just make sure that the sex scenes focus on the hot man. It can cross over—the first romance novel written for straight women and gay men."

"I think the hot man should be called Enrico," Maryann said.

"Ah, there it is," Susan said. "Maryann has a crush."

"You don't think Enrico is sexy?" Maryann asked tentatively.

"Of course," Susan said.

"Here, here," Katherine said, raising her almost empty glass.

"Come to mama," Edith said to her martini.

Katherine started by saying, "The hero will be called Enrico, and he works with his hands."

"In Syracuse," Edith added.

"Syracuse, like in New York?" Katherine asked.

"No, Syracuse in Sicily."

"There's no Syracuse in Sicily. It's in New York," Maryann said.

"I guess they don't teach geography at Vassar," Edith said to Maryann. "I don't know much about New York outside of the city, but my Syracuse is in Sicily. I know that as fact."

"Since when?" Maryann asked defensively.

"Summer of 1979. An exchange program, my junior year. I wanted to learn Italian, so I spent the summer in Italy and Sicily. His name was Giancarlo, and he was all that and a bag of chips."

"That won't do," Katherine said. "Exchange students are notorious sluts. No. I need someone innocent. Alice Bishop—that's it—she is a mousy secretary from Indiana who arrives in Sicily in July. She is dressed in white, I think."

"Like a virgin," Maryann added.

"Sing it, Madonna," Susan encouraged.

"Yes, like a virgin," Katherine continued, "because she is a virgin waiting for adventure. She is walking in a white cotton dress with...with little pink flowers woven into the cloth and is wearing cork-soled shoes. One of the heels snaps, and she starts to fall near the end of the pier, and Enrico sweeps in."

"Shirtless," Edith interrupted.

"Shirtless isn't sexy at first," Kate protested.

"It's sexy," Edith insisted.

"Is this my story or yours?"

"You're basing it on my life. Giancarlo was shirtless."

Katherine continued unfazed. "Enrico sweeps in. His unbuttoned shirt blows back in the warm wind, revealing his chiseled chest gleaming with sweat as he catches Alice before she falls. Alice becomes disoriented in Enrico's arms, growing dizzy from his masculine scent tinged with citrus, the latter from the lemons he grows on his family's land."

"*Femminello* lemons," Edith interjected.

"*Femminello*?" asked Kathrine.

"It's a type of lemon in Sicily," Edith responded. "Trust me."

"Alice becomes disoriented in Enrico's arms, growing dizzy from his masculine scent tinged with citrus, the latter from the *Femminello* lemons he grows on his family's land. She looks up at Enrico's handsome face and focuses on his dark green eyes glimmering like emeralds set in bronze. Alice tries to catch her breath, but in doing so, she inhales his intoxicating scent, and her lungs fill with the smell of citrus-infused sweat. She is hot now from the heat of the mid-morning sun, from the warmth of Enrico's strong, muscled arms that are enfolding her, and from the unfamiliar fire that is burning beneath her skin."

"I'll buy that story," Susan said.

"So will I," a tall Black man said as he walked past their table. "It sounds like a very sexy story."

"We were just making something up," Katherine said, embarrassed that outsiders heard their conversation.

"It sounded good, didn't it?" the tall Black man asked his dinner partner walking behind him.

"I didn't hear it, but I'm sure it must be good," he said. "Harry never gives compliments freely. Believe me, I know."

"He's right. I don't," Harry added with a smile. "Good luck with the story."

"Nice meeting you," the shorter man said. "Enjoy your evening." The two men headed to their table by the window, where Enrico was waiting to take their drink orders.

"They always make a fuss over that couple," Susan said, downing the last of her vodka martini.

"They are not a couple," Edith replied, finishing her gin martini.

"Of course, they are a couple. I can see it from here," Maryann added as she finished her Sancerre.

"I said the same thing when I came in tonight," Edith said with conviction. "I told Paolo they were his favorite couple, and he said they were not a couple."

"Men are such fools," Susan said.

"They are," Maryann agreed.

"I'm going to write it," Katherine said. "I won't try to publish it, but I think it will be fun to write."

"You will write it, Eleanor Lavish. You will get it published, and I will do the artwork for the cover," Susan said. "I'll ask Enrico to model for it."

"I want to come to that," Edith said.

"So do I," added Katherine. "That might be the incentive I need to write the book."

"We shouldn't objectify men," Maryann scolded.

"Why not?" Susan asked. "Straight men objectify women all the time. And gay men objectify men. Women shouldn't feel guilty about doing what is a natural part of being. Who do you think is sexy in here tonight?"

"What?" Maryann asked, embarrassed. "We could be everyone's mother."

"You can be everyone's mother," Edith said. "Age is just a number. We are still women in the game. Look, Maryann, you're planning to run a half-marathon."

"Yes, I am," Maryann said, startled at the thought and feeling suddenly empowered. "The guy two tables over. He's sexy."

The four women turned in unison to look.

"That's a former governor," Susan said.

"No," Maryann replied.

"Yes, it is," Kate said, agreeing.

"He's a pig," Edith added. "P-I-G. Pig."

"I remember that scandal," Maryann replied. "But he's still attractive."

"But lipstick on a pig..." Edith began.

"That would be fun," Maryann interrupted. "Tying him up and then applying lipstick."

"Is this going to be a romance novel or gay porn?" Susan asked.

"Wouldn't it be justice for a man who procured women to become the target of a woman, just once?" Maryann asked. "The hunter becomes the hunted."

"Where has this woman been hiding all these years?" Edith asked the table.

"Behind *The New Yorker*, like me," Katherine added with a laugh. "I'm convinced. I need to write a slutty romance novel for us, for Maryann, for all objectified women."

"That leaves you, Edith," Maryann said. "What dream have you delayed?"

"Are you ready to order?" Enrico asked. He had approached the table unnoticed.

"Saved by the boy," Edith said. "I mean, man, of course," she added. "We need some more time, but maybe another round of drinks. Yes, ladies?"

The other three women concurred. Enrico cleared away Maryann's, Susan's, and Katherine's glasses, leaving Edith's with the growing grove of olives.

"What's your delayed dream, Edith?" Susan asked. "Tell us, or you will have to pay."

"That's not fair," Edith said. "I can see that that five-figure check of yours has gone to your head."

"You're among friends, Edith," Maryann said. "If I am going to run a half-marathon, and Kate is going to write a slutty novel, you should tell us something."

"What about Susan?" Edith asked. "She hasn't told us an unfulfilled dream."

"She sold a painting and is picking up the check," Maryann added with surprising force. "Fess up."

Edith sat for a moment and then looked at her three friends. "I always get here fifteen minutes early to be alone. I tell myself it's because I want alone time, but it's really the opposite. I don't want alone time. I want to meet someone, and I guess I think that if I am here fifteen minutes early, I might meet a handsome or at least interesting older guy sitting at the bar, and I won't seem desperate because I am meeting three friends, and if he is interested, he will ask for my number. If he isn't, you will all be there soon. But I never meet anyone. I talk with Marina. I drink too much."

The three women didn't respond right away. Susan was first.

"You don't drink too much. We drink too little. We can fix that tonight. Drink up, ladies. To hell with Betty Ford."

"To hell with Betty Ford," Kate and Maryann chimed in.

"Edith," Susan began, "We have men, and we don't have men, but we always have each other. This is the hard time of life...there is less ahead than there is behind. But what's the choice, right? We're a team, the four of us. Look at us. We're amazing women. We've been through a lot before we met, and we have been through a lot these past twelve years."

"Tell us something that you want to do," Maryann said.

"I want to go back to Syracuse—Syracuse in Sicily. I want to go back to that same place I was in when I was an exchange student, and I want to find Giancarlo. I know, he's probably married or dead..."

"Or gay," Susan added with a broad smile.

"He's definitely not gay," Edith said.

"Ok," Susan replied. "He's either married or dead or... maybe, maybe he's still living in Sicily, single now and smelling of *Femminello*—that can't be real—lemons."

"I can't go to Sicily," Edith said.

"Why not?" Susan asked.

"It's a silly dream. I can't afford to do that."

"You can't afford not to, just like Maryann here must run her race before her hip replacement, and Kate must write a slutty novel before she goes senile, and I have to get Enrico to strip in a studio for the cover art before arthritis sets in. You know what? We're all going."

"What?" Edith asked.

"Look at what I just made on a single painting," Susan said, taking the bank receipt out of her purse again. "It's a lot of money. I'm taking all of us to Syracuse. Picture it: Sicily. Four post-menopausal women."

"You're crazy," Edith said.

"You're drunk," Maryann replied.

"You're a genius," Katherine said. "I'll write my slutty novel based on my own slutty behavior. I'm in."

"Well, then, so am I," Maryann said. "I want to be a slut, too."

"A bunch of old women are going to Sicily?" Edith asked incredulously.

"I don't see any old women at this table. Come on. Say, yes," Susan said, reaching out to Edith, who for once was not picking at an olive or holding a glass. She was completely without a fortress.

"Ok," Edith said. "Let's do it."

"Four women go to Sicily," Maryann said.

"Four friends go to Sicily," Susan corrected.

"Four good friends go to Sicily," Katherine said, completing the circle. The four friends joined hands around the table. Edith was the first to break the moment.

"Enrico," she yelled across the restaurant. "We need drinks. I'm dry."

To which the entire wait staff shouted back, "Not even in January."

A Perfect Day

"There's a parking spot over there, Vincent. Just ahead on the right."

"I don't think we will fit. It looks tight."

"Give it a try. I have a feeling we will make it. I will say a Hail Mary."

"Isn't that a little extreme? Do we need to bother her for a parking space? It seems like an overreach."

"Hail Mary, full of grace. Blessed art thou and blessed is the fruit of thine womb, Jesus."

Amelia continued her prayer as Vincent pulled up close to the car in front of the open space, then turned the wheel and slowly began parallel parking the sedan. "Holy Mary, mother of God, pray for us sinners now and at the hour of our death. Amen."

"Amen," Vincent repeated. He had parked the car in one attempt.

"You see?" Amelia said to her son.

"That was some great parking. It deserves applause."

"Now who's overreaching?" she said, smiling her most pleased-with-herself smile. Amelia was enjoying herself. It was not just proving the power of prayer, which was not a theory to her, but oxygen. She breathed in Italian Catholicism from the moment she left the womb. Italian Catholicism for women of a certain generation was a combination of Church teachings, traditions, and superstitions, pulled together by heavy doses of incense, guilt, and midweek, morning trips to a church with a rosary. There were variations, like the differences between Amelia's and Cousin Gracie's sauce—neither called it gravy nor could they understand why some people claimed Italians did. But the variations were not of such great consequence when it came to matters of faith.

The saints were on speed dial if speed dial had existed in the 1930s when they were being formed in the faith. You called the saints up at will.

The Hail Mary for the Virgin Mother was ubiquitous. It was the one-size-fits-all of prayers. But when you had specific needs, you called the experts—like the signs on septic tank cleaning trucks that traversed the suburbs of Long Island: "You tried the rest, now try the best." If you lost an object, call on St. Anthony. If you were lost, invoke St. Christopher. And poor St. Joseph! He got tucked head-first into the front yards of homes up for sale, usually just north of the small cement grotto where a Blessed Mother stood with outstretched arms. St. Jude was for hopeless causes. Amelia had him working overtime to find Vincent a nice woman, but St. Jude had limitations. Jude was being—if you excuse the expression—cock-blocked by St. Sebastian, whom Vincent had been calling for assistance in finding a nice man since he was seventeen.

This Saturday morning, it was less about the power of prayer for parking and more about the shared time with her son that put a smile on Amelia's face. The mother and son were close enough; Vincent stopped by most weekends to do laundry and help with small chores around the house. But the two never discussed anything of great substance. It was a recounting of the past week's events on both their parts. Occasionally, there were moments of levity, like the afternoon last October when they both stared out the front window to watch Nancy Cavatelli dig up part of her front lawn because she had forgotten exactly where she buried the small St. Joseph statue, and her sister Cecilia now wanted it back.

While those moments were special, they didn't bring Amelia lasting happiness. Today felt different. Vincent invited her to join him in searching for two matching wing chairs for his apartment at a Macy's sale. The sale was held in a large, ancient warehouse in Long Island City, before many of these massive industrial structures were replaced by glass towers, an attempt to evoke the allure of Manhattan. On this Saturday, the Macy's warehouse was just another aging brick building among many similar ones. The large sign painted on the rust-colored brick identified the destination.

Amelia and Vincent walked the two blocks to the building where the car was parked. There was a steady stream of shoppers ahead and behind them. Amelia knew Vincent was determined to find two matching chairs, and she was determined to be as amiable as possible.

"I think we should scope out the floors first," he said as they entered. "Let's see what is available."

"That sounds like a plan," Amelia said, following her son. She had two missions unbeknownst to Vincent: to scout out wing chairs and to look for any potential women who might be a suitable catch for her son, whom she did not realize was only interested in male fish. "That one's nice," she said. Amelia pointed to a chair that Vincent could barely hide his disgust for, but Amelia had a hidden motive. Standing near the chair was an attractive young woman walking alone amid the haphazardly displayed furniture across the massive floor.

"I don't think so," Vincent said. "I don't like red."

The chair was red, but so was the woman's hair, so Amelia thought to herself, "Ah, no redheads."

They continued across the first floor. Vincent, like his mother, had two goals: to find two wing chairs and maybe catch sight of a handsome man wandering alone in the fields of upholstery.

"Let's go over there," he said. "I want to look at that sofa."

"Aren't we looking for chairs?" Amelia asked.

"Yes, but that sofa looks too interesting to ignore. I want a closer look."

Amelia watched her son walk toward the sofa. She could see he was engaged in a brief conversation with a man standing near it. Vincent is always so at ease talking with men, she thought. I wish he would show the same focus when he meets women, she continued to muse. She was in no hurry to join her son because Amelia knew he would not buy a sofa, and he always seemed slightly guilty when she interrupted him while he was chatting with a stranger, usually a man around his own age. Amelia convinced herself they were talking about men's stuff, and since Vincent had no interest in sports or cars, she assumed it must be about women.

It was not the sofa that caught Vincent's attention. It was the man around thirty with a smile that could stop traffic. He was also tall, athletic, and broad-shouldered. The man was without question the best chest in a seven-floor building filled with bureaus.

Vincent pointed to the Chesterfield sofa. "It's nice. I like leather," Vincent added. He could have done better, but it was early in the morning, and his mother was nearby. What man excels at picking up stray men with his mother as a wing man? A wing chair, yes. A man, rarely.

"So do I," the man said. "I like leather, but my boyfriend doesn't. He says his legs stick to leather in the summer."

The mention of a boyfriend so quickly was like discovering a Manhattan had been made with bourbon and not rye. Vincent's disappointment was palpable.

"It is a nice sofa," Vincent managed. He did not want to appear obvious, but he was to everyone except his mother.

"Well, it's all yours," the man said with a polite smile as he moved on. By then, Amelia had caught up with her son.

"Do you think you want to buy this?" she asked.

"No, not at all. We came here for chairs, not a sofa. I just was curious, that was all."

"I didn't think you liked leather sofas. You always said your legs stick to leather cushions."

Amelia did not realize she was pouring salt into an open wound. Vincent smiled and nodded, and the two continued on the first floor. There were a few chairs here or there worth stopping for, but nothing special.

Vincent's mother had a thing for dining furniture. Besides wearing My Sin by Lanvin—and always mentioning the perfume and the company together—Amelia liked dining room furniture. She was constantly replacing it for a larger size—another thing Vincent had in common with his mother, but not quite in the same context. Vincent knew before they even reached a massive table that they were taking a detour.

"Look at this, Vincent," Amelia said, beaming. "It is so beautiful." She was touching the mahogany tabletop.

Vincent, who could be a jerk at times, wanted to say, "Mom, are you going to venerate it?" but he did not. He was having fun with her this morning. She was game for an adventure that he wanted to take, and that did not happen often. Vincent played along.

"It is beautiful, Mom. The finish on that is like a mirror. Look, we can see ourselves in the tabletop." Mother and son looked at their reflections and smiled.

"It's a pity we don't have a camera. We could take a snapshot of ourselves as reflected in the table," Amelia said.

"That would be nice, Mom. I didn't think of bringing a camera here."

"Of course not. Who could imagine people walking around with a camera in their pocket, taking pictures of themselves all day long? How boring would that be?"

"I agree. It would be like being trapped in a room with Cousin Giorgio and his Kodak Carousel slide projector. Remember last July 4th?"

"How could I forget. One hundred slides of him and Angela on a Circle Line boat up to Bear Mountain. You would think they were in Paris on the Seine."

"It was torture, Mom. But remember when the slide with him and Cousin Angela eating the hot dogs got stuck in the projector. The slide began to melt from the heat of the projector's lamp. Their faces started to dissolve."

"I had forgotten that, Vincent," Amelia said, laughing. She began contorting her face as if it was melting, gazing at her reflection in the tabletop. Vincent, who was rarely silly in public or private, joined her. They were having a grand time until a stern man came by and gave them a look. Amelia called it the Monsignor Shannon look, referring to her pastor. That look would stop a nine-year-old boy in his tracks, force a nineteen-year-old man to admit to impure thoughts, and send many an Italian matron running to confession to admit to sexual activity that would curl a man's hair—except for Monsignor Shannon's, who was completely bald.

The look was potent. Amelia and Vincent stopped laughing instantly. They both gave a Cheshire-cat smile to the stern man, but as soon as he was out of sight, burst out laughing.

"I should buy this table," Amelia said.

"Mom, it's beautiful, but it is so big. It won't fit in the dining area."

"It will fit. I just need to move some things around."

"Like the walls. If you put this table in the dining area and opened it up for the leaves, no chairs would fit. We would have to crawl under the table to get to the other side."

"You're exaggerating. It is not that big."

"Mom," Vincent pleaded.

"You're probably right. But it would be fun to watch Cousin Giorgio crawl under the table to reach the other side. That would be a picture!"

The two started laughing again, making contorted faces that were reflected in the highly polished mahogany dining table. They moved on.

Amelia felt closer to her son than she had in years. "I could just sell the house and buy one with a bigger dining room," she said, looking back.

"Yes, you could, Mom," Vincent said with genuine amusement. "You'll have to borrow Mrs. Cavatelli's statue of St. Joseph before you put the house up for sale," he added before grinning at his mom. She immediately got the reference to her neighbor across the street and started laughing.

"She never found it," she said.

"I know. She should have asked St. Anthony for help."

They both started laughing again. Then, mother and son sauntered across the first floor of the warehouse, eventually taking the stairs up to the second level, where they were greeted by another sea of chairs, sofas, and tables.

They split up, with Amelia looking for chairs and a woman for her son, while Vincent looked for chairs and a man. Vincent was the first to get lucky. It was the perfect wing chair. Not too big. Not too small. It was a country French-style wing chair with exposed fruitwood on the ends of the arms and the sides of the wings. The chair was upholstered in a tapestry fabric, with an off-white background and the deepest of blue stitching for the wide floral sprays that dominated the pattern. The blue was deep, warm, and rich. Vincent fell in love right there.

Amelia did not know about her son's quest for a man, but she did know when her son fell in love with a piece of furniture. He was smitten. She took genuine pleasure in seeing his delight. She had not seen that look since he was a boy, tearing at the Christmas wrapping from a GI Joe jeep and trailer. She, of course, had no clue what her son's fantasies were for two GI Joes in that trailer.

"It's a beautiful chair, and look at the price," Amelia said. "They are practically giving it away."

"I agree. I love this color," Vincent added.

"I can see that," Amelia replied. "It's a beautiful blue. I don't think I have seen that shade before. Do you want to find a salesperson?"

"Not yet," Vincent said. "I have a plan." His face lit up like the childhood Christmas tree that was next to the GI Joe jeep and trailer. "Stay here by this chair. Guard it, Mom. I will look for another matching chair. There's probably one somewhere on this floor. The odds are this was part of a display in some store. There should be two. If I find another chair, I will get a salesperson and have him put a hold on it and then bring him back here to you with the other chair."

"That sounds smart, Vincent," Amelia said. It seemed like a lot of work for a chair to her, but she had no desire to break the mood. And she could sit down while he wandered around. Perhaps a nice woman would come by, as well, she thought.

Amelia sat in the chair, admiring the fabric while Vincent went off on his quest. He walked briskly across the floor, passing imposter chairs left and right. He was so focused on his mission that he ignored the occasional man's chest that beckoned for a closer inspection. It was now all about the chair.

He went up to the next level, and then he saw it—the chair. He homed in like a pigeon, and then he saw the red tag. Sold. It was sold. How was that possible? A man noticed him looking crestfallen and approached.

"I hate when that happens," he said. "You see something you like, and it's already taken."

"I really wanted this chair. There is one like it on the floor below, and I need two chairs."

"There may be more," the man ventured. "It may have been a popular item that was on the display floor in several Macy's."

"You're an optimist," Vincent said. "What are the odds of that?"

"What are the odds of meeting someone interesting at a warehouse sale?" the man asked. "I'm Jake."

Vincent hadn't seen that coming. He hadn't even paid attention to what the man looked like; he was so focused on the chair. "I'm Vincent."

"Nice meeting you, Vincent. I'm looking for a sofa, myself."

"There are lots of sofas," Vincent said.

"There are lots of chairs," Jake replied. Gay men outside of gay bars are often as articulate as a herd of moose. "Maybe we could search together?" Jake asked.

"That would be great," Vincent replied, "but I should tell you up front that my mom's sitting in the matching chair on the level below."

"You're here with your mother?" Jake asked, laughing.

"That sounds lame."

"No, not at all. I'm laughing because I'm here with my mother, too."

"You're kidding me."

"No. She wanted to find a sofa for the family room and asked that I come along. She's standing over there." Jake pointed to his mother, who was about Amelia's age and height. She waved as if she were standing on the deck of the Queen Elizabeth 2, and it was leaving port. "She is going to come over here, now," Jake said. "And I should warn you that she is very Italian."

"Is there another kind of mother?" Vincent asked.

"You're Italian?"

"As Italian as St. Joseph," Vincent said.

"You know he's not Italian. He never went to Italy."

"I know. But Italians have appropriated him for their pastry table."

"Indeed."

Both young men sized each other up. If they could have heard their inner voices, the verdict would have been the same: Not too big, not too small.

Jake's mother joined them. "I'm Victoria," she said, extending her hand.

"Mom, this is Vincent," Jake said. "He's here with his mother, too."

"Where is she?" Victoria asked.

"On the floor below. She is sitting in this perfect blue wing chair, just like this one. I'm looking for a matching chair. I found this one, but it's sold."

"There may be another on the floor," Victoria said.

"Your son said the same thing," Vincent replied.

"Good. I raised Giovanni right. I have an idea. Why don't you two go off looking for another chair, and I will keep your mother company. She won't be hard to find. I will look for the matching chair."

"That is a great idea, Mom," Jake said. He and his mother were on the same page: a sofa for her, a boyfriend for him. Victoria went off to find Amelia.

"Giovanni?" Vincent asked as soon as they were alone. "What happened to Jake?"

"Jake is here with you. Giovanni left with my mom when I was still a little boy. I don't like that name."

"I think it's kind of sexy—Giovanni."

"I could grow used to it again," Jake said mischievously.

"Good to know. Shall we look for another chair?"

"My mother expects it."

"I wonder if our moms will get along?"

"Of course they will. They will talk about their parishes. Italian mothers always talk about their parishes to strangers."

"What do Italian men like us talk about?" Vincent asked as they started to walk across the floor.

"Our mothers," Jake quipped.

"True," Vincent acknowledged with a chuckle.

"Mothers aside," Jake said, moving a little closer to Vincent, "Italian men like us don't talk...we do." Jake gave Vincent's shoulder a slight squeeze barely noticeable. Vincent blushed. Noticing that, Jake said, "I like the color, it will go well with the chairs."

The two men went up to the next level, where Vincent spied another matching chair. "Look!" he shouted.

"I see it," Jake said. "Check it out quickly before someone pounces."

Vincent made a beeline for the chair. It was not sold, and it was in perfect condition. Jake joined him and said, "Sit down in it. I want to see you in the chair."

Vincent quickly obliged. The chair felt good. Jake's command felt good. It all felt good.

"We need to find a salesman?" Vincent said, standing up. "My mother will think I have forgotten her."

"She is with my mom. They are probably having a ball. I can go look for one. I think I saw one across the floor." Jake said, pointing to a salesman some distance away.

"Don't go. I can wave him over," Vincent said.

"Let me. I'm a little taller." Jake waved the same cruise ship wave as his mom had earlier.

The salesman came over.

Vincent told the salesman he wanted to buy the chair and a matching chair on the floor below. The salesman congratulated Vincent on his find—Vincent was unsure if the salesman meant the chairs or Jake—but it did not matter. A red "sold" tag was affixed to the chair, and the three men headed down to where Amelia and Victoria were waiting.

Amelia barely noticed Vincent approach. She was laughing loudly with Victoria. The two women had become fast friends. "Success?" she asked upon seeing Vincent with Jake and a salesman.

"Yes, Mom," Vincent said. "Thank you for staying here."

"It's been fun. Victoria and I went to the same all-girls elementary school. St. Agnes. I was three years ahead of her. We were talking about the nuns."

"Ah, the nuns," Jake said with a knowing smile. "It's all nun-sense."

"Don't make jokes, Giovanni, about the good sisters. They are great teachers, and they sacrifice so much. They are the brides of Christ."

"That always sounded like Jesus was a Mormon with so many wives," Jake said.

Vincent laughed.

"You'll have to excuse my Giovanni, Amelia," Victoria said. "I sent him to Fordham. Jesuits," she added seriously.

"Ah, the Jesuits," Amelia said, as she did the sign of the cross.

"I fear we are outnumbered," Jake said to Vincent.

"There are two of us and two of them," Vincent replied.

"Yes, but they are mothers," Jake said.

"We are outnumbered," Vincent agreed. "I've found my chairs, but your mom still needs a sofa. Maybe we should all go looking for a sofa?"

Amelia stood up and said, "I think that is a great idea. Let's find Victoria a sofa."

With that, the four—two moms and two sons—went off in search of a sofa, which they found on the fourth floor. It was not covered in leather.

After purchasing the sofa, Amelia suggested lunch, but there was no restaurant or diner in the warehouse district, so the moment passed. Amelia and Victoria exchanged pleasantries, and Vincent and Jake exchanged phone numbers.

They went out for almost a year, and back then, that was a long time. Amelia would have liked Vincent to have found a woman, but she was coming to terms with the probability that her son was not looking in that direction. Vincent noticed a change in his mother after that day of buying furniture together. Maybe Victoria had said something to her when Vincent and Jake were chair hunting. Vincent never asked. It didn't matter.

✳ ✳ ✳

"There's a parking spot over there, Vincent. Just ahead on the right."

"I don't think we will fit. It looks tight."

"Give it a try. I have a feeling we will make it. I will say a Hail Mary."

"Don't start up on that. You're not even Catholic."

"I've been with you for fifteen years. I'm honorary by now. How does it go? Hail Mary, full of grace, find me a parking space."

"That's blasphemous. You will go straight to hell."

"Not if you are driving. You get lost everywhere."

"I will let that pass because," Vincent paused to glance at his husband Brian in the passenger seat, "you are right. But I found you."

"Good answer, sweetie. Now, park this car."

Vincent pulled up to the car in front and began to parallel park. It took him four attempts. "I used to do this better," he said to Brian.

"You still do the important things well," his husband replied.

"Good answer," Vincent said, kissing Brian before they got out of the car. "Let's see Mom."

Vincent and Brian entered the nursing home and found Amelia in a wheelchair in the common room. She was sitting near a window, with sunlight bathing her face, that, while aged by time, had acquired a childlike innocence over the past three years.

Amelia was no longer able to speak or communicate; her dementia had progressed that far. She sat in the chair and vaguely watched Vincent, who attempted to catch her up on the events of his life. He did this once a month now. He used to go more often, but it had become harder for him to see her sitting there and not responding. As he spoke about work, the house, and his married life, Amelia fingered the fabric of his shirt. It made Vincent uncomfortable the more she played with it.

After an hour had passed, he stood up and said, "Goodbye, Mom. We'll be back soon."

Amelia smiled broadly, but there was no eye contact, no sign of recognition. Vincent was unsettled when he and Brian got back to the car. "She kept playing with my shirt," Vincent said. "She has never done that before. It felt weird."

"It is a beautiful shirt, Vincent," Brian said. "I don't think I ever saw such a deep shade of blue."

"I used to have chairs with this same shade of blue," Vincent replied, not having given the chairs much thought over the years. "Do you think she recognized me at all? She just played with the shirt."

"Does it matter? She looked happy."

"I guess that's all that matters," Vincent said. "I wanted more," he added honestly. "I wanted more." Vincent sighed, and Brian squeezed his arm. "Let's go home," Vincent said after a pause. He pulled the car out of the spot, and he and Brian drove off.

Amelia sat in her wheelchair, silent. An aide walking past noticed her contorting her face and was concerned that Amelia might be in medical distress. But when the aide approached Amelia, she started giggling. "What is she thinking about?" the aide said aloud. "Whatever it is, she is happy."

Amelia continued to giggle as she and Vincent made faces in the reflection of the mahogany table before they found the first wing chair.

The chair's fabric was a beautiful shade of blue. The deepest of blues she had ever seen. The blue was so vivid, she would never forget it. It was forever associated with that Saturday. She would have to remember to call St. Anthony to find St. Joseph later. She would have to remember that, but not now. She and Vincent were having a grand time in the warehouse. A grand time. It was a perfect day.

Conversations from Sicily

4:32 a.m., Thursday, New York City

"Did I wake you up, dear?"

"Mom, it's... I don't even know what time it is." Kenny squinted at his smartphone. "It's 4:32 in the morning." He switched on the lamp on his nightstand.

"I'm sorry, dear. It's 10:30 here in Sicily. It's a beautiful day. The sun is shining. Say hello to the girls."

"Mom, I'm in bed. Wait!" Kenny realized his mother had FaceTimed him and he was on camera. There was no time. Kenny's mother's three female friends and travel companions were now in the picture, waving. Kenny pulled the sheet up, partially covering his exposed torso.

"Don't be shy with us," one of the women said. Kenny had always found his mother's three closest friends interchangeable. At 4:30 in the morning, this was even more true.

"We saw you naked as a boy," another one added.

"Yes," the third joined in.

"You have filled out nicely since then," the first one said.

"Mom!" Kenny protested.

Edith moved the camera away from her friends who could be heard laughing in the background.

"Have you been drinking, Mom?" Kenny asked, sitting up fully in bed.

"Define drinking."

"Alcohol."

"That's a rather broad interpretation, Kenny. Many things have an alcoholic content. Vanilla extract, for example."

"When have you ever drunk vanilla extract, Mom?"

"Are you always this irritable in the morning these days? No wonder you can't find a husband."

"Mom!"

"I'm just saying," Edith responded.

"And you're just drinking."

"I haven't had a drink in...what time is it?" Edith looked at her Cartier watch.

"I rest my case."

"You are beginning to sound like your father...may he rest in peace."

"He's not dead."

"I'm just practicing what to say."

"You're incorrigible."

"Thank you. Finally, a compliment. So how are you settling in?"

"It's strange being back home."

"Atlanta was never right for you. You belong in New York."

"Maybe," Kenny said, stretching his six-foot-frame. "Atlanta was not working for me, and there are more job opportunities here. I'm talking to the people at Manhattan Stage tomorrow. They are looking for an artistic director, and they liked what I did in Atlanta."

"You see, it is all going to work out perfectly. And you have the apartment to yourself until the end of May."

"End of May? I thought you and the girls were coming back next week."

"Change of plans, dear. We are still hot on the trail of Giancarlo."

Edith Henderson, with her three closest friends, had left New York City three weeks earlier for a one-month trip to Sicily, ostensibly to search for Edith's first love, Giancarlo, the son of a lemon grower whom she met decades ago as a young woman traveling in Sicily. The trip was the fruit of an evening of drinking and soul-baring at their favorite restaurant a few blocks from her apartment. To Kenny, his mother's entire world had always revolved around a ten-block radius on the Eastside of Manhattan. Seeing her sitting outside, dappled in Sicilian sunlight, she looked surreal. That she was just a little tipsy before lunch, well, that was just a Thursday.

"Are you sure you want to continue this quest, Mom?" Kenny asked. "He's probably fat, bald, and married."

"First, Kenny, women do not go on quests. That is a totally male concept. Women have adventures. I am having an adventure—a grand adventure, dear. The girls and I are having a wonderful time."

"That I can see," Kenny said. "Where are you?"

"Right now, at the hotel. We are heading to an olive grove after lunch. I'm very excited."

"I can imagine, Mom. You know the olives do not grow in martini glasses."

"Very funny, young man. Or should I say, not so young man. Have you thought about a little Botox."

"Mom! I'm only 39."

"Your face looks 40 to me."

"It's the camera and the light in the bedroom in the middle of the night. If you would allow me to have a good night's sleep, my face will look 39."

"Kenny, sometimes I wonder if you are really gay. You don't want to look 39 when you are 39. You want to look 31 in great lighting, and maybe 33 in the shade."

"Where do you get this stuff from?"

"Someone's podcast. I can't recall."

"So, it must be true," Kenny said, disapproving.

"Don't give me that tone, young man. You sound like your father—may he rest in peace."

"Still not dead."

"Still practicing," Edith said, smiling in a way that even Kenny had to smile back. Edith and her husband George divorced some ten years ago. George left Edith for a much younger woman named Zinka, something that still irked Edith so she referred to him not as her ex-husband, but as her late husband. Kenny had always favored his mom, so he got a secret pleasure from her verbal digs at his father, whom he never wanted to emulate.

"I don't sound like Dad," Kenny protested. "That is a horrible thing to say, Mom."

"Now don't get all pouty. You did that as a boy, and see what happened? All those lines on your face. Botox. I can give you the number for my guy on Park Avenue."

"I don't want the number for your guy, Mom."

"He might be gay."

"Everyone might be gay."

"Not in Sicily. The place smells of heterosexual men. It's in the air, isn't it girls?"

Kenny could hear his mother's three friends loudly agreeing. One was shouting, "Viva, Mario!"

"*Che bel culo!*" Edith shouted.

"Did you just say, 'what a fine ass,' Mom?"

"I call them as I see them. Like an umpire in baseball—strikes and balls."

"*Che belli i testicoli!*" one of Edith's friends shouted.

"You are all going to get into trouble, Mom. You can't tell a man he has beautiful balls. You're all out of control."

"I'm your mother, Kenny. And a man doesn't wear swimwear that revealing unless he wants to be objectified. See for yourself. *Guardare, mio bellissimo figlio.*" Edith moved her phone in the direction of Mario, a tall, furry, bronzed man of about thirty years of age who was strutting along the terrace of Edith's hotel.

"*Che belli i testicoli,*" Kenny said appreciating what he saw. "Just be careful, Mom."

"I will. I have condoms, Kenny. *Preservativo.*

"Mom!"

"What did I tell you as a little boy?"

"Never shake a martini."

"After that."

"Use protection. I was seven. I had no idea what you were talking about."

"Yes, but by the time you were in your teens, you did."

"It is too early for this conversation. I need to get some sleep so I can look 39 or maybe 38."

"Dr. Garber, Park Avenue. He does wonders."

"I'm saying goodbye, Mom."

"*Ciao.*"

Kenny put the phone back on the nightstand, switched off the light, turned over in his bed, and fell back to sleep quickly. He dreamt of Mario's balls tightly packaged in a deep blue Speedo. *Che belli i testicoli!*

✳✳✳

2:15 a.m., Monday, New York City

"Kenny, were you asleep?"

"Mom, it's...wait." Kenny looked at the time on his phone. "It's 2:15 in the morning."

"I thought you would still be awake," Edith said, smiling. She was on the hotel terrace.

"At 2:15 a.m.?"

"I know all about you gay boys and your nights out in the bars. I read *The Advocate.*"

"Mom, I am not a gay boy. I am 39. I don't stay out all night."

"Well, if you called me more often, I would have known that," Edith responded. "How did it go at Manhattan Stage? Did they offer you the position?"

Kenny sat up in bed, turned on a light, and drank some water from a bottle on his nightstand.

"You should use a glass," Edith said, sipping an Aperol spritz.

"The bottle is fine. Why dirty a glass?"

"There's a dishwasher in the kitchen."

"I prefer the bottle, Mom."

"You did as a baby, as well. You wanted nothing to do with my breasts."

"Mom, this is so inappropriate."

"I knew then you were gay."

"Because I preferred a bottle?"

"A mother knows."

"Then if a mother knows, why is she calling me in the middle of the night? Aren't you on your quest...I mean your grand adventure?"

"The girls and I have decided to go to Syracuse."

"You could have done that in New York. It's closer."

"I know you know there is one in Sicily. It's where the great *Femminello* lemons come from. Giancarlo's family was from there. The lemons there smell just like Enrico. We want to go to an entire lemon grove that smells of Enrico."

"Have you no boundaries, Mom?"

"You're a grown gay man. You can't be embarrassed talking about men."

"With my mother, yes. And he's on to you, by the way."

"Who is on to me?"

"Enrico. He knows you love to flirt with him—you and the girls."

"That's not a secret."

"He rubs *Femminello* lemons on his chest just to excite the four of you."

"That's called being industrious," Edith said, nonplussed. "And how would you know?"

"How do you think?"

"Enrico is gay? Enrico is gay! How can Enrico be gay?"

"Do I need to spell it out for you? You, the originator of *che bel culo!*"

"Well, his ass is beautiful," Edith sipped her Aperol spritz, then it dawned on her what Kenny was telling her. "You've been with Enrico?"

"You're surprised?"

"Impressed, son. *Che bel culo!*"

"*Si.*"

"Another reason to stay in New York, then."

"That was long ago, Mom. Enrico was new to New York City, and I was having dinner at the bar on a slow night. We got talking, and then, it just happened."

"You young men are so casual about sex."

"This from my mother who is on a grand adventure to find a man she hooked-up with when she was like twenty."

"Hooked-up is so vulgar. It was a magical connection. Kismet."

"Kismet in Sicily—it sounds geographically daunting."

"You're sounding like your father, dear, may he rest in peace."

"He's still not dead."

"What time is it?" Edith said with a laugh as she looked at her wristwatch. "I am in the land of the vendetta, Kenny."

"My mother, Donna Corleone."

"That was sweet of you," Edith said approvingly. "So, tell me how it went with Manhattan Stage. The girls will be back soon, and I don't know how I am going to tell them that you deflowered Enrico."

"I did not deflower Enrico. His petals had been removed long before I arrived. And the meeting went well. They offered me the position."

"And?"

"I said yes."

"That is fabulous. Girls, girls!" Edith shouted across the terrace. "Kenny got the job. He's staying in New York."

Kenny could hear his mom's three friends approaching the phone. At least this time, he was wearing sleep pants.

"Congratulations, Kenny," one of them said.

"I should paint you," another one said. "You would make a great nude on the shore."

"Mom! Rescue me, here."

"You're perfectly safe in your old bedroom. Susie is a great painter. She's bankrolling this vacation, so think twice before refusing the sitting. You could be hung in a gallery."

For once, Edith didn't get the double-entendre that slipped from her mouth. Kenny did, and he just smiled.

"I don't need that kind of publicity. I want to be taken seriously."

"That is all well and good, but where does that get you on a Saturday night? You need to have fun. Call up Enrico."

"I can handle my own sex life."

"You're not getting any younger. Have you called Dr. Garber?"

"No, Mom. I have not. I have a lot to do with the new job. They wanted me to start today, and I wanted to be completely rested, except my mother called me at 2 a.m."

"Don't be so dramatic."

"I'm in the theater."

"Not at the moment."

"Why aren't you this fun in New York?"

"I am. If you spent more time with me, you would know that."

"You may have a point," Kenny said.

"Oh my god, girls. I am bonding with my son. I need something stronger than an Aperol spritz. I need a martini."

From a distance, Kenny heard a man with an Italian accent saying, "Hendrick's, in and out with the vermouth, and olives."

"You train them well, Mom."

"It's a gift, Kenny. I learned at a young age, if you want to get anywhere in New York City, you must have a good sense of direction—Hendrick's gin, in and out with the vermouth, and olives. Lots of olives."

"I'm not sure that is the kind of direction that most people are looking for."

"Please, don't be so provincial. You did not grow up in Connecticut. I raised you to be open-minded."

"You were a regular Auntie Mame—the Rosalind Russell version."

"That was kind of you," Edith said, smiling. "I always liked Rosalind Russell. So, what will be the first show of your season?"

"*Candide*. The season is already set through the summer, and I can only tinker with the last show for next year. Everything is planned so far in advance. I am meeting the director and set designer later today."

"*Candide*, I saw that in high school on Broadway," Edith said. "If I recall, it has a large cast of men. Maybe you can meet someone in the cast."

"Mom, I can't date someone in the cast. It would be unprofessional."

"Maybe the director is handsome?"

"You don't give up, do you?"

"I want to see you settled."

"So do I. It will happen."

"Sometimes, life needs a little push. I should know. Look how long it took me to go on my grand adventure. Don't waste time, Kenny."

"You sound like you are having fun without Giancarlo."

"I am. We are going to keep looking, but there are a lot of olives in the grove."

"And there are a lot of olives in that martini," Kenny said as he saw a handsome waiter in a white open cotton shirt and black slacks bringing his mother her cocktail. From the position of the camera on his mother's tablet, Kenny was certain the waiter was going commando.

"It's dirty," Edith said, taking a sip of the martini and looking up at the waiter. "I like it dirty."

"Mom!"

"He can't understand me, dear. That's the glorious part of being in another country."

"I am sure he understood you."

"Did you understand what I said?" Edith asked the waiter.

"No," the waiter said.

"You see, Mom."

Before Edith could respond, the waiter said into Edith's tablet's camera, "*Tua madre è una donna bellissima.*" Kenny was now completely sure the waiter had gone commando.

"*Gracia,*" Edith looked at the waiter's nametag. "*Gracia,* Enrico." She turned back to the camera and said, "Another Enrico. They grow on trees here like the olives and lemons. I may never come back to New York," she added, smiling at Enrico *di Sicilia.*

"You'll want to come back eventually," Kenny said, slightly distracted by Enrico's package. "You will know when the grand adventure is over."

"When did you get so wise?" Edith asked her son.

"I'm always at my best in the middle of the night."

"Something you want to tell me?" Edith asked with a mischievous smile.

"*Ciao, mama.*"

"I get the hint, and the girls are waiting. Talk soon. *Ciao.*"

Before Kenny could add, "talk when it isn't the middle of the night in New York," Edith had ended the call. He put down the phone, took another long sip of water, turned off the light, and rolled back into sleep. He dreamed of Enrico *di Sicilia. Che belli i testicoli!"*

❊ ❊ ❊

4:23 a.m., Thursday, New York City

"Kenny, dear, it's Mom."

There had been a two-week lull in his mother's calls, so Kenny was fast asleep when Edith Face-Timed yet again in the middle of the night. He switched on the lamp on the nightstand.

"Mom, can't you get the time difference straight by now?"

"You can always go back to sleep. As a child, something would wake you up, and then you would be back to sleep in a minute. It was like your body naturally produced Ambien."

"Now, I have a prescription," Kenny said, rising slightly in the bed. "Are the girls with you?" he asked as he adjusted his sheets for modesty.

"They are doing some shopping. We have been doing a lot of shopping."

"What did you buy, Mom?"

"An olive grove."

"What?" Kenny sat up from the bed, relieved he had arranged the sheets before his mother's announcement. "You bought an olive grove? Where? Why? When? How?"

"You left out 'who,' dear," Edith replied, smiling. She was sipping an Aperol spritz. "In order of your questions that remind me so much of your father, may he rest in peace," the latter said in unison with Kenny who knew the sequence by heart. "I bought it in the Valle del Belice, because I like olives, last Friday, and with part of the settlement I received from your father—may he rest in peace." This time, Kenny did not respond to the ending. He was in shock.

"You bought an olive grove in Sicily. I can't believe it."

"It's a lovely grove and it has a lovely villa on the property—you will have to come see."

"Are you moving to Sicily, Mom?"

"Not permanently, Kenny. But I need to enjoy life while I can. Do you know Noel Coward?"

"Mom, I'm a thirty-nine-year-old gay man who is now the artistic director of Manhattan Stage. I know Noel Coward."

"Well, my parents saw him in Las Vegas in the 1950s, and he performed this adorable song called 'A Bar on the Piccola Marina.' My mother used to play a recording of the performance on the record player all the time. The song is about me, dear. It's about an older woman whose boring husband dies—for real—and she goes off to Capri and has a ball."

"Mrs. Wentworth-Brewster," Kenny said.

"You know it."

"Yes, Mom. I'm a thirty-nine-year-old gay man who is now the artistic director of Manhattan Stage. I know the song."

"Smug is not attractive on you, Kenny. It wrinkles your forehead. You really should call Dr. Garber."

"Mom!"

"Just like your father, may he..."

"Stop," Kenny interrupted. "Explain how you are Mrs. Wentworth-Brewster, the repressed matron in the Noel Coward song. You have lived a fabulous life in New York."

"I have lived *a* fabulous life in New York, but I have not lived *my* fabulous life in New York. It's not just gay men who need to come out, dear. I have been trapped in a life that was planned out by my mother and her mother. I just want to have some fun."

"I've never heard you talk that way, Mom," Kenny said, now fully awake and focused on his mother, who looked truly radiant in the Sicilian sunlight. "If you want to have a grand adventure, you should have one."

"I want more than one, Kenny. That's why I bought the olive grove. Life is not about one grand adventure—life is meant to be full of grand adventures, many adventures. I came looking for lemons and I bought olives. What's that saying, 'When life hands you a lemon, make limoncello.'"

"It's lemonade, Mom. The saying is 'When life hands you a lemon, make lemonade.'"

"Really?" Edith asked with a twinkle. "Well, I was handed *Femminello* lemons and bought an olive grove, so I made vinaigrette." Edith laughed. Kenny had never heard her laugh quite like that before.

"You sound happy," he said.

"I am happy," Edith replied, sitting back in the patio chair and looking up at the bluest of skies. "I have decided, Kenny, to stay through the summer. The girls are going to help me get the villa in shape." She paused for effect and then added, "So is Marco Antonio."

"Marco Antonio," Kenny said. "He sounds epic or maybe tragic—I'm not sure."

"Neither am I. That's what grand adventures are about. He also owns an olive grove We met a few weeks ago. He exports olive oil to the United States."

"Donna Corleone."

"*Si*. So, watch your step. He's a lovely man, Kenny. A little older than me. He is very Sicilian—dark, virile, musky."

"Musky? We should stop there, Mom. There are some boundaries I want to keep in place."

"Don't be a prude, Kenny."

"I'm not a prude, Mom. Let me tell you about *Candide*," Kenny added, changing the subject. "I met with the director and the set designer. The director is very good, but the set designer George Montrose is such a character. He's an older gay man and he arrived for our meeting with his dachshund Otto. And Mom, he and the dog were dressed exactly alike."

"You're joking, yes?"

"No, he's famous for it—more than for his set work. He and the dog were in Burberry."

"I've seen many dogs wearing faux Burberry outfits."

"That's the classic check pattern. This was the newer look with the logo name extended on the clothing. George Montrose is a little portly, so while the look was young for him, you got the effect. Otto is a miniature dachshund, so the logo sweater was too long for his body. It read Burbe."

"Burbe? That's hilarious, Kenny."

"It was. I couldn't help staring at the dog, and now I'm wondering if the dog is not George Montrose's shtick, but a savvy way of diverting attention from his set designs in production meetings. I think he wants to put the production in a giant greenhouse, but as I said, I was distracted."

"Climate change is a hoax, dear."

"Very funny, Mom. I think the greenhouse is for the finale—'Make Our Garden Grow'—the final song. It seems a little ham-handed to me."

"Speaking of ham, dear. I should ship you some prosciutto. It is amazing here."

"Just don't buy pigs."

"Your father and I are divorced; I am done with being attached to anything porcine."

"I can't argue with that, Mom."

"I have to run, dear."

"So soon," Kenny said, surprising himself as soon as the words came out of his mouth. He was finding these middle-of-the-night talks with his mother strangely fun and comforting.

"Yes, I am having lunch with Marco Antonio, and I need to fix my hair."

"It looks perfect, Mom."

"Thank you, Kenny. That's the problem. Marco Antonio likes it a little mussed."

"TMI, Mom."

"Such a prude. Be sure to look for an attractive man in the cast and then bring him home to Sicily."

"That sounds so ridiculous coming from a woman who has spent her entire life in Sutton Place."

"Not my entire life, Kenny. It's not over yet, and your mama is going to have a ball. *Ciao, mio figlio.*"

"*Ciao, mama.*" Kenny placed the phone back on the nightstand, turned off the light, and went back to sleep. He dreamt of prosciutto.

✳✳✳

5:32 a.m., Saturday, New York City

"You're awake."

"You sound disappointed, Mom. I was checking some emails on my laptop when you called."

"Are you working out?"

"I go to the gym. I always go to the gym," Kenny answered, unconsciously tightening his muscles even though he was talking with his mother. Old habits die hard. "Let me get a T-shirt."

"Don't be silly. I'm your mother. You look relaxed. You finally visited Dr. Garber."

"No, I did not. I told you I don't believe in Botox."

"Kenny, don't believe in climate change, don't believe in free and fair elections, and don't believe in fake news, but always, always believe in Botox."

"Thank you, Mom. But I don't want to have someone inject my face with Botox."

"You can get it in your ass, as well."

"Mom!"

"Such a prude, just like your father, may he rest in peace."

"That is getting old."

"So is he, but I, on the other hand, am getting younger." Edith truly was. Her skin, while slightly tanned, appeared smoother. Her eyes sparkled, and Kenny could almost imagine what his mother must have looked like some forty-plus years earlier when she visited Sicily for the first time as a young woman.

"You look fantastic, Mom. There's no denying that. How is the olive oil business?" he added in a Marlon Brando *Godfather* voice as he stroked his two-day stubble with his right hand.

"Mine has yet to start in earnest. There is still a lot of paperwork to be completed regarding the purchase of the grove. I am more focused on getting the villa renovated. The girls are indispensable. Susie is going to paint a mural on my bedroom ceiling."

"I can only imagine," Kenny said, smiling. His mother's mood was intoxicating. "And Marco Antonio?"

"I thought you would never ask. He is amazing, Kenny. He treats me like I was Sophia Loren in a 1960s movie. I feel like a movie star. But more than that, I feel like a woman, Kenny—like my own person."

"That sounds extraordinary, Mom."

"It does, doesn't it? And do you notice anything different?"

"You look fantastic, but that is not different."

"That was very nice of you, but take a good look."

Kenny stared at the laptop's screen. He saw his beaming mother in a white cotton dress dotted with small flowers. Her jewelry was discreet, as always. Then it hit him. "You don't have a drink in your hand."

"Exactly."

"You've gone dry?"

"You've gone straight?" Edith replied quickly with a laugh. "Don't be silly. But I decided I don't need a drink until closer to dinner. There is so much to do here, why waste time sitting on a terrace with a cocktail waiting for life to happen to you? You have to get off the terrace, put down the cocktail, and grab life with both hands."

"I feel like I've heard that in a play."

"Maybe some version of that. But it's true, Kenny. You're still a young man. Get off the terrace."

"I get off the terrace."

"When? I call you every morning in the middle of the night, hoping you don't pick up because you are with someone, but every time I call, you are asleep in bed. Get off the terrace."

"I have. I did."

"When?"

"Well, I was out last night and he's older than me, but attractive and sturdy. We didn't even exchange names," Kenny began when there was a sound from the bathroom.

"There is someone there? He's there? Finally! Girls, girls," Edith shouted, "my Kenny finally has a man."

"Bravo!" Kenny heard from the terrace.

"You don't mind that I put the towel on the floor?" a man's accented voice asked as he left the bathroom and walked toward Kenny sitting at his desk.

"Wait a minute," Kenny said, panicking. "I'm FaceTiming."

"I'm not shy," the man said.

Kenny was about to say, "It's my mother," but it was too late. The older, but well-chiseled, naked man came up behind Kenny, giving Edith a full-frontal view.

"Oh my God!" Edith exclaimed.

"Mom, I'm sorry. He's very sweet and he's Sicilian," Kenny added with emphasis.

"I know he's Sicilian," Edith said. "Giancarlo."

"Edith!" Giancarlo replied.

"No," Kenny said, still trying to process what had just happened. "Your Giancarlo?"

Giancarlo and Edith both smiled. Neither spoke.

Edith's three friends, who had walked over to where she was seated with her tablet, broke the silence as they looked at the famous Giancarlo standing naked next to Kenny in his bedroom in his mother's New York City apartment.

The three women proclaimed in unison, "*Che belli i testicoli!*"

Ulysses on Riverside

Part 1 – In Port

Charles walked out of the lobby of his apartment building on Riverside Drive much as he had for the past 40 years. Slower, yes, but still steady.

The chillness in the air felt more like late April rather than mid-May, and Charles buttoned up his sweater—a grey cashmere cardigan bought when he was still working full-time and could afford such spontaneous and expensive purchases.

Michael would tease him as soon as he walked into their apartment and saw the purple Bergdorf Goodman bag. "You don't need another sweater," he would say. "All over India, there are naked goats shivering because of you," Michael would add for dramatic effect.

"Let them wear cotton, the fabric of life," Charles would reply as he walked over to Michael, who was undoubtedly lying on the couch wearing a pair of cotton lounge pants and nothing else. "And what's so wrong about being naked?" Charles would add as he yanked the legs of the pants, pulling them down in a single, well-practiced move. Later, as they lay in a comfortable tangle on the couch, Charles would pick up the lounge pants from the floor and say, "Yes, cotton is the fabric of life." He would then get up from the sofa and walk back to where he left the Bergdorf bag with the new sweater on the floor and add, "But cashmere, sweetie, is the fabric of living."

Charles would follow that with a finger snap, which prompted Michael to shout from the sofa, "You are such a drama queen, but I love you anyway." Charles would turn, make a little bow, blow a kiss, and say, "What I do for my art."

For 32 years, that was their routine. Charles would never take the tags off a newly purchased sweater until the final negotiation with his spouse had been successfully completed on that sofa. Charles remembered the day he bought the sweater he was wearing today. It had been their 10th anniversary, and he wore it when they went out to dinner just north of Lincoln Center to celebrate.

Lorenzo's was the restaurant—their restaurant. Just like Michael, Lorenzo's and its owner, Lorenzo Malifiore, had been gone for some time. And like Charles's newer neighbors, who had no knowledge of when Charles and Michael were fixtures in the building, most Westsiders today had no awareness of there ever having been a neighborhood place where couples came for the veal, the homemade Limoncello, and Lorenzo's endless stories about the Amalfi coast, where he grew up.

Lorenzo and Lorenzo's are gone. No plaque marks the spot. Instead, a chain drugstore stands there now. "What was that song so long ago?" Charles would ask an old friend when they walked past where the restaurant once was. Before they could reply, Charles would add, "They paved paradise and put up a CVS."

Not that Charles had an axe to grind with CVS, it's just that there was no veal chop Milanese down Aisle 4. And there was no Michael anywhere except in Charles's memories.

That was why the couch, which had witnessed much of Charles and Michael's life together, was not replaced, but reupholstered. Michael's spot is no longer discernible in the seat cushion to anyone but Charles. Some things only get clearer with aging vision.

The traffic signal turned green, and Charles crossed Riverside Drive heading toward the park. Twenty years ago, Charles would have crossed 108th Street and walked down the stone steps into the city park that runs parallel to the Hudson River. Riverside Park was Charles's favorite park, not just because of its closeness to his apartment, but because it was as comfortable as one of his well-worn cashmere sweaters—familiar, warm, and full of memories.

However, Riverside Park had a huge drawback for octogenarians: it was less accessible than Central Park. You had to be able to navigate stone steps at most entrances and handle steep inclines to get to the mature trees that blocked out the view of the city to the east and, in enough areas, the highway below to the west.

These glorious towering trees, Charles would think, were the opposite of people. They became stronger and wider as they aged, while he and his friends—the ones still living—had become weaker and smaller. It made Charles wonder if these now-majestic trees had been hidden inside the small saplings when first planted, and that perhaps the majesty of youth remained, but hidden, inside the bodies of old men like himself.

When he was still able to do the steps, Charles would cross the street at 108th, just as he does today, and climb the stairs down into the body of the park. He had a routine: he would head north to where the path curved right at the tennis courts, and then up a winding path leading back to Riverside Drive just south of Grant's Tomb. Once at street level, Charles would stop briefly at the tomb before circling back down into the park slightly further south than where he had first entered.

There he would find a pavilion where he could buy a coffee, and then walk back just south of 108th, find his bench, sit down, sip his drink, and stare out at New Jersey.

Charles called it playing "chicken" with the Garden State. He would stare at Jersey, and Jersey would stare back at him. In all the years that Charles had sat on his very specific bench, neither side had blinked.

Whether the people of Fairview, Guttenberg, or whatever Jersey town looked across toward 108th Street in Manhattan were blinking now, Charles did not know. He could no longer manage the stone steps down to that wide expanse that had become as daunting to him as the Mississippi had been to Huck and Jim. The park itself had become another river—a metaphorical body of something so wide that it prevented Charles from reaching the other side. Age taunted Charles with each passing year because he was still who he was, despite the growing physical infirmities.

It always brought him back to his thoughts on the park's towering trees—could the vigor of youth still exist within an enfeebled body?

As Tennyson wrote: *Tho' much is taken, much abides; and tho' we are not now that strength which in old days moved earth and heaven, that which we are, we are.*

After Charles had crossed Riverside Drive, he gazed longingly at the park entrance and the daunting steps, muttering to himself, "that which we are, we are," before heading north through the tree-lined promenade that runs street level along the park below. Taking the same walk he did years ago—north to Ulysses' and Julia's final resting place, a stately granite memorial to the nation's 18th president—he stops in front of the neoclassical structure.

Inscribed above the entrance are the words, "Let us have peace," the closing of Grant's letter to the president of the 1868 Republican National Convention accepting the Republican Party's nomination for president of the United States.

Charles would ponder what that meant—"Let us have peace"—given its placement on Grant's Tomb. Was it the hope for a nation recovering from the Civil War, as Grant must have meant in his original letter? Was it a prayer for Ulysses and Julia, who were laid inside? Could it even have been a little bit of irony, given the fierce competitive bidding among several cities following Grant's death to claim his remains and construct the secular temple that now stands high above the Hudson River? In New York parlance, "Fuhgeddaboudit, Illinois, and Arlington; New York City won out. Let us have some peace!"

When you are retired and alone, you have time for such considerations. And Charles had time. Charles still had time.

He walked slowly back just south of 108th Street to his bench on the east side of the street-level promenade that ran parallel to the park. He faced the park, and another row of benches across the width of the promenade. There would be people to entertain him as he sat. In a few weeks, many young shirtless men from Columbia University would be running past. There might even be some today, Charles thought. Young athletic men didn't mind the cold. Charles still enjoyed the eye candy— that which we are, we are.

But there was more to the show than that. The leafy trees gave the sidewalk an almost Parisian feel. The parade passing his front-row seat was crowded with mothers pushing strollers, toddlers exploring their newfound mobility to the consternation and wonderment of their nervous parents, teens being loud and silly, couples in love, couples in the process of becoming uncoupled, and an inordinate number of New

Yorkers with dogs. Dogs of every size, breed, and, since it was New York City, political persuasion.

Charles could tell the political preferences of a dog by how it walked, where it peed, and, of course, by the bark. Republican dogs strutted, peed with impunity, and barked at everything—particularly at things no one could see. Democratic dogs tended to saunter, sniffing around for a while before lifting a leg or squatting in the spot where they had started their search. They barked at other dogs, perhaps questioning the state of city government, the influx of Republican dogs, or the lack of universal health care for canines. Unaffiliated dogs most often ran ahead of their person—unaffiliated dogs would not admit to having an owner since they believed that living creatures cannot be owned, although it is well known that cats of all political stripes will prostitute themselves for some cream or kibble, but that, again, was their choice. The unaffiliated dog also liked to be off-leash, and they had never been fixed.

Such a dog zoomed in on Charles—if a dachshund could be said to be zooming—with his leash trailing behind him, and his person trailing behind the leash. The dog came right up to Charles and shoved his nose into Charles's leg, demanding attention. The dachshund's tail wagged furiously before the dog grabbed onto Charles's right leg. This dog is most definitely unaffiliated, Charles thought.

"Ollie, stop that," the dog's person shouted as he hurried over to Charles's bench. "You don't do that. It's not polite."

"You have never been to The Rambles," Charles said with a wry smile. The dog's person, an attractive, clean-shaven young man in his late twenties, was wearing a T-shirt featuring a popular gym's logo, with a rainbow flag in one of the vowels of the name. Charles assumed the young man had to be gay and knew of the notorious cruising spot in Central Park.

"I have not," the man said. "Why do I now feel embarrassed?"

"Because if you had been to The Rambles and admitted it, you would have thought that a total stranger thinks you were a slut. *But*," Charles continued like a detective near the conclusion of a murder-mystery story, "you didn't question why I mentioned The Rambles, so you clearly understood what I was referring to. You might not have been to The Rambles, but you know what goes on there. Ergo, you're embarrassed."

The young man looked baffled. This greatly pleased Charles.

"I'm Charles," he said, extending his right hand to the young man.

"I'm Pete, and you already met Ollie here. His full name is Oliver Wendell Holmes, but I call him Ollie."

"Oliver Wendell Holmes is a lot of names for such a little dog."

Ollie barked at Charles. "I meant no offense, Ollie," Charles said to the dog. "Even dogs are size queens," Charles added with a smile. "I have a good friend who has a dachshund, Otto. That's the dog's name. My friend's name is George. But his dog, Otto, has a lot of issues. They say dogs and owners transfer personalities."

"I don't hump random legs in the park."

"My aging joints are gratified to hear it," Charles replied with a smile.

"May I join you?" Pete asked. "I was about to sit down somewhere in the park, but Ollie has a mind of his own. It's pretty on this side of the park."

"Well, young man, you can certainly join me on this bench. I welcome the company and conversation, but it is prettier on the other side—on the inside."

"Why don't you sit there?"

Charles pointed to his legs. "These legs are not good for vigorous exercise—aside from the occasional dog humping," Charles added with a chuckle. "I used to go down to the park all the time—before I met Michael, when Michael and I were together, and for a few years afterwards. But the steps are too hard. I miss the view."

"I'm sorry," Pete said. "Didn't mean to bring up sad memories."

"Young man," Charles began, "memories are rarely sad. It's the present that can make you cry." Both men remained silent for a moment. Ollie lightened the mood by trying to climb up onto Charles's lap.

"He really likes you," Pete said. "He's never this friendly with strangers."

Charles picked up Ollie, who started licking Charles's face. Charles laughed as he petted Ollie and settled him down on his lap. "I haven't been licked like that in public since David Dinkins was mayor."

"Who was that and when was that?"

"BG," Charles said. "Before Giuliani. Dinkins was the mayor before him."

"That's a long while back."

"Yes, it is," Charles said. He looked a little sad. "This is where you offer me a Lifesaver."

"What?"

"A tagline from an old TV commercial for a candy you probably have never eaten. Something bad would happen, like the high school basketball player missing the key shot and losing the big game, and his father would offer his gutted son a Lifesaver as a consolation prize."

"You're kidding?"

"No, it was a different time. We found that droll—there's a word for you. We found that droll."

"Well, I don't have any Lifesavers. To be honest, I don't think I have ever seen them."

"That's perfectly OK, Pete. They are a multicolored candy."

"Like gummies?"

Charles chuckled. "I *am* old. Yes, just like gummies. And that observation, my young man, was very droll of you."

"Do you come here often?" Pete asked as he sat down and turned to face Charles. Pete's long, hairy legs stretched out well beyond the edges of the bench.

"To the park, for more than five decades. To this bench, probably ten or twelve years."

"Always the same bench?"

"Yes, always the same bench. We don't get to pick our spot in life, but we can certainly pick our spot in a New York City public park. This is my bench. Well, it is also Austin P. Chambers' bench." Charles pointed to the bronze plaque on the bench. "You can adopt a bench to memorialize yourself or someone you know in various parks across the city. It helps fund the parks."

"That is very cool," Pete said. "I wondered what the deal was. How much does it cost?"

"I think it's $10,000, but I could be wrong, and it's not forever, but a good long time."

"It would be nice to be remembered on a bench," Pete said.

"I guess," Charles said. "I would rather be remembered for more than that, but I suppose enjoying the park is something to be remembered for. I never really thought about how I will be remembered."

"I'm sorry. I keep hitting on sad subjects. It comes with my job."

"Don't tell me. You're a mortician."

"Worse."

"You're in public relations," Charles replied with a smile.

Pete laughed loudly. "Almost as bad. I write obituaries for the Times."

"You're a journalist? Good for you. I have great appreciation for people who embrace dying professions, and even more for the irony of you writing about dying in a dying profession."

"Should I pull out the knife now," Pete said, clearly amused, "or should I let you twist it a little more?

"Please let me twist. It will bring back the 1960s."

They both laughed.

"I want to be friends," Pete blurted out. "You are such an original."

"You're not from New York, are you?"

"How can you tell?"

"I'm not such an original. Eccentric old gay men—particularly on park benches—are as common in New York City as pretzel vendors. And we often have the same smoky aroma."

"I moved here late last fall for the job. I like the beat—bringing dead people back to life."

"Who knows? You could win a Pulitzer. You could be the next Sanche de Gramont."

"Lifesavers, I do not know. But I do know that story. It's a legend that anyone who starts writing obits has heard. He was the *Herald Tribune* journalist assigned to run to the old Metropolitan Opera House and cover the onstage death of the baritone Leonard Warren."

"I am impressed," Charles said. "Right on the money. Leonard Warren was one of the greatest baritones of his time. He died right after singing the aria, "Urna fatale del mio destino," from Verdi's *Forza del*

Destino. The aria's title translates to 'fatal urn of my destiny.' Warren sang it and then collapsed on stage. Now that is the force of destiny."

"Crazy stuff—destiny," Pete said. "Opera star dying on stage, being the guy who is called to rush to cover the scene, and then winning a Pulitzer for writing the obit. Destiny."

"Maybe you can win a Pulitzer on the obit desk."

"The old Met on 39th Street is long gone. You can't dash up to Lincoln Center from the Times' building. It would have to be a Broadway star in a Broadway theater."

"We could talk about that," Charles said, with wicked glee. "Who's really old and ready to die on stage?"

"We can't talk about that," Pete said, mildly shocked. "What if they died?"

"They are all going to die. We are all going to die. I'm just saying, be prepared."

"I am. I'm working on..." Pete stopped himself. "I shouldn't say. It's advance material on someone famous who is really old."

"I could get it out of you. You Pennsylvania boys are so easy to break."

"I didn't say I was from Pennsylvania."

"Your shorts have a Penn State logo. It's not rocket science."

"I guess I still read like an outsider," Pete said, blushing.

"And that is a good thing. Being outside Riverside Park, not so good. Being an outsider—new to a place—that's a horse of a different color."

"Like in *The Wizard of Oz*," Pete chirped.

"Friend of Dorothy," Charles replied, and then added, "and friend of Ollie's.

Ollie wagged his tail in agreement.

✳✳✳

Charles had turned south at Grant's Tomb when he spotted Pete and Ollie walking west on 120th Street. Charles waved across the street. When Pete and Ollie were within earshot, he said, smiling broadly, "Fancy meeting you here."

He had come to enjoy his not-so-random encounters with Peter and Ollie. In many ways, Pete reminded Charles of himself nearly 60 years ago, when everything wasn't just possible, but limitless. The hard stop that would eventually come for Charles was nowhere in sight then. Yet, that young man was still inside him.

Tho' much is taken, much abides; and tho' we are not now that strength which in old days moved earth and heaven, that which we are, we are.

For Charles, at this final stage in life, aging was more than inevitable; it was something to be embraced. Young people may think it is a terrible thing to grow old, with wrinkles and infirmity. True enough, these are not the joyous parts of aging. But to see the shell is to miss the thing itself—the good, the bad, the extraordinary highs that come without warning and the lows that temper the soul like chocolate, giving it a sheen as radiant as the star atop your childhood Christmas tree.

Charles had his shares of lows and highs—the bullying as a child for being gay when he did not even know what gay was; the pain of false steps with too many men; the fear of AIDS; the finality of AIDS, as friends died long before they acquired the tempered sheen of old age; and the joy of meeting Michael, learning him, loving him, and the pain of losing him. And now, two new characters have arrived in the final leg of his voyage home—Pete and Ollie.

They did not make him feel young because that is asking for the moon, but rather, Pete and Ollie made Charles remember what being young was like. That was not the moon, but the stars, as Bette Davis said to Paul Henreid at the end of *Now, Voyager*. It is not the fairy tale ending. It is the best outcome for your very specific scenario. And it can bring you great joy.

The moon is elusive, but joy is within reach, easier to find, and yet, often rejected in the search for the moon. Charles had been to the moon. The stars were fine enough now.

"I was hoping we would see you today," Pete said as he and Ollie joined Charles. "Ollie could think of nothing else."

To prove Pete was telling the truth, Ollie wagged his tail and demanded attention from Charles, which he immediately received.

"You see how pleased he is to see you," Pete added, laughing.

"The feeling is mutual, but I haven't wagged my tail since they closed Studio 54," Charles said.

"I wish I had known you back then," Pete replied.

"No, I don't think so. I had no depth. I was like veneer on a cabinet."

"I don't believe you."

"I was. Trust me."

"I think you were always a nice man."

"Ah, well," Charles said as they walked south, "nice is not necessarily all that deep. Nice is often the partner of shallow. There was little behind my smile in those days," Charles added, and then, taking a beat, said, "Except my real teeth."

"I think you are selling yourself short. People don't change that much."

"I won't try to change your mind. I will take the compliment like a box of chocolates."

"Are you going to get all Forrest Gump on me?"

"God, no. Life is like a box of good chocolates? Phooey! Where I buy my chocolates, they make the box up for me with what I want—so I always know what I get."

"You've ruined one of my favorite movies," Pete said with a smile, so Charles understood he was not really upset.

"See! I am not even nice anymore," Charles added, poking Pete slightly in the arm. "I am an old curmudgeon."

"No, you just have good taste in confections."

"Confections," Charles repeated. "Now that's a ten-dollar word."

"When you write obits, it is not a word that comes up often." Pete, deepening his voice like a clichéd TV news anchor, continued, "Henry Jones III died at age 86. He was found slumped in his library, an open box of confections at his side."

"Not a bad way to go—in a chair with chocolates," Charles replied wistfully.

The two men and the dachshund walked in silence for a few minutes.

"You know, you have me reading the obits every day," Charles said, breaking the quiet rhythm of their walk.

"Found anyone you know?"

"No, they are all too famous in the Times."

"They are not."

"Believe that if you want. Drink the Kool-Aid. They pay your salary."

"I'm not drinking the Kool-Aid. I want all my real teeth when I am your age," Pete added playfully. "There's a process. Non-famous people are featured. They just have to be pitched to the Obit Desk correctly."

"Pitched? Well, if that's the case, I'm a Mets fan. My bullpen is empty. The odds are low."

"Even they have an occasional good year."

"It's always in the future, and when you reach my age, 'there's always next season' becomes a less believable scenario. I'm content with my life. I don't need the editors of *The New York Times* to validate it with an obituary."

"I believe that when we write about non-famous people, we are not validating the deceased, but the everyday people reading that person's obit. They see themselves in the story."

"You really believe that?" Charles asked, stopping.

"Yes."

"Damn, *you* are the nice one. And since you are, let's sit down. I'm getting tired."

"Sure. But your bench is further down."

"My bench is further down, but my energy ended here, so this will have to do for now. We can move later—assuming you have time."

"I have time. I have lots of time," Pete said.

"Yes, you do," Charles replied. "Yes, you do."

❋ ❋ ❋

Weeks passed. The temperature rose and, to Charles's delight, the Columbia men's shirts came off. Dozens of young athletic men ran either with T-shirts tucked into the waistbands of their shorts or without them at all. It had become Charles's favorite season—like Christmas without any wrapping paper—the gifts were all exposed around the tree.

"You're enjoying the show, aren't you?" Pete said, catching Charles off guard. He had just run up to Charles's usual bench. Pete, like the slightly younger Columbia men, was shirtless.

"I am now," Charles said. "You've been holding out on me. I had no idea you were in such great shape. I've never seen you without a shirt or Ollie, for that matter."

"I left both in my apartment. Too hot for a shirt, and dachshunds just can't jog."

"I'm definitely going to be distracted."

"Good. I like to think the time I spend at the gym is paying off."

"It is. You're gay Bitcoin."

"You know what they say—better crypto than creepy."

"At my age, I avoid any word with 'crypt' in it. But you are distracting me from my distraction, which is your chest. I didn't think you were that defined."

"My chest is defined—my life, not so much. It has been a rough day. That's why I decided to take a long run and show off my body. I needed some attention. I am *so* gay," Pete added, stretching out "so" like taffy.

"Needing attention is not a gay thing. It's a guy thing. Women are so much more evolved than we are. We, on the other hand, are always preening in the barnyard. So, what happened today that made you rip off your shirt and play to the masses of old men on park benches? Not that I am complaining," Charles added, with a laugh.

"You're going to make me blush."

"With all that fur, no one would notice."

"You like a man with chest hair? Some men prefer smooth."

"Scotch should be smooth. Men should be men. Michael was like a carpet. I loved it."

"Devin didn't have a carpet. It was more like a little mat at the top of his chest."

"Devin? You've never mentioned Devin. In fact, you have never mentioned any man. I was beginning to think you were celibate."

"Sadly, the last part has been true for some time. Devin is my ex."

"What happened?"

"He was carried away to Paris by this French guy named Claude Marcel."

"They are always called Claude Marcel," Charles said, smiling.

"Make fun if you wish. He was...he *is* a dancer. A ballet dancer. I went to a ballet benefit, and Devin was dancing. He was smooth. He had waxed the thatch. There was not a hair to be seen, or at least not visible to me at that point. Long story—he left me for Claude Marcel and sent me an email this morning about a sweater he left in my apartment. He wants it back."

"A boyfriend is a boyfriend, but a sweater is forever," Charles said, grinning. "Buck up, Pete. We have all lost men. It's part of the journey."

"I know. But it doesn't make it any easier."

"You want it easy, and you moved to New York City? You don't need a boyfriend, you need a shrink, young man."

"Cruel," Pete said, laughing. "I must sound pathetic."

"No, just young, but you brought your 'A-game' torso, so I am going to indulge you. But I feel so *Death in Venice* looking at you."

"I never liked Thomas Mann."

"Who does?" Charles chuckled. "You will meet a wonderful man, Pete."

"Someone like your Michael?"

"Yes. But I met Michael when I was older than you. We both had been around the block long enough to understand what the confusing parking signs on the curb meant. You still don't know when it's time to move or be towed away."

"From Mann to parking regulations."

"Just another day in New York City."

"I want romance," Pete said longingly, and a little too loudly. A man slightly younger than Pete overheard him as he walked past, turned around, and grinned. The man was attractive.

Charles gave Pete a nudge, signaling that an opportunity was presenting itself. Sensing that Pete needed more than just a nudge, Charles said to the man, "My friend is a hopeful romantic. I think it comes from too many endorphins after running."

"I believe in romance, but I don't run. I walk," the attractive stranger said. He had blue eyes that reminded Charles of a day long ago with Michael in Malibu. They were on vacation in California and were staring out at the ocean. The sunlight hit the water just right, or maybe it was the wine they were drinking, but the young stranger's blue eyes took Charles back to that forgotten moment. It threw Charles off his purpose of forcing Pete into a conversation with the stranger. It was not necessary. The stranger was not shy.

"I'm Hal," he said.

"I'm Pete," Pete said as he shook the man's hand. Pete stood up, towering over Hal, who was no more than five feet seven. "Sorry, I'm probably still a bit sweaty. I was running earlier."

"No apologies needed," Hal said, with a smile, impressed by Pete's toned physique. "I feel like a sloth compared to you. I should be running."

"Do you like to run?" Pete asked.

"Honestly, not at all," Hal responded.

Pete laughed. "I respect that answer. No one ever says that to me. Or no guy around our age says that to me. They all want to sound like they live in the gym or are out running at dawn. Walking is fine."

Charles, who by now had left the memory of Michael and Malibu, rejoined the conversation. "Pete loves to walk, as well. Why don't you join Hal on a walk, Pete?"

"I can't leave you," Pete said, not entirely convinced he should just go with the moment.

"We'll always have Paris," Charles said dramatically.

"Everybody says *that*," Pete replied. "And we never had Paris."

"We have shared French fries. That's close enough," Charles added. "Go. Walk. I am fine. Come back later."

"You won't be here," Pete protested.

"And you won't come back later. So, it's settled. Go forth, young man, on an adventure with young Hal here. He may be your Henry V."

"You're embarrassing me," Pete said. "I'm going to blush."

"With all that fur, no one would ever know," Hal said, unknowingly echoing what Charles had said earlier.

"It's a sign," Charles said to Pete with a knowing wink. "Walk."

"I'll be back," Pete replied as he left with Hal.

"Not today," Charles said quietly. "Not today."

✳✳✳

A week passed before Charles saw Pete again. He was walking with Ollie and Hal. Charles could not tell who was more enamored with Pete: Ollie or Hal. But it was obvious from the way they stayed close to Pete that he was the master of both. While Charles felt joy for his young friend, it was mixed with the sadness of knowing he would remain on shore while his young friend set sail.

"I was wondering when I would see you," Charles said, concealing his sadness. "You look quite the 'throuple,'" he added.

"Maybe we are," Pete said, tugging at Hal's hand. "It has been a wonderful week."

"I can see it has," Charles said. "Good to see you, Hal. Or is it Henry V?"

"When anyone mentions St. Crispin's Day, I always think of Krispy Kreme. I think that kills all Henry V aspirations," Hal said.

"I love Krispy Kreme," Pete said playfully. He lightly kissed Hal on the cheek. They were in that early stage of a gay relationship where new lovers wear their emotions openly—on their sleeves, shirts, and, if overly excited, on their trouser fronts. It usually sickened Charles to watch in public, but there was something sweet about Pete and Hal. Charles could not mock that. "So does Ollie," Pete added, as if Hal needed further validation. He did not.

Ollie was playfully tugging at Hal's trouser leg. Charles noticed it was a demure tease, not the full-on humping he had experienced when first meeting Ollie. The dachshund understood his boundaries now that his man had a man. It made Charles smile.

"You look happy," Pete said, sitting next to his older friend. Hal sat on Pete's other side. Ollie jumped up on Charles's lap.

"I am happy," Charles said. "This is nice. Isn't it nice, Ollie?" Charles asked the dachshund before Ollie started licking his face. "This is very nice."

"I'm sorry, Charles. I've been busy this past week," Pete said.

"I'm sure you have," Charles replied knowingly.

"Don't look so smug," Pete said. "It was a busy week. I've been working on an advance obit."

"Whose?"

"I can't tell you."

"You're like a member of the Illuminati," Charles protested.

"They have great costumes," Hal said.

"Don't encourage him," Pete said to Hal teasingly. "He does not need encouragement to pull out some secret from me. He is very good at it."

"If that's the case, he should be applauded," Hal said, kissing Pete on his cheek. "I want to keep you honest."

"You will have no issues with me on that score," Pete said. Turning back to Charles, he added, "I really have been busy at work. I will find time for you. I have enjoyed getting to know you this spring and summer. I really have," Pete emphasized, squeezing Charles's hand.

"Look at you," Charles said. "A few months back, you were still the new kid in town, and now you are sitting in public holding the hands of two men."

"And they are both very nice hands." Pete lightly kissed Charles's hand first, and then did the same to Hal's hand, quickly following with a kiss on Hal's mouth. "Life is good. Friends. Sunshine." Ollie barked. "Excuse me, Ollie, and a gay man's best friend."

"Savor this," Charles said. "Beginnings are special. Beginnings are what we remember. The first kiss. The first time you make love together. The first fight. It all should be savored—even the first fight, which will be over something silly. The beginnings we can identify—the last times not so easily."

"I remember every breakup all too well," Pete said.

"Have there been many?" Hal asked. "I can't imagine anyone breaking up with you."

"That is very sweet," Pete said. "But when you have a man leave you for a Frenchman named Claude Marcel..."

"They are always called Claude Marcel," Hal interrupted.

"What is it?" Pete asked in disbelief. "Do the two of you compare dialogue notes? You say the same things. It is uncanny."

"I think it is rather charming," Charles said. "But back to my point about last times. I was referring to the last time we did something special with a person we loved who is no longer in our lives. I remember so many wonderful things about my years with Michael, but I don't remember the last time we had a perfectly normal dinner. Or the last time we kissed without a sense, it might be the last time. We don't remember those moments because they aren't special when they occur. They are lost on us, lost in our vast memories of many things."

"*Do any human beings ever realize life while they live it?—every, every minute?*" Hal interjected.

"*No. The saints and poets, maybe they do some,*" Charles answered. "Thornton Wilder's *Our Town*. I'm impressed."

"I love that play," Hal said. "It says everything important about life in a very sparse way."

"It does. He's a keeper," Charles added, looking at Pete. "He's a keeper. Savor these new moments together because, with luck, you will remember them, and they will flood your later years like an ocean that does not separate you from home, but rather, is the path to home.

"And with luck, that will make up for not remembering the last time it was wonderful. You will take comfort in knowing it began gloriously—as all journeys should begin—and you will take comfort in knowing there was a journey, and you and someone whom you loved more than yourself were once on that journey with you. They say it's not the destination, but the journey. I don't agree. It's both. The destination without the journey is meaningless, and the journey without landfall is not epic, but tragic. We need to reach land with all the regrets of what we can no longer do, but also with all the joy of what we did. The sadness comes with knowing that joy is behind us, and that while we want one more voyage, we cannot leave land anymore. It is here that we stay."

"Would you like one more journey?" Pete asked Charles.

"I am too old for a journey," Charles answered.

"No, you are not," Peter replied.

"*'Tis not too late to seek a newer world,*" Hal said.

"Tennyson!" Charles exclaimed. "He is a keeper, Pete."

"He is. So where do you want to journey to, Ulysses?" Pete asked. "I read Tennyson, as well."

"Never said you didn't," Charles responded, with a wistful smile. He was beginning to ponder whether there was a journey left in him. "Troy," he finally said.

"You're taking the poem way too seriously," Pete said with a laugh.

"Not that Troy. Troy, Michigan."

"Troy, Michigan. What's in Troy, Michigan?"

"My childhood. Or it was there. I grew up outside of Detroit, when Detroit was a city of great possibilities. Troy is a suburb about 20 miles from the city. It's become fancy now, but it wasn't when I was a boy. My parents are buried there."

"Do you want to visit their graves?"

"I don't know what I want. But I think I would like to see where I began before I come to my end," Charles said, before trying to dismiss the possibility of one more adventure. "Maybe it's all meaningless," he added.

"It has meaning to you, Charles," Pete said, "so it has meaning. I say we take a road trip—all three of us."

"Do you even have a car?" Charles asked, not convinced about the proposal.

"They have these businesses that rent cars. It's kind of new," Pete said.

"Don't be a smart ass," Charles replied with a smile.

"He has a nice ass," Hal added.

"This is what I would have to deal with on a road trip?" Charles asked.

"A little inappropriate gayness will do you good," Pete answered.

"What about Ollie?" Charles asked.

"Ollie hates cars. I can let him stay in one of those fancy dog boarding places. If he's lucky, he can knock up another dog while we're gone."

"You want to get Ollie laid?" Charles replied. "We don't need to travel for that. There are plenty of slutty dogs in New York."

"This is not about Ollie getting laid." Ollie barked and wagged his tail as if he understood. "But it would be a nice bonus," Pete said, petting Ollie. "This is about you having a new grand adventure, Charles."

"I don't know if I am up to such a journey, and I don't know what it is I would expect to find. I haven't thought about Troy in years. It just came to mind when you pushed me on the topic."

"I didn't push that hard. You will know when you find it."

"Jesus! You *are* young. No one ever knows when they find what they were looking for. Life doesn't work that way. We are always searching for the wrong thing, so if we find that thing—that wrong thing—it doesn't give us the satisfaction we wanted because it was the wrong thing."

"Maybe you need some observers who will tell you when you find the right thing," Hal ventured.

"Keep this up, young Hal, and I will demand the St. Crispin's Day speech," Charles said.

"I will work on it in the car on the drive to Troy."

"Are you up for the trip?" Pete asked. "Take a leap, Charles."

"Do I have a choice? I feel like I am being forced on a trip to Bountiful."

"If that were the case," Hal said, "We would make you wear drag."

Charles burst into a deep, uncontrollable laugh at the thought of being in drag as an old Southern woman. He wasn't even sure why he found it so funny, but he did, and so he laughed, an infectious laugh— silly and unstoppable, until Pete and Hal couldn't help but to join him. If dachshunds could laugh, Ollie would have joined in. Charles hadn't laughed with such abandon in years, and he realized he needed this adventure. He was not done with life.

"To Troy?" Pete asked through chortles.

"To Troy," Charles said with conviction.

"To Troy," Hal added.

"To Troy," they said in unison.

Part 2 – The Odyssey

Pete and Hal both arranged to take five days off work. Ollie was checked into Poochie Plaza, an establishment that guaranteed every dog a good time. If the female dogs only knew what awaited them, their owners would be looking into doggie birth control.

The three men left the city early Saturday morning to avoid the traffic. Pete had rented an SUV that would give Charles plenty of room in the back seat. Charles was standing outside his apartment building when Pete and Hal pulled up.

"You didn't have to wait outside," Pete said as he got out of the car. "One of us would have come up and helped you with your bags."

"I don't have much. It's only a week—just this small suitcase and a tote bag with a book."

"There will be no time for reading this week," Hal said as he stepped out of the passenger side and opened the back door. Pete took Charles's suitcase, opened the back hatch, and put Charles's bag in the trunk.

"We are on an adventure!" Hal exclaimed.

"He's a perky personality," Pete said, closing the back hatch. "You might as well get used to it now."

"Michael used to say the same thing about me. My percolator has slowed with time to an intermittent drip."

"We'll change that," Hal said, helping Charles into the car. "Do you need help with the seat belt?"

"No, but you can cut my meat for me later," Charles replied sarcastically.

"You have met your match, mister," Pete said to Hal, as he walked over to his side of the car and kissed him. "Charles is very self-sufficient— and not shy about letting people know it."

"The message has been delivered loud and clear," Hal said, smiling. He was not easily offended. "I will wear the tire treads across my chest with pride."

"Good," Charles said, satisfied that he had made clear he wanted no special treatment. "I may be old, but if I have embraced this trip to Bountiful, I intend to be independent."

"I completely understand," Hal said, as he reached down to the floor mat in front of the passenger seat. "I bought you this for the trip." He pulled up a wide-brimmed woman's hat identical to what the main female character wears in the film version of *The Trip to Bountiful.* "Wear it with pride."

Charles looked at the hat and laughed. "But I'm not putting on a dress," he said, donning the hat.

"It's you," Hal said.

"He doesn't have to wear it," Pete told Hal, unsure if Charles was offended by the ribbing.

"It's my hat, and I will do with it what I choose," Charles said playfully. He leaned over to Hal, now sitting in the front, and added, "Well played, young man. You are a keeper."

"I don't understand what just happened," Pete said, settling into the driver's seat. "Are you buckled in, Miss Daisy?"

"It's Watts," Charles and Hal said in unison.

"Her name is Carrie Watts," Hal said to Pete. "What kind of gay are you?"

"The kind who has never seen *The Trip to Bountiful.*"

"We could get out now?" Hal teased.

"We could, but he has the car keys. And I think he is too big for us to overtake. Besides, I have not driven a car in 40 years."

"Is it going to be like this all the way to Troy?" Pete whined.

"Ulysses said the same thing to his crew. Stop complaining and drive on," Charles said with newfound vigor. He started to sing, "California, here I come."

"I want to be Ethel," Hal said.

"I'm Ricky," Pete said. "And clearly, Fred is in the back seat. We don't need Lucy. She couldn't sing anyway."

The three men sang "California, Here I Come," the song from the end of the classic *I Love Lucy* episode where Lucy, Ricky, Fred, and Ethel start their cross-country drive from New York to Hollywood. No one needed to explain the reference. It was like *La Marseillaise* to a Frenchman. They kept singing it until they were west of the George Washington Bridge.

✳✳✳

"You know what the best thing is about New Jersey?" Hal asked, as they were approaching the Pennsylvania state line.

"It's not in New York," Charles suggested.

"You've heard that one, I take it," Hal replied.

"Everyone in the four boroughs has heard that," Charles said.

"There are five boroughs in New York," Hal answered.

"I can't hear you," Charles replied.

"I said, 'There are five boroughs in New York,'" Hal repeated louder.

"Nothing. I hear nothing," Charles said again.

"Am I being gaslit?" Hal asked Pete.

"Let's just say, Miss Ingrid Bergman," Pete began, "that some people in this car believe Staten Island is just the extreme east side of New Jersey."

"That is snobbery," Hal said. "I love Paramus."

"I rest my case, Ingrid," Charles said.

"What about Princeton?" Hal continued.

"It's an anomaly—like Berlin was in the old East Germany."

"There are many beautiful places in New Jersey. It's the Garden State. Thomas Edison had Menlo Park. New Jersey gave birth to Meryl Streep."

"I thank them for the light bulb, the phonograph, movie pictures, and birthing Meryl, but you will not change my mind," Charles said.

"You started this," Pete said, pointing ahead to the state line sign. "We have now officially left the State of New Jersey."

"I think the sun is shining a little brighter," Charles said as he looked out the window.

"It feels cloudy up here in the front," Hal pouted.

"Sweetie, you are my sunshine," Pete said, squeezing Hal's hand.

"I'm going to be sick," Charles complained from the back seat. "I will concede New Jersey has some value… small, but some. But please, put a lid on the ick."

"You are just as much a romantic as I am," Pete said.

"Maybe," Charles said wistfully. "Been too long to remember."

"Tell us a 'you and Michael' story," Pete said, as he gave Hal a knowing smile.

"Yes, I want to hear about Michael," Hal agreed.

"Michael. You want to know about me and Michael? Where to begin?"

"Wherever you want," Hal responded.

"Here's the deal. I tell a Michael story, and then both of you tell me a story about a past love. We have two days to get to Troy. Agreed?"

"Agreed," Pete and Hal replied.

Charles leaned back into his seat, playing with the brim of the Carrie Watts hat. He looked at it as a conjurer might a book of spells, knowing it held the power to make magic if he said the words right. They were an hour west of the New Jersey-Pennsylvania line when he began.

Charles's Story

"We were new—Michael and me—just like the two of you are," Charles said, looking wistfully at the hat brim. "A couple of weeks in, and lots of sex—I had forgotten how much sex you can have in your thirties. Let me correct that—how much good sex you can have in your thirties.

"We still didn't know what we were to each other. There was a connection beyond deciding 'I'm going home with you' near closing time inside a bar, but we hadn't realized that we would become each other's home. That came later, much later. Maybe that's a waste of time, but we spend a good amount of our lives wasting time," Charles added. "It was summer, around this time of year, so it was hot. We were in Michael's Mustang. It was vintage, which is a fancy way of saying it was old and used—just like I am now."

"You're not old," Pete shouted from the front seat.

"Sure, and you're not gay," Charles replied. "There's nothing wrong with being old. Let me tell my story, my way."

"Yes, sir," Pete said.

"That's better," Charles said, pleased with himself. He continued. "Michael lived in Queens, near the Nassau County line. It was like going to New Jersey, taking the subway, then a bus, and finally, I think, a mule. I should have realized sooner that Michael was a keeper because I took that subway, a bus, and a mule to see him, but I didn't."

"There are no mules in Queens," Pete shouted from the front. "You made that up."

"I remember seeing a mule," Charles replied. "It's my story. Maybe it was Joe Camel."

"Who?" Pete and Michael asked.

"You're ruining my story with these fact checks. I am adding a little poetry—something you know little about when writing obituaries, Mr. Journalist."

"I think that was a hit, a palpable hit," Hal chuckled.

"OK, you took a subway, a bus, and a mule," Pete said. "I concede the point."

"Thank you, now may I continue?"

"The floor, so to speak, is yours," Pete said, smiling. He was enjoying riling up Charles.

"Michael and I were going to drive out to the East End. No Fire Island for us. We wanted to go somewhere with fewer gay men. We weren't looking for that gay scene. Back then, the entirety of the East End wasn't an extension of the Upper East and Upper West sides of Manhattan. The Hamptons were fancy, but if you drove all the way toward Montauk, you could find motels that were inexpensive, close enough to the ocean, and escape reality.

"Michael's Mustang was ten years old and had 150,000-plus miles on it. Some scratches, too—some inherited, and some added by Michael. He couldn't park to save his life. I don't know how he ever passed a driver's test. He was fine on the road, but give him a curb, and he could never judge the distance. Tree bark became his friend.

"It didn't matter to us. We didn't care about scratches and dents on the side of a car. That came later, as well. Michael liked having a car in the city until the very end. But this was not the very end—this was the beginning. So off we went in Michael's bark-scratched, fire-engine red Mustang toward the LIE. That's the Long Island Expressway to you newcomers.

"Michael's Mustang was not a convertible, and it didn't have air conditioning, so we cranked the windows all the way down and sweated like pigs, even as the car did 60-plus on the road. The air pushing through the windows was still hot.

"It was sexy watching Michael start to glisten like a furry Christmas tree, the hair on his arms and legs matted and formed vertical and horizontal patterns on his body. I can vividly remember how turned on I was by the sight of Michael sitting next to me in that sweaty car as we flew down the LIE.

"We talked about everything and nothing—eventually, about favorite music. He loved opera. I had never seen or heard an opera until Michael entered the picture. I had no desire to. I was all about pop music. I loved Queen. 'Bohemian Rhapsody' was big then. It came on the radio, and I started singing 'Mama, just killed a man. Put a gun against his head, pulled my trigger, now he's dead.'

"It probably was the first telling moment between us—I felt comfortable enough to channel Freddie Mercury in front of this incredibly hot man—did I tell you how hot Michael was? He was so sexy. He never lost that. You never lose that because the sexy part isn't the veneer—the sexy part comes from inside.

"Anyway, I was singing 'Bohemian Rhapsody,' and he was smiling, but not really reacting. I'm thinking that he must be saying to himself, 'How am I going to get through this weekend with this guy?' But I am now fully committed to singing 'Bohemian Rhapsody,' and the song gets to the lyric, 'Easy come, easy go, will you let me go?' So, I sing that, and then as I begin the next line, Michael chimed in, 'Miss Miller, no, we will not let you go.'

"It was perfect. Not the way he sang. Michael couldn't sing his way out of a paper bag, but he was so uninhibited, with a huge grin on his face, glistening with the sweat from the heat. My knees went weak, and I was sitting in a car! What I felt at that moment was profound—the freedom Michael had singing out, 'Miss Miller, no, we will not let you go'—it was intoxicating.

"The lyric is 'Bismillah,' not Miss Miller, but it sounds like Miss Miller because who knows that Bismillah means 'in the name of God,' so I joined in singing 'Miss Miller.' It made it all more hilarious and special at the same time.

"We sang the rest of the song louder and louder, the intensity growing like Ravel's *Bolero*, another piece of music I didn't know until Michael, but it doesn't take a genius to figure out what *Bolero* is about.

"Something changed after that. Other songs played on the radio, and we sang and laughed. Then we started talking about where we grew up, and who we had sex with. It was pre-AIDS, so we were not concerned about that—it was more to gauge who was the bigger pig. In case you're interested, I was. Michael was like a sculpted god with fur, while I was more of a regular guy in shape, but not the kind everyone would look at when he entered a bar. That never mattered to me. I didn't need you to look at me when I came into the room. I just needed you to exit with me when I was ready to go.

"Hard for you to see me as I was fifty years ago," Charles said, more to the hat brim in his hands than to Pete and Hal. "Funny, I still see that guy from time to time when the light is just right, and the mirror has lost enough of its silver backing to reflect the past better than the present.

"By the time we got off the LIE onto Route 27, it was late afternoon, and we still had a good hour of driving ahead. It's called *Long* Island for a reason. As we got closer to Montauk, we saw a roadside motel. Nothing upscale. We got a room with two beds because it was still the 1970s, and you had to be careful. The guy checking us in—he couldn't have been more than seventeen—didn't have a clue. Michael was athletic and tall, and I was nondescript. We looked like two buddies heading out to the East End for some sun and surf.

"I had barely closed the door of the motel room when Michael grabbed me—almost lifted me up—and kissed me hard on the mouth, our tongues quickly finding a rhythm. Soon, we were pulling at our sweat-soaked T-shirts. I remember that day so well. I can't tell you much about yesterday, but that day, I remember. After we finished having sex, we showered, changed, and went in search of dinner.

"We found a little roadside seafood shack with a view of the water. We ordered lobster rolls and corn on the cob. Michael had slathered his corn with gobs of butter, and it dripped all over his mouth. I told him he had butter all over his chin.

"'Do you want to do something about it?' he asked. He was smiling, his lips glistening with melted butter.

"I said that I did, but I knew we couldn't there. 'It wasn't safe,' I told him as I handed him a wad of paper napkins.

"'Safe is overrated,' he said. 'We have a lifetime to be safe. We can be safe when we're old.'

"I replied that I didn't want to end up a statistic in my thirties—we had to be safe, if we wanted to be old. I was referring to the random gay bashings that happened back then.

"'Look around,' Michael said in a confident voice. We were sitting by the window, and the restaurant was partially full. As I said before, Montauk was not the prime destination then, as it is now. There were a few young couples—straight, of course. And an old man who looked a little like Ernest Hemingway in the corner. He was smoking a Marlboro—the pack was on the table. People could smoke inside restaurants then. He gave us this knowing look.

"I repeated to Michael that it wasn't safe—there was a guy looking at us.

"'Papa Hemingway?' he asked. I hadn't told him I thought the smoker looked like Hemingway, so I was impressed.

"Yes, the old man and the cig, I said, trying to be clever.

"'Jesus, you're a punster,' he responded, with an exaggerated look of surprise. 'I have fallen for a punster,' he repeated.

"I didn't hear what Michael said next. I got stopped at 'I have fallen for.' So, you've fallen for me, I asked him.

"'Isn't it obvious?' he responded.

"I am bad with signals, I replied. And I was. Like I said earlier, we spend most of our lives wasting time. What a stupid thing for me to have said to Michael—you've fallen for me—like I was being coy."

"Just like a fish in a pond," Hal interrupted.

"Oh, my God! *I've* fallen for a punster!" Pete exclaimed.

"It's a sign, Pete," Charles said. "It's a good sign," he repeated, before returning to his story. "After I told Michael that I was bad with signals, he said, 'Let me help you with that.' He leaned over the table and kissed me in front of the straight couples, Papa Hemingway, and the waitstaff.

"I had never been kissed by a man in a public restaurant. In bars, yes, and outside of safe places in the Village, but never in a public restaurant.

"'We can be safe when we are in our 80s,' Michael said, as he leaned back in his seat with his wide smile and lips still glistening from the butter.

"We can be safe when we are in our 80s," Charles repeated, his voice wavering with emotion. "We almost got there." Charles looked out the car window. "We almost got there."

Neither Pete nor Hal could see Charles trace his fingers along his lips, remembering the taste of Michael's lips, warm and covered with butter from the fresh corn. Charles could still smell the fresh corn. And as Charles looked out the window of the SUV as it sped along I-80 through Pennsylvania, all he saw were waves pushing up against the sand below the piers of a seafood shack near Montauk.

Pete and Hal exchanged looks, not knowing what to say. Hal turned on the radio. He found an opera station, thinking Charles would like that. It was Puccini's *Suor Angelica*, a beautiful, sad short opera, part of a trio of one-act operas called *Il Trittico*. Hal didn't know that; neither did Pete, whose knowledge of the Metropolitan Opera was limited to the obituary for Leonard Warren.

Charles could have identified the opera after decades with Michael and seasons at the Met, but all he heard were the waves pushing and tugging against the underpinnings of a seafood shack.

The three men were quiet until they stopped for lunch.

❊❊❊

Lunch at a McDonald's perked Charles up. It wasn't the food—a Happy Meal can only go so far when you're over eighty—but rather the sight of Pete struggling to find something healthy on the menu.

"Have a Quarter Pounder with cheese," Charles suggested. "Nothing is as satisfying as a Quarter Pounder with cheese."

"Do you know how much sodium there is in a Quarter Pounder with cheese?" Pete asked.

"Sodium?" Charles replied. "Do you know how large a sweat stain you have on the back of your shirt. The Westside Highway during a blizzard isn't spread with that much salt."

"I sweat efficiently," Pete said. "It's a runner's thing."

"You're not running, now," Charles said. "You're in a rest stop off I-80. And you are sweating like a pig—have some sodium."

"Are you going to help me out here?" Pete asked, turning to Hal.

"Not on this one," Hal said. "Relax. Your blood pressure is fine. You won't bloat. Have the Quarter Pounder with cheese. And," Hal added, "you might want to change that shirt."

"I thought you liked me sweaty," Pete said, moving closer to Hal.

"Not in this context," Hal replied, noticing the girl behind the counter make a disapproving face.

"She'll get over it," Pete said. "It's the 21st century."

"Not in western Pennsylvania," Charles interjected. "They are clinging to the mid-twentieth century like two socks in a dryer. Order the Quarter Pounder and buy yourself a fresh T-shirt in the gift shop. I'll pay for the food, and Hal will help carry it to a table. Now go."

"You win. And you've gotten mighty bossy outside of Manhattan," Pete said, resigned to the fact that he lost the battle and his shirt. "I'll be back."

Fifteen minutes later, Pete returned wearing a new T-shirt emblazoned with "Rust Belt USA." The shirt was a size too small.

"There was nothing in my size that didn't have a truck or a gun on it," Pete said as both men looked up from their burgers and fries. "If you say anything, I will make a scene."

"Honey," Hal said, "That T-shirt is making a scene all by itself."

"Leave him alone," Charles said, smiling between mouthfuls of burger, cheese, pickles, and bun. "Respect a man who is willing to humiliate himself in public."

"Honey, I respect you," Hal said, laughing. "I respect you so much that I will fight the urge to take a picture of you in that shirt."

"Too late," Charles said, taking out his phone and snapping a shot.

"Are you done shaming me?" Pete said, sitting down.

"For now," Charles replied. "I will make a final decision after I hear your love story."

"You'll have to wait until we get back into the car. I want to consume my pound of salt." Pete bit into the Quarter Pounder with cheese. "Damn, these things are good."

Charles and Hal exchanged satisfied looks. The three men ate, joked, and eventually ambled back to the rental SUV that was stifling from sitting in the sun.

"You know I will sweat through this shirt in less than two minutes," Pete said, opening the driver's door and turning on the air conditioning. "And it is so constricting. I will have to rip it off."

"That's my job," Hal said playfully, as he climbed into the front.

"I will just watch," Charles said, sliding into the back.

"You two are incorrigible," Pete said. "I should withhold my story."

"We love you like our luggage," Charles said, imitating Olympia Dukakis in the film version of *Steel Magnolias*. "Tell the story. I want to hear all about Claude Marcel."

"I'm not going to talk about Claude Marcel or Devin," Pete said, driving the SUV back onto the Interstate. "In the grand scheme of things, Devin was just a footnote."

"Smelly and a heel," Hal said.

"The puns! The puns!" Pete complained.

"Learn to live with it," Charles said to Pete. "There are worse things than bad word play."

"I know that, Charles," Pete said, smiling at Hal.

"Like bad foreplay," Hal added, with a twinkle that made Pete think of Christmas.

"You can't resist a pun, can you?" Pete asked.

"Just like I can't resist you," Hal replied.

"Ick! Ick!" Charles shouted. "Tell the story, already."

"My story is about a boy I knew in high school," Pete began.

"Your first time can be special," Charles said.

"He wasn't my first time. I hope that doesn't shock you?"

"Was that directed at me or Hal?" Charles asked.

"I was thinking of you, but I guess I should add Hal," Pete said. "I'm not a hound."

"I like dogs," Hal said.

"And you can't shock me," Charles said. "At my age, nothing surprises me except waking up each morning. And maybe," he added, smiling broadly, "seeing you in this T-shirt."

"Enough about the T-shirt. OK, this is my love story. It's about a boy named Mark, not my first time, but the first time someone mattered."

Pete's Story

"We were in the same homeroom, senior year in high school," Pete began. "Mark sat in the next row, one seat up. I could see the back of his neck, which usually had a trail of light brown hair that grew quickly between haircuts. I don't know why I remember that specific feature, but I followed the trail like Lewis and Clark if they were homosexuals—and please, no comments from the peanut gallery," Pete said, looking up at the rearview mirror.

"We had different schedules and interests," Pete continued. "I was on the school newspaper. Mark was in the drama club. I was assigned to cover the spring musical, *Pippin*. Mark played Pippin, and he spent a good part of the show shirtless. I was easily distracted. I had spent most of the year looking at the trail at the back of his neck, and then there was all this great stuff in front.

"I'll bet," Charles chuckled.

"That's not what I meant," Pete said. "And you were going to be silent?"

"Me thinks the lady doth protest too much," Charles replied. "Nothing wrong with a good front."

"OK. I noticed everything," Pete continued. "Mark had this amazing smile—he was having so much fun up there. It was clear he was doing what he wanted to do with his life. I wasn't assigned to review the show, but instead, to just write a feature on the rehearsal process.

"I spent weeks watching the show in rehearsal and seeing how it all came together from the beginning to the end. I interviewed all the kids in the cast, but I was drawn to Mark.

"We started talking about things other than the show. He had been accepted into Carnegie Mellon, which had a great theater program, and he dreamed of a life on stage. He didn't want to be in film or TV. Instead, he talked endlessly about being on stage, describing what it felt like to be in front of an audience, and how it was different every time.

"I asked him whether film was better because you could do it over and over until it was perfect, and then that perfection was what was captured on film. Plus, the money was better.

"That last part lit him up like a firecracker. He said money wasn't important. And I said something like 'it wasn't now, but when you add ketchup to hot water and call it soup, it will be.' I know, I should have come up with something better than ketchup soup, but it was all I could think of because I had some extra ketchup packets in my backpack."

"Extra ketchup packets?" Charles interrupted. "Extra ketchup packets from where, Mr. Sodium-free?"

"I take the Fifth," Pete said. "Look, I was seventeen. Don't judge me."

"Of course, we will," Hal said. "That's our job—to judge. Too bad we don't have Oliver Wendell Holmes. That would give us three judges like on a circuit court appeals panel."

"What exactly do you do?" Charles asked Hal. "You come up with all these bizarre references."

"I am a man of mystery," Hal said. "If I told you, Charles, I would have to kill you or at least force you to wear drag."

"May I continue with my story?" Pete complained.

"No one is stopping you," Charles said. "Continue. You told Mark that he needs to make money, so he doesn't have to make soup from ketchup packets—is that about right? It's a good thing, Pete, that you just write obituaries. Dead people can't complain about your lack of creativity."

"That really hurts," Pete said. "I was only seventeen."

"We know," Hal said, smoothing out the sweaty hair on Pete's arm. "Go on with your story."

"I will," Pete pouted. "Mark and I talked about acting. He said the great thing about live theater was that it's rarely perfect. It's whatever happens in the moment—good or bad—it isn't frozen like on film. Mark was intense for seventeen."

"I hope you didn't just talk," Charles said. "I need a little excitement. Maybe you did something with the ketchup packets?"

"I'll ignore that," Pete responded. "Mark and I talked a lot—at first. I talked about wanting to be a journalist, and I said it was the opposite of theater. When you write something, you want it to exist exactly as you wrote it. Your words are *your* words...I was a little intense back then, too."

"Just back then?" Charles asked.

"Busted," Hal said. "But I wouldn't change that."

"I'm trying to tell a story here," Pete whined.

"*Trying* is the operative word," Charles replied. "Continue—and don't forget the ketchup."

Hal chortled; Pete continued.

"Eventually, I stopped interviewing him when we met up," Pete said. It started when the two of us would go to a diner after rehearsals. We never discussed being gay. I was out, I guess. I just didn't walk around with an alphabet chart of where I fit in the rainbow."

"Nice metaphor," Charles said.

"You're incorrigible," Pete replied.

"Keep your eyes on the road," Charles replied. "And I'm really enjoying looking at the hair on the back of your neck." Charles started singing the old Roy Rogers song, "Happy Trails."

Neither Pete nor Hal knew where the song came from, but the lyric— *"happy trails, to you"*—fit. Hal laughed as he ran his fingers along the back of Pete's neck. "Very nice," he said, chuckling.

Pete, amused by the ribbing and aroused by Hal's touch, continued. "Thinking back, I must have thought Mark was gay, or at least curious— he wanted to be a theater major, right? I know that sounds like a cliché, but clichés are often true. And there was something between us—the more he talked about acting, and I talked about writing, the more I wanted to know about him.

"This went on for weeks until the weekend before the show opened. We were alone in my car. And it was not a Mustang, Charles. It was a Honda Civic. That night, we went to the diner after rehearsal with other cast members. I was driving Mark home.

"We talked about where I was going to school and my plans to major in journalism. Mark said I should branch out, and maybe one day he could be in a play that I wrote. I said theater just wasn't my thing—I couldn't write dialogue. After I said that, he asked me if I listened to people, and I replied that I did all the time. He said, 'Then you can write dialogue. Dialogue is just people talking like they were talking.'

"It can't be all that simple, I said. I have seen so many bad movies. Mark looked directly at me and said, 'It's simple, Peter.'

"He called me Peter. No one had ever called me Peter. I was always Pete. But when Mark said it, it felt right. His eyes were locked on mine, and he said, 'Just let people speak like themselves. A good writer lets the characters speak for themselves. They lose themselves in the story just as actors do. They trust that if they are true to their characters, the result will be fabulous.'

"He was so intense and focused on me, like I really mattered to him. I wasn't sure how to respond, so I said, I just want to be a journalist.

"'It doesn't matter,' he said. 'Write, Peter, write. Let the characters say what they say. Get out of their way and let them speak.'

"What if they don't want to speak? I replied. What if what they want to say doesn't need words?

"Mark moved closer to me and said, 'You mean like this?' He leaned in and kissed me gently on the mouth. I was on fire. I had never been kissed that way. The guy I had sex with the summer before was all business. We kissed, but there was nothing romantic about it, and I did what he told me to do. This was different. Mark was asking me if it was OK. I didn't say anything. I just nodded. He kissed me again, this time not gently.

"We started making out in the front seat of my Honda Civic in the back of the Century Diner. Some people must have seen us, but we were in our own world. I was afraid to break the mood, but I wanted to go further, and we couldn't do that in the front seat of a Honda Civic.

"'I have an idea,' Mark said. 'We can go back to school. I have keys to the auditorium. I'm the president of the Drama Club. I have keys to the auditorium *and* the prop room.'

"I said, that's convenient, and he grinned. I didn't understand what Mark had meant by letting people sound like themselves, but that grin—

I understood that grin completely. The invitation to the prop room was not spontaneous. Mark had thought about this.

"You planned this, I said to him. He said that a good actor reads the entire script before learning the role. This is what happens to us in Act Two. He kissed me again. Full mouth. Tongue. The whole enchilada.

"I asked him if there was an Act Three, and he said, no. That confused me, until he said, 'Peter, right now it's a two-act play. If you want another act, you're going to have to write it. Are you up for that?'

"He was so confident, so in charge, just like when he was on stage. He squeezed my crotch. His grip was firm. I almost lost it right there. How am I supposed to drive a car like this, I asked. We'll never make it back to the school.

"'We will, Peter,' Mark said. 'I'll get you there.'

"He did. We drove back to the school, which was empty, and he pulled out an impressive set of keys from his backpack. There is something sexy about a man with a substantial keychain.

"And there was something exciting and forbidden about being in an empty school building. Mark had a key to the rear of the auditorium, and we walked through the darkened backstage area to the prop room. He unlocked that door, led me into the room, and flipped the light switch.

"There were parts of sets from other shows, odd pieces of furniture, and props everywhere. I remember a large ornate birdcage. I have no idea which play that came from, but I can still see it—this Victorian birdcage painted gold. It was on the side of an old yellow sofa. Looking back, it was not the kind of sofa you want to get naked on, but at the time, it was exactly the sofa for sex.

"We started kissing, removing our clothing, and then we were on the sofa with our shirts and underwear underneath us. Our jeans were on the floor. It was nothing like it had been with the guy from the summer before. There was nothing controlling about the sex. It was glorious."

"Glorious?" Charles said, ready to engage in conversation. "I haven't heard anyone describe sex as glorious in decades. People have good sex. Or great sex."

"Or bad sex," Hal said.

"Or bad sex," Charles agreed. "Glorious, though. That is a horse of another color—a deep, passionate color. Michael and I had glorious sex—not always, but there were times like that night in Montauk when it was glorious. Bravo, Pete."

"It was special," Pete said. "I have had glorious sex since," he added, looking at Hal. "And in a bed, not on a ratty sofa."

Hal smiled. He was smart enough to stay silent. There was no need to compete with Pete's past because the past is in the rearview mirror and life is not lived in Reverse, or even Neutral. It's always in Drive, speeding like their SUV on I-80.

"So, is that it?" Charles asked.

"Isn't that enough?" Pete asked.

"What happened? Did you see him again?"

"We saw each other through the rest of our senior year and that summer. He went to Carnegie Mellon. I went to Penn State. We started to drift in our freshman year in college. Nothing dramatic happened—no pun intended," he added, looking at Hal. "There was no breakup scene, just two young people drifting in different directions."

"Did he become an actor?" Hal asked.

"I am sure he did, but we lost contact over the years. If he is working somewhere, he hasn't made it big yet."

"Funny thing about big," Charles said. "It is all relative—size, that is. No bad joke. If he is doing what he wants, he's made it big. Making it big has nothing to do with fame. When you reach my age, you realize that the only size that matters is how big you have lived your life. The two of you should remember that. I never made it big in my career, but I made it big in life because Michael and I found one another, and we never let go."

"You want to make me cry?" Pete asked.

"Yes," Charles said. "If you cry, you'll stop whining about too much sodium."

"Incorrigible," Pete said.

"Absolutely," Charles added.

Hal turned to Pete and, thinking about what Charles just said about living big, said, "I love you, Peter."

Pete mouthed back, "I love you." He felt like he did in the Honda Civic with Mark at his side as they drove from the Century Diner to the prop room of their high school auditorium.

Charles relaxed in the backseat contented as Dolly Levi with a turkey dinner at Harmonia Gardens.

✳✳✳

While it was possible to make it to Detroit and then on to Troy in a day, they planned to stop over somewhere in Ohio and then drive the rest of the trip the following day. Pete didn't want to tire Charles, and if he was honest, he didn't want to push himself to do a long drive, either. He never enjoyed driving, and traveling across Pennsylvania, through Ohio, and then northward into Michigan was a long, tedious stretch.

Pete and Hal discussed finding a hotel with a pool. That was something they did not have access to in Manhattan, and a hotel pool on a late afternoon in the dead of summer would be like an oasis in the desert.

The three men were silent as they pulled into the hotel parking lot. Charles wanted to nap before dinner. Pete and Hal said they were going to the pool. Charles didn't sleep, and Pete and Hal never made it to the pool. The two men found the shower and a large bed a better substitute.

Pete and Hal knocked on Charles's door at 6 pm. Getting no response, Pete called Charles on his cellphone.

"Where are you?" Pete asked. He could hear loud splashing in the background.

"I am by the pool, looking at half-naked men and, sadly, half-naked women. Where are you?" Charles asked.

"I thought you were going to nap," Pete said.

"I thought you were going to swim," Charles replied.

"We changed our plans."

"So did I."

"We will meet you by the pool."

"I'm the cute one with the hat," Charles said, then hung up. He was enjoying himself—there was something invigorating about being away from Riverside Drive. He felt twenty years younger.

Pete and Hal came down five minutes later. Pete was wearing a white polo shirt, tan shorts, and classic navy Converse sneakers. Hal sported a brightly colored, unbuttoned camp shirt, blue-and-white striped shorts, and flip-flops. They joined Charles, who had changed into a simple linen shirt, linen pants, and a pair of canvas shoes. He was wearing the Carrie Watts hat.

"Look at you," Pete said. "That's a statement."

"A good statement," Hal added.

"It says Quentin Crisp was an amateur," Charles said. "I think this hat works."

"It is working overtime," Pete said, sliding into a poolside lounge chair next to Charles. Hal took the chair on the other side of Charles, stretching out his tanned legs and letting his unbuttoned shirt fly open wide, exposing his equally tanned chest.

"Aren't we a trio?" Hal said. "The sun feels good at this time of day. It's hot, but it's not *hot*."

"Are you ready for dinner, Charles?" Pete asked. "We're near a small town, and they probably have a restaurant that serves folks who venture off the Interstate."

"Folks?" Charles teased. "When did we fall from the Mayberry tree? Who says 'folks?'"

"Would you prefer dudes, Miss Daisy?"

"Carrie Watts!" both Charles and Hal shouted at Pete. Before Pete could come up with a funny retort, Charles spoke.

"We're about an hour from Cleveland. We can find a place nearby that will be fine, and I bet not all that 'folksy,'" he added, making air quotes. "I'm in the mood for something greasy like burgers."

"We had Quarter Pounders for lunch," Pete protested.

"And they were yummy, but they don't count," Charles said. "They were fast-food burgers. They had no juice."

"They were burgers. How much beef can you eat in one day?" Pete asked.

"Is that a rhetorical question?" Charles asked.

"Submit," Hal said. "Charles will win. You can work it off later this week."

"My arteries are clogging as we speak," Pete said.

"Then it is settled," Charles said, ignoring Pete's protest. "But before we can have dinner, we are still one story short of a combination platter."

"That is true," Pete said, happy to change the subject and hoping a little more time would improve Charles's mood for more burgers. "We both have told our stories. It's Hal's turn. Tell it."

"I don't feel like it now. After dinner," Hal said, stretching.

"Listen, mister," Pete said, "I can pick you up and throw you and that fancy shirt of yours into the pool. Charles can help."

"I always loved a good pool toss," Charles said, his mischievous grin revealing a side of himself that the two young men could not easily imagine. Charles, to their even greater surprise, got up from his chair and grabbed Hal's legs. "Grab his arms," he said to Pete.

"Wait, wait," Hal said, laughing. "I will tell the story. This shirt is silk."

"I have no respect for silk," Charles said. "If it were cashmere, that would be another story."

"I say save the shirt, but throw him in," Pete said, getting up and joining Charles by Hal's chair.

"No, no," Hal said, enjoying the moment more than his protestations conveyed. "I will tell you the story—and I will pay for dinner."

"If he's willing to pay for dinner," Charles began, "I am willing to keep him dry. But the story better be good."

"It will be," Hal said. "Now, go back to your chairs."

Hal's Story

"Ethan. His name was Ethan, and I met him at a Starbucks. It wasn't exactly a meet-cute moment. We were in a very long line for the bathroom. It was not moving quickly, and we caught each other's eye. First, it was almost like cruising in a club, except there were moms with kids mixed in with straight people, and there was us. At some point, I said, I wonder what the holdup is, and he smiled and said, 'We probably don't want to know.'

"I said he was probably right, but there were at least seven people between us and the bathroom door, and a lot of air could change before we ever got to the restroom. I wasn't sure where the conversation was heading, but he was smiling at me, and I read that as encouragement.

"He said that they should have a fast-track line for bathrooms, like they do for the security lines at the airports. 'We need Pre-Check,' he said."

"You mean pre-cum," Charles interrupted.

"Your mind is in the gutter, Miss Watts," Hal replied. "You're ruining the mood."

"I think I am *reading* the mood. I know where this is heading. In my day, I was around the block so often they put my name on an honorary street sign."

"You must have been something in your youth, Charles," Pete said.

"I was more than something," Charles replied. "I was something *else*." Charles finger-snapped for added effect. "Continue the story, Hal. You were on the bathroom line wanting pre-cum."

"Pre-Check!" Hal protested. "It was Pre-*Check*, and that was what I told him in the Starbucks—I wanted Pre-Check."

Charles and Pete did not even try to control their chuckling. "Settle down, boys," Hal said. "Let me continue. We were starting to flirt. Ethan suggested that maybe we should go somewhere else with public bathrooms.

"Do you have a suggestion? I asked, hoping he did.

"'There's a bar two blocks from here,' he said. Ethan was referring to The Crow, that small dive bar in the Village. I knew it well, but I still asked whether it was open at that hour. I knew it was open, but I didn't want to sound like a total drunk.

"He looked at his watch—he wore a watch which I thought was very old school—and said, 'The Crow opens at 4 p.m. I don't know from experience, of course,' he added, which was encouraging because that meant he was as big a drunk as me. He asked if I wanted to ditch the bathroom line. I did, and we sprinted to The Crow. We both really needed to pee."

"I am not feeling any romance in this story," Charles said. "If this doesn't heat up, I say we still throw him in the pool, Pete."

"I agree completely," Pete said, motioning as if he were getting up from his chair.

"You two are a hard audience," Hal said. "The romance comes later."

"I'm in my eighties," Charles whined. "I don't have much later left."

"After we got to The Crow and peed—and not together for your information," Hal added, looking at Charles, "we sat at the far end of the bar and ordered beers. The Crow isn't a fancy place. It was early, and it was empty except for one old guy. The bartender, a big, bearish man, came over and took our orders. When he came back with the beers, he asked us our names. Ethan and I looked at each other and laughed because we hadn't introduced ourselves yet. The bartender, whose name was John, made a joke about us meeting on an app, and we explained that we met online waiting to pee.

"He said he had a similar experience back in the day at the Limelight, the legendary club carved out of an old church. It's a mini mall, now.

"The three of us kept talking, which was strange because all I had wanted before we got to The Crow was to pee and then hook up with Ethan, but instead, John was pushing us into real conversation. He kept asking questions: Were we originally from New York? What did we do for a living? Where did we live in the city?"

"Ethan and I lived not far apart in Brooklyn. He was in Cobble Hill, and I was near Prospect Park. We kept talking as the bar filled up. John left us to tend to his patrons.

"I asked Ethan about his watch. He said it belonged to his father, who had died when he was a boy. The memory of his dad wearing the watch remained strong, and Ethan said it connected him to his dad. It was at that point that we clasped hands.

"There was a growing sexual energy between us, but I didn't think we would hook up that day. Ethan showed me a picture on his phone of him and his dad. His father was handsome, probably not more than thirty-five in the photo. Ethan was five. His dad was crouching behind him, giving him a big hug. They both had huge grins, and I could see the watch on his dad's arm.

"It was such an odd moment because Ethan, still a virtual stranger, shared something so intimate, so personal with me. He trusted me. It was the first time I felt intimate with another man, where it wasn't about the sex, but about the man—the person in front of me.

"Ethan said, 'Let's get out of here.' I said sure, but I had no clue what he had in mind. He led me to the subway, the A train, and said we're going up to Columbus Circle. It was past 6 p.m., but it was late spring, and the days were long, so it was still light out. He told me we're going to walk through Central Park.

"I always liked Central Park—it's not intimate like Riverside Park—but it's a grand public space, so off we went walking. I had no clue where we were heading, but Ethan had my hand, and I liked the way it felt, and I allowed him to lead me. We walked across to the east side of the park, near the zoo. Ethan stopped and pointed up at the Delacorte Clock, the mechanical clock with all the whimsical animals that look like they're playing music. It was just 7 p.m., and the clock came to life. It played, 'What the World Needs Now.'

"Ethan's face lit up like a boy's as he watched the animals move around the clock. When the animals stopped, he took out his phone and showed me the picture of him and his dad again. When I saw it earlier, I hadn't realized it was taken right where we were standing."

"'It was a perfect day,' he said.

"Just like today, I replied. We kissed, and then we took a selfie, matching the one he had of him and his dad. It was perfect. We didn't hook up that night—that came two days later. We were together for almost a year."

"What happened?" Pete asked.

"We met in the spring of 2019," Hal said. "The spring of 2020 happened."

"COVID?" Charles asked.

"He died in April, right in the beginning. He had asthma, so he was more susceptible to the virus. I wasn't with him when he died. He was in a hospital with everyone else who was dying."

"I'm so sorry," Pete said, getting up to sit next to Hal. "That must have been hard."

"It was, but it was a long time ago—a lifetime ago."

"Time helps," Charles said. "I'm sorry, too."

"I'm not sure why I told this story," Hal said. "I knew when I started how it ended, but it is a great love story. Just a short story…a sad, short story."

"It was a love story," Charles said. "Length isn't important when it comes to love. It's a limitless thing, so short or long doesn't affect it."

"I feel honored that you shared this with us—with me," Pete said softly.

"I had to, Peter," Hal said, squeezing Pete's hand. "I think we need to get out of here and get some dinner unless you still want to throw me in the pool."

"He's a keeper, Pete," Charles said, getting up from his chair. "He's a keeper."

The three men stood, hugged, and went in search of dinner.

✳✳✳

They found a burger place about ten minutes from the hotel. It was a local place, not a chain, which suited their collective tastes. The burgers were large and messy, and Charles enjoyed watching the younger men eat with gusto, ketchup and juices sliding onto their chins, and them handing one another wads of paper napkins. It took Charles back again to the roadside shack in Montauk. He could see himself and Michael sitting there with the melted butter. It made him smile.

"What are you smiling about?" Pete asked. "Do we amuse you?"

"You do—immensely. This is a moment for you two to remember. It's not romantic or fancy, it's just real. Unlike my teeth," Charles added.

"Enough about teeth," Pete said. "Your teeth look just fine."

"So does the rest of you," Hal said.

"I think your boyfriend is trying to get in my pants," Charles said, sipping a Coke. "If he gets inside them, maybe he can tell me if there's still anything down there."

"I'm sure you still function fine," Hal said.

"Maybe," Charles said. "Not going to find out anytime soon or later."

"None of that," Pete said. "This is going to be a fun night. We need to do something."

"Like what, Peter?" Hal asked, using Pete's full name for the third time in a day.

Pete smiled lovingly at Hal and said, "Something interactive."

"I told you I'm not going to have sex," Charles said.

"Point noted," Pete said. "Karaoke!"

"Karaoke?" Hal asked. "Where are we going to find a karaoke bar?"

"We have phones," Pete said. "We have search engines. We have a full tank of gas."

"I have never done karaoke in my life," Charles said.

"Never?" Hal asked.

"In my day, we went to piano bars, and did it live without any video help," Charles said. "We didn't need karaoke."

"I've been to The Edwardian," Hal said. "They still do it live there."

"I know," Charles said. "Michael and I went there years ago when the place was new. Michael liked to listen to the show queens sing. He couldn't sing his way out of a paper bag," Charles paused. "I said that earlier, didn't I?"

"I repeat myself all the time," Pete said reassuringly. "It has something to do with always saying things worth repeating."

"I vote for karaoke," Hal said, looking at his phone. "There is a place about 20 minutes from here that has karaoke on Saturday nights, and it's listed as LGBTQ friendly."

"It sounds like our kind of place," Pete said. "Are you up for this, old man?"

"Who are you calling old?" Charles said, taking the bait. "I could take you."

"Really?" Pete said, lifting his Diet Coke.

"I didn't say where I could take you," Charles added.

Pete and Hal groaned, and then the three men lifted their sodas and toasted: "To us."

The karaoke place was nondescript from the outside. It was a smallish brick building that must have once been a factory. There was a small sign that read "Tin Pan" above the entrance, lit by a row of four, black bell-shaped light fixtures. Parking was on the street and Pete found a space a few minutes' walk from the door.

Charles, who was feeling young and silly, grabbed the Carrie Watts hat. "For courage," he said.

"*Cry God for Harry, England, and Saint George!*" Hal said, placing his hand on Charles's back as they walked to the entrance.

"It's not St. Crispin's Day," Charles said. "But at least you're getting closer."

"The two of you are quite a pair," Pete said, bringing up the rear. "You should do a duet."

Charles and Hal exchanged looks. Charles winked at Hal and said, "I think we should do a trio."

"I don't sing," Pete said. "I like to watch and listen."

"If you can wear that ridiculously tiny T-shirt, you can sing," Charles said.

"If you can paint, I can walk," Hal added, batting his lush eyelashes. "I love that movie."

"What gay man doesn't?" Charles said.

"At least I have seen *An Affair to Remember*," Pete said. "But I am not singing."

"You suggested karaoke—you can't just sit and watch us," Charles said. "You will sing tonight—this is your 'fatal urn of destiny moment,'" he added, referring to the aria Leonard Warren sang at the Metropolitan Opera before he dropped dead on the stage.

"I have no intention of dying on stage."

"Then sing well, my young friend. Onward!" Charles shouted as he led the way inside.

Tin Pan was more welcoming than its exterior suggested. It was one big room with posters of old movies, pop stars from the eighties and nineties, and an entire Cher wall. There was a bar along one wall with orange vinyl-covered diner stools lined up like the dancers in the opening of *A Chorus Line*. Small tables were scattered across the middle of the room, and a stage, surrounded by three video screens, had been built into the left back corner.

For a place in the middle of nowhere by New York City standards, there was a good-sized crowd of about thirty people. Pete was driving, so he was not drinking. Hal and Charles had no limitations.

While Pete drank Diet Cokes, Charles ordered several Jamesons with ice, and Hal insisted on vodka martinis, which were only seven dollars until 10 p.m. if made with the well vodka.

"Is that any good?" Pete asked Hal. "Well vodka is usually not great."

"It's doing the trick," Hal said. "It is lubricating my pipes. How about you, Charles? How's the whiskey?"

"I'm lubed up," Charles said.

"I'm going to find us a song," Hal walked over to Miss Oval Teen, the drag MC sitting at the bar. He chatted her up while he browsed the song lists. He selected one and added their names to the list of performers.

"What are we singing?" Charles asked when Hal returned.

"It's a surprise," Hal said. "Just one question for the table—have you both seen *The First Wives' Club*?"

"Yes," Charles said.

"Yes," Pete answered. "I will watch Maggie Smith in anything."

"Good to know. Good to know," Hal repeated, with his most wicked smile. "Drink up, boys. Screw your courage to the sticking place. We will be up soon."

And they were. Miss Oval Teen called their names and then the name of their song, "You Don't Own Me."

"It's the finale of the movie," Hal said, as they walked toward the stage.

"Can't I just put that T-shirt back on and call it a day?" Pete asked. "Wasn't that humiliation enough?"

"I will lend you my hat," Charles said.

"No, I draw the line at the hat," Pete said.

"Suit yourself," Charles said, putting the hat on. The room loved Charles's energy and was cheering the three men before they made it to the stage. "They *love* me," Charles said, taking a small bow, like he used to do for Michael after a sweater purchase negotiation had been finalized. "I will be in the center. You two can be to my left and right."

"A star is born," Hal said.

"I regret this already," Pete complained.

"What was it that boy, Mark, said to you, 'get out of your own way,'" Hal asked. There was no time for Pete to respond.

The music started. Charles was in his element. It was not a piano bar, but there was an audience, and he was having the time of his life. Hal was game for anything, and he was not without talent. Pete, on the other hand, wasn't lying when he said that he couldn't sing, and being much taller than Hal and Charles, he literally stood out. But as the song progressed, and he tried to follow the improvised choreography, Pete realized that being ridiculous is exactly how relationships are forged.

The more the three men struggled with the movement and lyrics, the more fun they had, and the more the audience loved them. When they finished the song, the room stood up. Charles was exuberant. He had not had this much fun in years.

Miss Oval Teen bought them a round of drinks, and they laughed for a good hour at the table, cheering on other would-be singers. It was a mixed crowd of straight and LGBTQ people, but everyone was the same—they were there to have fun, to sing along with a recording, and, somehow, in the process, to find their own unique voices.

The men were still laughing loudly as they walked back to the rental car. Charles had fully embraced wearing the Carrie Watts hat. The friends were lost in their own private world and did not hear the footsteps of three young, big, drunk men behind them. These men didn't like any man wearing a woman's hat, or the fact that this industrial section of their town had become a haven for LGBTQ people.

One of them grabbed Charles's hat from behind, and as Charles, Hal, and Pete turned around, the other two took swings at Pete and Hal. Hal, being shorter, evaded the swing, but Pete was not so lucky. A fist landed hard on his face, and he fell backward onto the pavement.

Hal tried to fight back, but he was not up to staving off three men. Charles, who had seen his share of gay bashing as a young man, looked around for anything he could use as a weapon. There was a piece of discarded wood beside the building. He grabbed it and swung it as hard as he could at one of the men, hitting him square in the face.

That man crumpled to the ground, giving Hal an opening to take a swing at one of the others. It wasn't as forceful as Charles's, but it knocked the second man down. Charles took his piece of lumber and lunged at the lone remaining standing man's arm. He could hear the bone crack.

As quickly as it started, it ended. One man had a broken arm, one man's face was bleeding, his nose probably broken, and the third, while not seriously hurt, decided that Charles was a dangerous, crazy old man. He helped his two injured friends up, and they ran.

The scuffle outside was noticed by patrons exiting the club, who called 911. Pete lay motionless on the pavement. He looked up at Charles, wearing the Carrie Watts hat, and holding his piece of lumber like a weapon, as a young Ulysses might have.

Pete was trying hard not to lose consciousness. Before he did, he managed to say, "Thank you, Miss Daisy," to which Charles, now kneeling next to his friend, quietly whispered, "It's Carrie Watts."

Police arrived within minutes. Pete was taken to the hospital; the responding EMTs suspected he had a concussion. Hal, who was bruised and scraped, went with Pete to the hospital.

Charles, remarkably, was unscathed. Police wanted his statement before taking him to the hospital to be with Pete and Hal. Before he could leave the scene, a camera crew from a local TV station arrived. Once they learned that Charles, an octogenarian, had beaten off the attackers, they wanted to interview him on camera.

His linen shirt and pants were wrinkled, but Charles—his face flushed from the adrenaline still pumping through his veins—was more than ready for his close-up. When he saw the reporter approaching, he was eager to talk.

"I understand you beat off three young men with a stick," the reporter asked.

"It was a very big stick," Charles answered, emphasizing "big," and then added, "Teddy Roosevelt used to say that to me."

The reporter was young and dim. "You knew Teddy Roosevelt?" he asked.

"Absolutely," Charles said, enjoying the deception.

"Can you tell me what happened?" the reporter asked, clueless that Charles was playing with him.

"I was leaving the karaoke place with my two good friends," Charles began. "We had a great time in there. We sang, 'You Don't Own Me,'" Charles added, even though he was sure the reporter didn't want to hear about what happened before the attack. But Charles wanted to give the story added color, and for the first time in years, he was awash in brilliant reds, purples, blues, and gold.

"We were walking back to our rental car," he continued. "We're passing through from New York City. We didn't hear anyone behind us. We were laughing. It had been a great night. Then, out of the blue, someone knocked off this hat."

Charles was going to put it on for added effect, but as he looked at the hat, he noticed blood. He wasn't sure it was Pete's, Hal's, or from one of the attackers, but it sobered him instantly. This was not a time to enjoy the camera; it was a time to use it.

"You know, young man," Charles said in a changed tone, "when I was your age, gay men were targeted in New York City. It was all random. Baseball bats. Bottles. Fists. I thought that was in the past. We're a quarter-way through the twenty-first century, and it's still the 1970s and '80s. After one of the guys knocked off my hat, we all turned around—me, Pete, and Hal—those are my two good friends.

"The other two attackers—they were big, and I could smell beer on them—they started throwing punches. One of them, as big as Pete—and Pete is a tall man—sucker-punched Pete. He hit him hard on the left temple, and Pete went down for the count. He never saw it coming.

"I didn't really think—my friend was lying on the cement. My reaction was automatic. I needed something to defend myself, and I saw a piece of old wood leaning against the brick wall of the club. I grabbed it, and I swung it at the big, beer-smelling guy who had hit Pete. I swung that piece of wood like I was Roger Maris.

"You should have seen the expression on that guy's face as the wood hit him. It was the best moment of my life. I may be an old man, but I still have fight in me."

Charles took a deep breath. "That which we are, we are," he continued, but because Charles couldn't resist one more dig at the young reporter, added, "Teddy Roosevelt said that to me, as well." The reporter nodded before Hal continued.

"Hal was fighting the other guy, who was almost as big as the one I hit. Hal's guy was wearing a tank top, and I could see his arms were huge and covered in tattoos. He smelled, too. Hal, who is not that big, needed help, so I swung again—Roger Maris back at the plate. I think I broke that motherfucker's arm."

Charles had refrained from using profanity all his life, but he was so high on adrenaline that the words rose from a place buried deep inside. It felt good, so Charles said it again, this time with more intensity. "He was a *fuckin' motherfucker*.

"Well, that was it for them. The big one with his face bleeding, the smelly one with a broken arm, and the other one, scared shitless." There was no stopping Charles now from using profanity. "They ran with their tails between their legs. They will think twice before messing with an old man and his friends.

"Let me tell you something about gay men, young man. We stick together. We're brothers, shipmates bound together on the same voyage to Troy."

"I don't understand the last part," the reporter said. "Troy?"

"It's a metaphor," Charles answered. "It's also in Michigan."

The adrenaline rush was fading; Charles was starting to crash. He was tired and wanted to go to the hospital to see Pete and Hal. "I'm tired, young man," he said. "I need to see my friends, Pete and Hal."

Charles abruptly turned away from the reporter, who now had to talk to his producer about having "fuckin' motherfucker" edited out of the interview. A police officer drove Charles to the hospital, where two other officers were taking statements from Pete and Hal.

Hal had the beginnings of an impressive black eye and some scrapes on his arms. The fancy silk shirt that had been saved hours earlier from the over-chlorinated water of the hotel pool was splattered with blood. Charles thought it looked better now that it was stained by adventure. The shirt revealed the champion who had been waiting to be tested in combat. The blood was not so much a badge of honor as a sign of being honorable.

To sacrifice yourself for someone else—well, that was the bond among warriors, both mythical and real. Pete, Hal, and Charles were bound together as if they had traveled on a galley ship rather than in a rented SUV.

Charles realized they would not make it to Troy, but he saw no failure in that. Epic journeys are beset by tragedies; they often end badly. But if they end nobly, as this one had, well, that was what mattered.

Tennyson understood Ulysses' pain sitting on his little island yearning to set sail once more with shipmates still brave and fearless, despite the physical limitations of age. Charles wanted more than to sit on his island watching strangers pass by—he wanted to journey on to one last adventure. That wasn't narcissism; it was destiny. It was *their* destiny—his, Pete's, and Hal's.

Charles watched as Hal spoke to a nurse at Pete's bedside. Charles was Ulysses, old, but still proud and strong on the deck of his ship, and these two fine young men were his crew—his arms, his legs, his eyes, his voice—his most magnificent voice that had not risen before as it had today.

Charles whispered, barely audibly, "fuckin' motherfucker," and then chuckled at the absurdity of it taking eighty-plus years for him to say that out loud.

We three, Charles thought, will return to home port. Let the sea rise against us, let the heavens erupt, and let three fuckin' motherfuckers try to stop us; we will return home. As Tennyson wrote, "Some work of noble note, may yet be done, not unbecoming men that strove with Gods."

Thinking now of the young reporter, Charles said loud enough to catch the attention of a passing nurse, "Damn, that Teddy Roosevelt could write!"

The following day, Pete was released from the hospital. The three men spent another two days at the hotel to give Pete and Hal more time to recover. On Tuesday, Charles got behind the wheel of the SUV, the first time he had driven in decades. Hal did not drive, and Pete was not up to the task. With Hal to his right as navigator, and Pete stretched out on the back seat, the old man took the wheel, and they headed back to New York City.

They reached the city near sunset, with the Hudson River reflecting the fading orange sky. No one sang as they crossed the George Washington Bridge; no parade greeted the returning warriors. After returning the rental, Hal took Pete home, and Charles took a cab up to his apartment. He was tired, but he needed to walk along the side of Riverside Park to remind himself that he was, indeed, home.

As Charles walked up to Grant's Tomb and looked at the façade, the words above the entrance finally made sense. Charles smiled with satisfaction. There was no need to explain them out loud; the meaning was clear to him, and he was the only person who needed to know it: Let us have peace.

Part 3 – On Riverside

Three days passed before Charles saw Pete, Hal, and Ollie on the elevated side of Riverside Park. The doctor at the hospital in Ohio told Pete he should rest for the remainder of the week, and, much to Pete's surprise, he found it to be wise advice. He also liked staying in Hal's apartment, which was bigger than his and with better light. The only drawback was that he hadn't retrieved Ollie from Poochie Plaza; Hal thought that would be too much excitement for Pete.

Three days after their return, Pete and Hal walked to Poochie Plaza to pick up Ollie, who was excited to see his man. Whatever sexual adventures the young dachshund had had would remain unknown to Pete; whatever happens at Poochie Plaza stays at Poochie Plaza.

There was no question that the two men and Ollie would head first to Riverside Park. Pete had texted Charles to ask if he could meet them there. Charles quickly agreed.

He had not been idle over the past three days. The story of his most glorious victory over homophobic thugs in Ohio had made him a celebrity of sorts. Charles was flooded with requests for interviews by both local stations and national networks. An octogenarian fighting off three young thugs was great theater.

At first, Charles was excited about the prospect of becoming the story of the day, but by day three, he had doubts. He did not want to hog the glory; he wanted Pete and Hal included, but the news outlets were not interested in a threesome. They just wanted Charles.

When Charles saw Pete, Hal, and Ollie approach his bench, he was overjoyed, but he also wanted to discuss what he should do.

Ollie wasted no time pulling the leash from Pete's hand and running to Charles, who immediately picked up the dog, reveling in the affection.

"I come in second place, now," Pete said, walking up to Charles. "I am first loser." He sat down on the bench to the left of Charles and stretched out his long legs.

"Not to me, Peter," Hal said, sitting to Charles's right.

"Well played, Prince Hal," Charles said.

"I would think by now, I would have been elevated to Henry V," Hal replied. "Look at my black eye."

"It's impressive, I give you that. But no St. Crispin's Day speech—not even a Krispy Kreme. Hal you were, Hal you are, Hal you will be."

"You are a hard man to please," Hal said, teasingly patting Charles on the knee.

"You have no idea," Charles said. "I was a handful for Michael, but so was he to me, so it evened out in the end."

"So, they want you on two of the national morning shows," Pete said.

"Yes, I am quite in demand. But no Oprah."

"She doesn't have a show anymore," Pete said.

"That doesn't matter. I would like to meet Oprah. She is the only woman who I wish had been born a gay man because she would have been the next Harvey Milk. She understands the limitations of the people around her, while recognizing that she has no limits at all. That has allowed her to redefine what a woman can do, what a woman of color can do—if she were a gay man, believe me, she would have been our Harvey Milk for this century."

"I'm sure she would appreciate your adoration," Hal said.

"It's not adoration...it's respect," Charles said. "All the other media requests pale in comparison."

"That may be," Pete said, "but you must go with what is offered. You should do them all."

"I agree," Hal said.

"They only want me. They don't want you two."

"That doesn't matter to us," Pete said as Hal nodded in agreement. "You were the hero. This is your moment in the sun."

"I don't want to hog the glory. I don't want to be one of those gays."

"One of those gays?" Pete asked rhetorically. "You are nearing eighty-five...there aren't any other gays in your league."

"I didn't swing that piece of wood for glory," Charles said. "I did it because I love the two of you like you were both my brothers and my sons."

"That sounds like Faye Dunaway in the film *Chinatown*—my sister, my daughter, my sister, my daughter," Hal said.

"Hah, hah, hah," Charles responded. "That's why you're still Hal, not Henry V," he added, patting Hal on the shoulder, "And I love you for that."

"Look, Charles," Pete said, "You are our brother. We owe our lives to you. Without you, things would have ended badly for us. They would probably have ended—like 'we're all dead' ended. Embrace the celebrity. It's your moment in the sun. Bask in it."

"Like a pear," Hal joked.

"That's Bosc, but I appreciate the bad pun," Charles said, laughing. "If it weren't for you, Prince Hal, I would not have had the Carrie Watts hat. It had a magical power."

"Thank you," Hal said, "but you had the power all along."

"If you say I am like Dorothy in *The Wizard of Oz*, I will find a piece of wood and slug you right here and now," Charles said, regaining some of the feistiness of their trip. "You two are like a tonic. You bring me back to my youth."

"I am glad to hear it," Pete said. "You make us feel alive, as well."

"It's a pity we met so late in my life. You bring me back to my youth, but it can't be a long stay. It doesn't work like that."

"Enjoy the moment," Pete said. "And we have news."

"Hal is pregnant," Charles said matter-of-factly.

"How did I become the bottom?" Hal asked, clearly amused.

"Do you really want me to explain that?" Charles said, laughing. "Maybe Ollie can. I would put money on him getting laid recently. He looks like he got laid."

"How can you tell if a dog has had sex?" Hal asked.

"If an eighty-four-year-old gay man can't tell whether another male has had sex, he has not been paying attention. This dog has had some fun," Charles added emphatically. Ollie wagged his tail. "You see," Charles said. "I rest my case."

"All very interesting," Pete said, "but our news is that I am going to move in with Hal, and before you say it's too soon, I don't need more time. What happened in Ohio proved this is my person—this is my Michael."

Pete moved over to the other side of Charles to sit next to Hal. They joined hands.

"There's no arguing with that," Charles said. "I will go to Bergdorf Goodman and buy a sweater to celebrate. I haven't been in that store in years. It is time for a new sweater."

"Something that looks good on camera," Hal said. "You're about to become a celebrity. You need a fabulous sweater."

"Hal, baby," Charles added with playful affection, "all cashmere is fabulous...it's just the goats that are boring as hell."

"We should do something today," Pete said. "Something that celebrates your newfound celebrity and my moving in with Prince Hal, here."

"I'm not Henry V—even to you?"

"Well, still no St. Crispin's Day speech for Charles. He was my friend first."

"That's the stuff," Charles said excitedly. "Now, you're beginning to sound like a real couple—one with some legs."

"Peter does have good legs," Hal said, firmly grabbing Pete's knee. "Very good legs."

"Ick," Charles replied. "You want me to take back the compliment already? We need to do something before you get sloppy in public."

"Yes," Pete said. "Something interactive."

"Karaoke!" Hal exclaimed.

"Not on your life," Pete said. "I will never do karaoke again."

"Never say 'never,' my young, long-legged friend with no musical talent," Charles replied. "Life throws all of us many surprises. I have an idea. It's a beautiful day. We don't need to do anything but sit."

Two shirtless Columbia men ran past Charles, Pete, and Hal, who instinctively turned their heads in unison to follow the runners' progress.

"Aren't we the trio?" Hal said, laughing. "I have an idea. Let's rate the runners, like at the Olympics. We can text the numbers to each other and compare scores. Texting will be more discreet than holding up signs."

"Digital objectification," Charles said. "I like it. But one of you will have to show me how to send a group text."

Hal took Charles's phone and sent a test text to Charles's and Pete's phones. "You're all set now. We rate them on a scale of one to five."

The runners flew past, and the trio texted their scores to each other, debating the merits of each runner. When a very large man passed, Charles texted, "Eight inches."

Hal and Pete laughed, and soon Charles joined them. Passersby couldn't figure out what was going on with the three men who were uncontrollably laughing.

A young man approached them. "Can I have some of whatever you guys have been smoking or eating?"

Not missing a beat, Charles said, "Here, take these." He pulled something from his pants pocket and handed it to the young man. "Enjoy."

The young man looked perplexed, but assuming it must produce a great high, he said, "Thank you."

"Don't mention it," Charles said.

Once the young man was out of earshot, Pete asked, "What did you just give him, Charles?"

"Lifesavers."

✳ ✳ ✳

Weeks passed. Charles had not seen much of Pete and Hal, who were settling into their new life as a cohabitating couple. While Charles missed his two friends, the media attention had not yet waned, and he was reveling in it. But when Pete suggested they meet in the park to catch up, he immediately said yes and walked to his bench. Pete was there waiting.

"Is that a new sweater?" Pete asked. "It's almost cool enough for a sweater."

"It's September, and I have no circulation—just like print newspapers, Mr. Journalist," Charles said, as he sat down. "Where's Ollie?"

"Sorry to disappoint you. You just get this hairy beast," Pete said, patting his stomach. "Ollie is with Hal at home. I wanted to get in a run. Can't get fat."

"Little chance of that. How is married life?"

"Funny you should put it that way. I'm going to ask Hal to marry me. Is it too soon?"

"Never ask an old man if something is too soon. We will always tell you that the only thing that is too soon is death. No, if you love Hal, go for it.

"I'm glad you said that. I do love Hal. I don't think it is possible to be happier."

"Ah, I remember that feeling. Here's a great thing about life, Pete—it can get better. As happy as you are right now with Hal, I promise you that a few years down the road, it will be better, richer, and more exciting."

"Was it like that for you with Michael—even at the end?"

"The short answer is yes. Happiness is always different from what we imagine it to be, but you'll understand that when you are an old man wearing sweaters."

"I like your sweaters."

"I bet you do, but you can't have them—you're too big. It would be like that rest stop T-shirt all over again."

"Will you never let me forget the T-shirt?"

"No. Now, tell me about work. How's that going? Anybody good die lately?"

"I thought you read the obits daily."

"That was before we went to Ohio. Now I don't care who died. I'm too busy living. You saw me on channel 2?"

"Yes, I did. You looked great."

"And I came so close to meeting Oprah, so close. She was in the studio earlier that morning. I haven't been that disappointed since missing Jeff Stryker in a Las Vegas hotel lobby in 1996."

"Only you can put a 1990s gay porn star in the same sentence as Oprah."

"And that is why I was on channels 4 and 5, as well."

"You are a changed man, Charles."

"Not changed, as much as who I was when I was your age—except that I'm not as shallow. *This* is the version of me I wish you could see in a younger body. Confident, but not arrogant. Optimistic, but realistic. When we're young, we get caught up in our successes and think the world should grovel at our feet. Or the opposite is true, and we wallow in defeat. Now, I see it all clearly—the good and the bad. Who knew I would figure all that out without going back to Troy?"

"Do you wish we had made it to Troy?"

"No, not at all. I chose Troy as a destination because it was the first place that came to mind when you asked where to go for a final adventure. But it was never about going to Troy, Pete. It was about going somewhere—anywhere. It was about setting off from this island one last time.

"Troy was my past. There's nothing there for me now. So, no, Pete, I don't wish we had made it to Troy. But I would regret it to my dying day if we had never gone to Tin Pan and sung the song Hal picked." Charles began to laugh.

"What's so funny?"

"The memory of you singing and trying to do the choreography. You were as bad as Michael."

"I'm glad I bring you joy."

"You do. You're like a second Michael in my life, without all the romance and stuff that comes with the man who's your husband and lover. You're the part of him that made me feel so much more than just alive—I felt like I was living life when I was with Michael. Everything was an adventure. Yes, Pete, you bring me joy."

"This is where Ollie would jump up and hump your leg, and we could stop being serious."

"A man's best friend," Charles said, clasping Peter's hand. "This is nice."

"Yes, Charles. This is nice."

The two men sat silently on the bench for a while before Pete got up to start his run. "Leaving me so soon?" Charles asked.

"I'm a gay man. What did you expect?"

"Good answer. I'm getting greedy. I enjoy spending time with you and with Hal. You have so much ahead of you. Sometimes, I want that again, that feeling that there is more ahead than behind. Greed, that's what it is."

"I wouldn't say that, Charles. We all want more. Young or old, we want more. I promise not to be a stranger. I will make time for us—just me and you. We'll go to a McDonald's and order Quarter Pounders with cheese."

"Now, you're messing with me. You in a McDonald's? What about the sodium? What about the bloating?"

"What about spending time with someone who matters more than 730 milligrams of sodium?"

"I'm worth more than 730 milligrams of sodium?"

"Charles, you're priceless. This Saturday—you and me, and Mayor McCheese."

"What about Hal?"

"Who do you think will be in the costume?"

"That's evil, and I love it. It's something I would say."

"I know, Charles. You've changed me—just a little bit."

"It's not me. It's the Carrie Watts hat."

"Hal already told you that it was never the hat. Anyway, you're not wearing the hat. It's you."

"I've come to love you, Pete. Not in a sexual way—so don't get any ideas."

"I understand, Charles. I understand what you meant. I love you, too."

"Go along, now. I don't like "ick" even when I start it. Go and run. You have Quarter Pounders to eat."

"With cheese, no less."

"Yes, with cheese. I will see you Saturday."

Pete started to jog and quickly picked up his pace. Charles watched Pete run south until he could no longer see his tall, muscular frame. He wiped away the tears that had begun and stood up slowly, smiling through the effort. It had been a good afternoon.

✳✳✳

Late October had been unseasonably cold, so the spell of warmer weather in early November was welcomed by all New Yorkers. It was sweater weather again, and that was just fine with Charles. He walked out of his apartment wearing a new one—a fern-green crewneck he had purchased to celebrate his newfound fame. It was notable for the large dachshund woven into the fabric, spanning the middle of the front and extending to the back.

The past months had been a wonder to Charles. Pete and Hal had filled his days with laughter and life, something he knew he had lacked since Michael was alive, but something he had not realized until these past months, that he acutely missed. Like a runner who finally has surgery to correct a knee injury, he had forgotten what life was like without a constant, numbing pain.

Today, Charles wanted to see the river again. He wanted to go down to the once-familiar level of the park, walk to where the path narrowed and wound up toward the tennis courts, and then finally back up to the street to Julia and Ulysses' final resting place.

More than anything, though, Charles wanted to sit on his bench—not the one that had served as a substitute these past few years—but the one he had sat on for more than four decades, and stare at New Jersey, daring it to blink first. That was his plan, and Pete and Hal would offer the assistance he needed. He saw them waiting with Ollie as he crossed the street.

"You look great," Pete said after hugging Charles.

"I do. And look, I brought Ollie a friend," Charles said, pointing to the dachshund on the sweater. He turned around for added effect. "The dog goes all the way to the back."

"Look, Ollie, you have a brother," Pete said. Ollie wagged his tail more from the sight of Charles than from the sweater.

"It's good to see you, Charles," Hal said, kissing Charles on the cheek.

"What was that for?"

"Nothing and everything." Hal sat down and picked up Ollie.

"Ollie has taken to you," Charles said.

"So has Ollie's person," Pete said. "We have a favor to ask."

"You don't have to say, 'yes,'" Hal added, "but we want you to say 'yes.'"

"How many times do I have to tell you that I won't do a three-way?" Charles replied.

"It's not a three-way," Pete said. "We're getting married at City Hall. We want you to be our witness. You can give Hal away."

"You finally popped the question?" Charles asked, looking at Pete.

"You knew he was going to propose to me?" Hal asked.

"I know everything. Your future husband cannot keep a secret from me."

"That is so true," Pete said. "I told Charles weeks ago."

"Don't be concerned about that, young Hal," Charles said. "I couldn't be happier for the two of you. I would be honored to be at the wedding."

Pete and Hal both kissed Charles on each cheek.

"Still won't do the three-way," Charles said. "Now, I want a favor. I want to go down into the park. I want to walk where I used to walk. I want to show you my bench—my real bench."

"Can you manage the steps?" Hal asked.

"If the two of you just keep me steady and we go slow, it should be fine. If I need to be carried, make it sexy."

"Understood," Hal said. "Lay on, Macduff."

"You got the quote right," Charles said. "No one gets the quote right."

"He is a man of many hidden talents," Pete said.

"Yes, he is, Pete. Lay on, Macduff."

The three battle-tested warriors walked slowly down the stone steps into Riverside Park. The large trees had not yet shed their leaves, so there was a stunning display of reds, golds, and yellows.

"Let's go that way," Charles said, pointing north. I want to go as far as the path that leads to the tennis courts, then we can head back and, if I feel up to it, to below the Soldiers and Sailors Monument further south."

The men walked, and Charles talked. He talked about his old job, something he never did. He talked about youthful adventures. Mostly, though, he talked about Michael. First, when they were young and new, then as they moved through middle age, and finally, at the end.

Pete and Hal savored it all. Charles had shed the funny asides that often broke up moments of personal honesty. Today, Charles was as excited as a newborn child by everything he saw, but with the added benefit of having seen it all long ago. He was tired, but not yet ready to sit on his beloved bench. They passed a restaurant concession as they walked toward the Soldiers and Sailors Monument, and Charles said that after they finished walking, and he was settled on *his* bench, he would like Pete and Hal to go back there and get him a glass of wine. By the time they reached Charles's bench, the sun was already low on the horizon.

"Here it is," Charles said, pointing to a bench that looked like every other bench in the park. "This is where I sat. I know it by its placement between those two big trees and the dog park up there."

Charles sat down and patted the wooden slats, as if he was greeting an old friend—which he was. "I can't thank you enough for this. I never thought when we first met, that we would become so close—my sons, my brothers."

Hal stood before Charles and began:

> *"'This story shall the good man teach his son;*
> *And Crispin Crispian shall ne'er go by,*
> *From this day to the ending of the world,*
> *But we in it shall be remember'd;*
> *We few, we happy few, we band of brothers.'*

"It is not the whole speech, but I memorized a small part for you," Hal said.

Charles was moved by the ending of Henry V's St. Crispin's Day speech. "To you, King Henry. You are no longer young Hal."

Hal hugged Charles. "Thank you."

"So, Henry, take care of young Peter." It was the first time Charles had referred to Pete as Peter. "Now, get me some wine so we can toast your upcoming nuptials. I will watch Ollie."

Pete and Hal left Charles with Ollie. The sun was setting, and Charles stared at New Jersey. Lights were coming up across the river. It would later be understood as a transformer overload, but there was a temporary power loss in the New Jersey town of Guttenberg across the river, giving Charles the impression that he had finally won—New Jersey had blinked first.

Charles turned, hoping Pete and Hal were near so he could share the moment, but they were not in sight. It was just him and Ollie. He tried to recall the part of the Tennyson poem that applied to the sunset, but he couldn't recall the exact text. He went on his phone and found the poem.

Charles read the section aloud.

> *'The lights begin to twinkle from the rocks:*
> *The long day wanes: the slow moon climbs: the deep*
> *Moans round with many voices. Come, my friends.*
> *'T is not too late to seek a newer world.'*

"Damn, Ollie, that Teddy Roosevelt could really write." Charles laughed.

When Pete and Hal returned with the wine a few minutes later, Ollie was agitated, tugging at Charles' trouser leg.

"Stop that, Ollie," Pete said. "Let Charles nap." He approached Charles, tapping his shoulder. "We have the wine. Let's toast." Charles didn't react. "Charles, Charles," Pete repeated.

Hal put down the wine and gently touched Charles's shoulder. "We need to call 911, Peter." Ollie began to bark. The sun had set, and the lights had come back up in New Jersey.

✳✳✳

A month after Charles passed, Pete and Hal married at City Hall. To Pete's surprise, Charles, who had no living family, had named him his heir and left him the apartment he had shared with Michael. It gave Pete and Hal great joy to begin their family in the same place where Charles and Michael had lived. There was love in the floors, the walls, and the sometimes-challenging plumbing.

Two years after they married, they had a son; naming him after Charles was a given. Pete was the biological father, and Charlie looked like a miniature, non-hairy version of his father.

On almost every good-weather day, Pete and Hal would take Charlie to Riverside Park. It was late spring, and the air was warm, perfect for play.

"Charles, not so fast," Hal said loudly.

"Don't bother," Pete said. "He has a mind of his own, and we can see him from here. Give him a little independence."

"He can have independence when he's eighteen. This is New York City. I don't want him that far away. Charles, you get back here now."

Charlie stopped in his tracks. He knew the tone, and his parents only called him Charles when they were angry. He didn't want that; he was an amiable six-year-old. He was just having fun with Ollie, who, despite his advanced age, still enjoyed a frolic in the park.

"How many times have I told you, you can't get too far ahead of us?" Hal asked as he scooped up his son. "We want you to be safe, always."

"I am, Dad," he said. Charlie called Hal "Dad" and Pete "Papa." "It was Ollie's fault," Charlie continued. "He wanted to go further."

"Ollie?" Pete asked. "Ollie just wants to walk far enough to pee. He's getting old, Charlie."

"Ollie is OK, Papa."

"I think we should sit down for a bit," Pete said. "It will do you and Ollie some good."

"Are you old, Papa?"

"Why did you ask that, Charlie? I am just entering my prime."

"What's your prime?"

"Your prime is the space between young and old," Hal said. "I am younger than Papa, so I am not in my prime yet."

"Don't listen to Dad, Charlie," Pete said. "Dad is only a year younger than me. We are both young enough. I wanted to sit here."

"Is it because of the sign?" Charlie asked, pointing to the plaque on the bench.

"Yes, Charlie," Pete said. "It's because of the sign, the plaque."

"He was your friend?"

"He was more than a friend, Charlie," Hal said. "We named you after him. I hope you have someone like him in your life."

"I have you two. I don't need anyone else."

"You will always have us," Pete said, "but I hope you have a Charles in your life, too."

"That would be weird," Charlie said, "having a friend with the same name as me."

Pete and Hal laughed. "Yes, it would be weird," Pete said.

"Can I go over there?" Charlie asked, quickly changing subjects, as only children can.

"What happened to 'I have you two?'" Hal asked.

"I just want to go over there," Charlie said, pointing to the bench directly opposite. "Please!"

"OK, Charlie. Just across from us," Pete said. "Ollie will protect you. He can be fierce," Pete added for Hal's amusement.

"Ollie couldn't be fierce if his life depended on it," Hal said, snuggling next to Pete on the bench. "No dachshund is fierce."

"Good point," Pete said. "You are always right."

"But you are the writer."

"Those puns, those puns."

"Well, I don't have a Pulitzer like someone on this bench."

"It means little in the bigger scheme of life."

"The prize, maybe, but not what you wrote about Charles. It was beautiful."

"It was what had to be said. I wanted to prove Charles wrong—you don't have to be famous to be featured in the *Times*."

"He was a little famous after the Ohio adventure. Charles was not wrong."

"Look at our son," Pete said, pointing toward Charlie, letting the comment pass. "He is amazing."

"Charles would have loved him."

"And that we named him Charles. Charles wanted to be remembered."

"And he is—by us, he will be by our son, and by anyone who reads the plaque on this bench. This illegal plaque, I might add."

"I couldn't get this bench. There's a waiting list, and it had to be *this* bench. Who will notice that there is an extra plaque on a park bench? The plaque police?"

"Just don't tell our son you committed an act of vandalism."

"No bench was harmed. Shall we get our son and head home?"

"Yes, Peter, let's go home."

The two men got up and pretended to run toward Charlie, who started to laugh. He loved his two fathers, and he loved to play. It was a good arrangement all around. Each father took hold of one of their son's hands. Hal also held Ollie's leash.

"Lay on, Macduff," Hal said.

As the family walked toward the 108th Street steps to street level, the last bit of sunlight hit Charles's plaque. Below his name and his dates was a single line from Tennyson:

"To strive, to seek, to find, and not to yield."

About the Author

Alfred P. Doblin has spent most of his professional career working as a journalist, most notably as the Editorial Page Editor of *The (Bergen) Record* in New Jersey. Writing a twice-weekly column and editorials, he has been recognized by numerous state and national journalism associations, including the American Society of News Editors (ASNE) award for excellence in editorial writing, the Society of the Silurians, NLGJA: The Association of LGBTQ+ Journalists, and was nominated four times for the GLAAD Media Award for Outstanding Newspaper Columnist. He was a finalist in both the 2024 and 2025 Saints and Sinners Fiction Contest, part of the Tennessee Williams & New Orleans Literary Festival. His debut book, *Tales of the Lavender Twilight*, a collection of 11 short stories, was published in 2025. He is also the grandson of the German novelist Alfred Döblin. Currently working in communications, Doblin lives in Brooklyn, NY. This is his second published book.

www.ingramcontent.com/pod-product-compliance
Lightning Source LLC
Chambersburg PA
CBHW030918060726
47591CB00005B/1586